W9-AMB-595

SIBLEY PUBLIC LIBRARY
406 Ninth Street
SIBLEY IOWA 51249

A PROMISE
TO BELIEVE IN

A PROMISE
TO BELIEVE IN

Brides of Gallatin County

BOOK ONE

TRACIE
PETERSON

BETHANY HOUSE PUBLISHERS

Minneapolis, Minnesota

A Promise to Believe In
Copyright © 2008
Tracie Peterson

Cover design by Andrea Gjeldum
Cover photography by Karen Woodburn

All rights reserved. No part of this publication may be reproduced, stored in a retrieval system, or transmitted in any form or by any means—electronic, mechanical, photocopying, recording, or otherwise—without the prior written permission of the publisher. The only exception is brief quotations in printed reviews.

Published by Bethany House Publishers
11400 Hampshire Avenue South
Bloomington, Minnesota 55438

Bethany House Publishers is a division of
Baker Publishing Group, Grand Rapids, Michigan.

Printed in the United States of America

ISBN 978-1-60751-138-0

To Deb and Brian,
who give me hours of
radio listening,
laughs, and encouragement!

Books by Tracie Peterson

www.traciepeterson.com

A Slender Thread • *I Can't Do It All!***
What She Left For Me • *Where My Heart Belongs*

ALASKAN QUEST
Summer of the Midnight Sun
Under the Northern Lights • *Whispers of Winter*

BROADMOOR LEGACY*
A Daughter's Inheritance
An Unexpected Love

BELLS OF LOWELL*
Daughter of the Loom • *A Fragile Design*
These Tangled Threads

LIGHTS OF LOWELL*
A Tapestry of Hope • *A Love Woven True*
The Pattern of Her Heart

DESERT ROSES
Shadows of the Canyon • *Across the Years*
Beneath a Harvest Sky

HEIRS OF MONTANA
Land of My Heart • *The Coming Storm*
To Dream Anew • *The Hope Within*

LADIES OF LIBERTY
A Lady of High Regard • *A Lady of Hidden Intent*
A Lady of Secret Devotion

SHANNON SAGA†
City of Angels • *Angels Flight* • *Angel of Mercy*

WESTWARD CHRONICLES
A Shelter of Hope • *Hidden in a Whisper* • *A Veiled Reflection*

YUKON QUEST
Treasures of the North • *Ashes and Ice* • *Rivers of Gold*

*with Judith Miller   †with James Scott Bell
**with Allison Bottke and Dianne O'Brian

TRACIE PETERSON is the author of over seventy novels, both historical and contemporary. Her avid research resonates in her stories, as seen in her bestselling HEIRS OF MONTANA and ALASKAN QUEST series. Tracie and her family make their home in Montana.

Visit Tracie's Web site at *www.traciepeterson.com*.

CHAPTER ONE

MAY 1879, MONTANA TERRITORY

"Miss Gwen! Miss Gwen! You gotta come quick!"

Gwendolyn Gallatin looked up from her sewing and cocked her head to one side, unknowingly imitating the family dog, Major Worthington. The sounds of occasional gunfire and celebrating from the saloon next door had been frequent this evening, but she was surprised to hear her name above the ruckus.

A young boy of fourteen burst through the open front door, panting. Sandy hair fell across his dirt-smudged face. "Miss Gwen!" He could scarcely get out the words.

"Goodness, Cubby, whatever is the matter?" Gwen put aside her sewing and got to her feet as her sisters, Lacy and Beth, joined her from the kitchen.

"It's your . . . your pa," Cubby said, regaining his wind. "He's been shot clean through. My pa says to come quick."

Gwen's hand went to her throat as she exchanged a frantic look with her sisters. Lacy, who was the youngest of the three and not yet twenty, raced to the front door. She wore a long split skirt that allowed her easier movement, but Beth, dressed very ladylike, was right behind her.

"Take us to him, Cubby." Gwen felt as if the words were forced from her throat as she moved leaden limbs to follow her sisters.

"He's in the street. Just in front of Pa's saloon." Cubby followed the girls out the door, Gwen at his side.

A small crowd had already gathered when Gwen arrived. Lacy was kneeling in the dirt beside her father, and Gwen watched as Beth touched a lace-edged handkerchief to the older man's chest. When Gwen approached, the crowd parted, as if on cue. She could see the ashen color of her father's face and hear the whispered murmurs among the rough cowboys, who smelled of sweat and beer.

"Gwennie," her father whispered as she knelt beside him. She put her hand to his head. He already felt cold. "Let's get him to the house," she told her sisters.

"Don't," her father said, straining to breathe. "I'm . . . done for."

"Nonsense, Pa. People get shot all the time," Lacy said, pushing back an errant strand of her cinnamon-colored hair.

Beth wept softly, causing their father to give a slow shake of his head. "Don't . . . be . . . cryin', Bethy. I'm heaven-bound." He gave the girls an awkward smile and closed his eyes. "Don't . . . make . . . the coffee . . . too weak, girls." And then he was gone.

Gwen looked at her father as if expecting something more. Surely he'd just succumbed to the pain. He couldn't be dead.

Beth looked up at Gwen. "He's not breathing."

Lacy was calling him. "Pa! Pa!"

The entire event unfolded like a bad dream. People were saying things, bustling about, but Gwen was frozen in place, unable to move or hear them clearly. Their father was dead. What were they going to do now?

"I'll take care of this," Simon Lassiter said, helping Gwen to her feet. His brother, Nicholas, was right at her side. The Lassiter boys had always been good friends to the Gallatins.

Gwen looked at him, noting the sorrow in his eyes. "What should we do?" she asked softly.

"We get the sheriff, that's what," Lacy declared. She looked at the gathering of cowboys. "Which one of you shot him?"

"Nobody shot him, Miss Lacy," Cubby said, shaking his head. "Leastwise, not on purpose. The boys—they was shootin' it up, celebratin'."

"Cubby's right," his father replied. Rafe Reynolds puffed on a cigar for a moment, then motioned to the gathering of drunken men. "Nobody was aiming to hurt George Gallatin."

"But he's dead, just the same," Lacy said, looking to Gwen. "Someone needs to get the law out here." She began to cry. "Pa deserves justice." Beth put her arm around Lacy and nodded.

"You ladies go on back to the roadhouse," Simon instructed. "We'll take George on over to the shop. Nick can ride for the sheriff while I get George . . . well . . . get him ready to . . . ah . . . bury." Simon wore a look suggesting he'd just as soon be wrestling a grizzly.

"I'll bring his suit," Gwen said without emotion. The shock of the situation washed her in a numbing sensation. Lacy and Beth were crying, but tears wouldn't come to Gwen's eyes. It was senseless to cry. Her father was dead, and it was clearly her fault as much as the man who'd fired the gun. After all, she was the one who'd sent him out that evening. And she was the one who'd been cursed.

∞

"I can't believe this has happened," Lacy said as she stood beside the still-open grave of their father.

At nineteen, Lacy was the youngest of the Gallatin girls, as they were often referred to. She was more tomboy than lady and generally shocked social convention by donning boy's britches to ride astride or climb up on the roof to reset a shingle or two. She was the son their father never had, and Gwen relied on her for the heavier work around the Gallatin House.

"Dave Shepard said it was an accident," Gwen said, looking off past the grave to the crowd of people.

"Dave would say that," Lacy remarked, the sarcasm thick in her voice. "I talked to him and to Sheriff Cummings. Neither of them think it's anything more than an unfortunate incident."

Beth dabbed her eyes. "There's no way to prove who did it. The men were rowdy, and everyone was shooting it up. At least, that's what Rafe said."

Lacy crossed her arms. "I believe him about as much as I would believe the Major incapable of killing chickens."

Gwen cast a sidelong glance at the family dog that had sat faithfully beside the grave of his master for over two hours. "Talk like this won't get us anywhere." She looked at her sisters, read the deep pain in their eyes, and wondered if they blamed her for their father's death. God knew *she* did.

"Well, I'm gonna go give Deputy Shepard a piece of my

mind," Lacy said, stomping off and pulling her skirts up high enough to avoid the better portion of the muddy path.

Beth looked at Gwen. "I'd better go with her."

"Yes." Gwen knew Lacy's penchant for taking umbrage with Dave Shepard and any other man who stood in her way. Having been only five when their mother died in childbirth, Lacy seemed to carry a perpetual grudge against the world— but especially toward the opposite sex.

Beth hurried after Lacy as Simon Lassister made his way to Gwen's side. "Sure sorry about your pa, Gwen."

Gwen nodded. "I know you are, Simon. I appreciate the casket you made. Let me know what I owe you."

"Nothin' at all. Nick and I wanted to do it by way of payin' our last respects." He lowered his gaze to the dirt. "He sure didn't deserve to get shot down like that."

"No," Gwen admitted. "He didn't. If I hadn't sent him over to your place to get the knives sharpened, it probably wouldn't have happened."

Simon looked back up. "This wasn't your fault, Gwen. You can't go blamin' yourself."

"I know," she replied, knowing this was the answer he expected. She didn't want to get into a lengthy discussion on why he was wrong, so she just nodded.

Gwen gazed at the man who was four years her senior. He wouldn't understand, even if she tried to explain it. Her life had been consumed by the death and dying of the people closest to her.

"Did you hear what I said?" Simon asked.

Gwen shook her head. "No, I'm sorry. I'm afraid I was lost in my thoughts."

"I asked if I could walk you back," Simon repeated. "Nick

and I are going to tend the grave, and I'd rather you not be here for that. It might be difficult to watch."

Gwen glanced at the open hole in the ground. The wooden box that held the earthly remains of George Gallatin rested alongside the grave. She shook her head and turned to go. "No. You just do what you have to, Simon. I'll be fine."

Gwen couldn't resist, however, glancing over at the grave to the right. *Harvey.* She thought of how much her father and husband had enjoyed each other's company in life. Perhaps now they would also share that companionship in death. Yet sadly, she couldn't cry a tear for either one. A lifetime of loss and sorrow had taken its toll, and there were no tears left.

Gwen bowed her head and walked toward the house as she heard Simon and Nick lowering her father's casket into the ground. She'd left a piece of her heart in that grave, just as she had with all the others. Sometimes she worried that there wasn't any heart left inside her.

Harvey would have told her she was just being silly. Harvey had been so full of life; he didn't believe in curses or bad luck. He just believed in living life in a hurry. Maybe that's why he'd died at such a young age—he'd just lived up his life too soon.

"Sometimes I just want to punch that man in the nose," Lacy declared as she and Beth came alongside Gwen.

"What's Deputy Shepard done now?" Gwen asked softly, pushing aside images of the man she'd once loved.

"It's not what he's done," Lacy retorted. "It's what he's *not* doing. He's not even looking for our father's killer."

"Be fair, Lacy. There were a dozen men around that night, drunk and celebrating roundup. You cannot expect Deputy Shepard to know which stray bullet struck Pa."

Their little sister stopped dead in her tracks. "Well, someone's gotta do it. Guess it'll have to be me."

Gwen took hold of Lacy's arm. "Please. Can this wait? They haven't even laid the dirt on Pa's grave yet. Mrs. Shepard is at the house preparing a funeral dinner, and we have to at least try to keep up appearances."

Lacy's hard expression softened. "I'm sorry, Gwen. Of course it can wait. I wasn't thinking."

Patting Lacy's arm, Gwen began to walk toward the house. "We have so much to figure out. Pa left us everything, but the real question is, do we want it?"

"What do you mean?" Beth asked.

"I mean the stage stop. Gallatin House. Do we want to go on with it? It's the only thing Pa was ever any good at. The only thing . . ." Her voice broke as she struggled to continue. "The only thing that gave him any success."

Beth put her arm around Gwen's waist. "He was good at it. People liked him, and he liked serving them."

They approached the log structure from the muddy stage road and paused. Last night's rain gave everything a look of being freshly washed. Droplets of water still glistened on the new grass and sparkled like diamonds in the midday sun.

The girls had watched their father fail at one job after another—attempts to strike it rich, to be accepted. Yet George Gallatin was nevertheless a thoughtful and gentle man who loved his daughters dearly. He brought the girls to the Gallatin area of the Montana Territory, certain that sharing the same name would bring them good fortune. Gallatin House was his only endeavor that had really thrived.

"He was a good man," Gwen finally said.

"He was always kind and never raised his voice," Beth replied.

"Pa never knew a stranger," Lacy added, her anger

appearing to have passed, at least momentarily. She gave a heavy sigh.

Gwen squared her shoulders. "Well, it's not like we have to decide anything right now."

"I don't mind if we do," Beth replied. "I think we should stay. I mean, where would we go—three women, all alone?"

"Being three women all alone is also a good reason to consider going elsewhere," Gwen countered. "Remember what Mrs. Shepard said that one time: 'A single woman alone in the territory is like water to a thirsty man.' I suppose that would make the three of us like a water hole to a herd of parched cattle."

"I don't think I appreciate being likened to a water hole," Beth said with a frown. "Besides, it's not like we're destitute. We have a good home and friends, even if we do have to tolerate Rafe's Saloon and his desire to sully the reputation of everyone in the area."

"And we make good money from the stage contract," Lacy added. "We have a solid agreement with the freighters, too."

"Until the end of summer," Gwen replied. "The stage contract was to be renegotiated this August, don't forget."

"Then maybe that's the answer," Beth countered. "It's only May. Summer is just getting started, and the heaviest flow of travelers will be coming through. Why don't we just see what the summer brings and how hard it is to handle all the work on our own?"

"I agree," Lacy stated with a determined air. "That will give me time to investigate Pa's death and seek out his killer."

Both Beth and Gwen stopped and looked at their sister. "What?" Gwen questioned before Beth could speak.

Lacy looked at her with a shrug. "If the law won't see to

it, I will. I'm not afraid to root out the situation and learn the truth."

Gwen frowned and shook her head. "I doubt fear is the reason the sheriff is less than enthusiastic to stretch this matter out. There's simply no way to know who shot Pa."

"Then hang them all," Lacy replied.

"You don't mean that." The shock of Lacy's statement registered quite clearly in Beth's tone. "You can't want innocent men to die."

"No. I didn't want Pa to die either, and he was the most innocent of them all. He wouldn't even take a drink, much less get drunk. Someone deserves to pay for this, and I intend to see they do." Lacy stormed off to the house, not giving either Beth or Gwen a chance to speak.

Beth looked at her older sister and shook her head. "You don't suppose she'll really do anything, do you?"

Gwen sighed. "Knowing Lacy, we'd better hide all of our rope. I could see her becoming a one-woman vigilante movement."

"Yes," Beth said, nodding as they began walking toward the two-story log house. "I'm sure you're right. I think Pa probably had the best idea when he suggested we put a lock on Lacy's door. One from the outside—not the inside."

Gwen smiled. "We may have to ask the Lassiter brothers to check into it."

∞

That night after her sisters had retired to their bedrooms, Gwen crawled into bed and tried hard to forget the events of the day. She was grateful that the next stage wouldn't be through until Wednesday. That gave her another day to focus on the matters at hand.

She snuggled under the down comforter, feeling half frozen by the chill of the room. May in Montana meant the need for additional heat once the sun went down, but Gwen hadn't bothered to light the stove.

It started to rain again and the sound against the windows and roof made a rhythmic beat that comforted Gwen. She thought about praying, but it had been a long time since she'd given it much effort. After all, could God even deal with someone who was cursed? She'd often tried to find hope in the Scriptures, but verses continued to haunt her and give her reason to believe her cause was lost. She couldn't deny that there were nearly whole chapters that spoke of curses being real—that cursing people, even entire nations, was something God had done frequently.

It also looked to be that once God cursed someone, He turned His back on them, as well. Gwen could hardly expect that God would listen to her prayers if He had also cursed her.

She slipped deeper beneath the covers and curled up with her knees to her chest, just as she had done as a child when situations became too frightening. How she longed for comfort—for hope that things might be different. But nothing ever seemed to change.

"And now Lacy wants to take on the world—or at least the territory—and find Pa's killer. Poor Beth is up in arms over Rafe's soiled doves, and I'm stuck here, not knowing what to do about any of it."

Life in the Montana Territory hadn't been all bad, she had to admit, but there were some definite obstacles—mountains to climb and conquer. She thought of Harvey Bishop and smiled.

Harvey had been her knight in shining armor—or at least her wandering troubadour with a passion for life. Harvey had come into her life so quickly and had exited in much the same way. The day he and Gwen had married, he fell ill with measles. Ten days later, it was his grave Gwen stood beside.

She stared up at the ceiling and tried to remember Harvey's face, but the image was fading. Everyone had suggested she keep her own name rather than take Harvey's. After all, the marriage had never been consummated. That alone had been a tremendous source of embarrassment for Gwen. Prior to marrying, she had worried about the merciless teasing that followed new brides. But everyone knowing and pitying her for not ever experiencing her marriage bed somehow seemed even worse.

"Don't worry about what those folks say, Gwennie," her father had told her. *"Ain't no use listening to 'em or even givin' 'em the time of day. Our Harvey was a good man, and that's all that matters. You keep my name or his—don't make much difference to me. You're loved just the same."*

Gwen was certain that her decision to retain her maiden name had been the right choice. Not many knew her here or in Bozeman. It was less confusing if three sisters all bearing the same last name showed up. There was no need to explain the past that way, and this suited Gwen very well. She wondered from time to time if Harvey would have been offended that she cast aside the name of Bishop, but it wasn't something she dwelled on.

As sleep finally took her, Gwen pondered the future in her dreams.

Across the hall in her own bedroom, Lacy paced the floor until well past midnight. She might have failed at many things in life, but she would not fail at this.

I will find Pa's killer. I promise to find him, and I won't rest until I do. If I have to lie or cheat, then so be it. It will be justified in the end.

She knew her father and sisters would never have approved of such an attitude, but she didn't care. The house felt empty without the large, boisterous man who'd raised them. The future seemed tenuous knowing he was gone.

Reaching down, she gently stroked the flannel cloth of her father's nightshirt. She hadn't told Gwen or Beth that she'd taken it, but she knew they would understand. Wrapping her more feminine robe around her, Lacy crept from her room and went downstairs. Major Worthington was no doubt asleep at the foot of Gwen's bed. Gwen had taken over their father's bedroom, where their dog always slept. She said she'd done this so she and Beth wouldn't have to share a room. Lacy believed, however, that Gwen desperately wanted privacy to deal with their loss.

A harsh yowl could be heard out on the porch. Calvin J. Whiskers, their buff tabby, was letting her know that it was too cold to spend the night outside. Lacy opened the door and looked down at the cat. He yowled up at her as if to say it was about time she opened the door.

"Well, it's not my fault you were out playing Romeo to the Lassiters' Juliet. I swear, you have a better love life than anyone in a ten-mile radius."

Calvin walked past her, not making so much as a comment one way or another. Lacy smiled and left the door open as she stepped out onto the porch. The night air had turned cold with the rain. She hugged her arms to her chest and shivered.

Walking to the far side of the porch, she could see that even the saloon had quieted down. Without the weekend cowboys or stage travelers, there weren't too many regulars to keep Rafe or his girls busy.

Lacy studied the street, fixing her gaze on the very spot where her father had died. She tried to see in the night darkness, but there was nothing to see.

"Nobody cares," she whispered to the air.

CHAPTER TWO

∽

The Gallatin House, as it had come to be called, sat at a stage crossroads that took traffic from Bozeman to Butte and Helena, or south to Norris and Virginia City. It wasn't impossible to get around the vast expanse of Montana Territory—it was just time-consuming and dangerous. The Battle for the Little Bighorn was not even three years past, and the Indian wars spurred on by that horrible defeat were still vivid memories.

The Gallatin family had a good reputation with the stage line and with the local freighters. They offered clean beds free of lice, good meals with plenty of food, and pretty girls who were happy to listen to the rambling stories of weary travelers. And for an extra dollar or two, a fellow could even get his shirt and socks washed out and freshly pressed before the stage left the next morning. There were few establishments that could boast that kind of service. Not to mention the place had its own hot springs. For a saddle-sore cowboy or stage-bruised traveler, a long soak in the warm, healing waters exceeded expectations. It made the Gallatin House a much sought-after refuge, especially by the local drivers.

There wasn't much else to this wide spot in the road. Rafe's Saloon was positioned only about a hundred feet away—much to the girls' displeasure—while the Lassiters had a fine blacksmith shop and stables another twenty feet to the south of that. The Lassiters held the stage contract for service to the horses, as well as the responsibility to keep a fresh team. It only stood to reason that, over the years, the men had added more stock and had developed a reputation for having some very fine horses for sale or rent.

There were several close ranches and a handful of small homesteads in the vicinity, enough so that there were constant rumors of how they should encourage a mercantile, doctor, and regular town committee to be formed. The place didn't even have a name but was simply referred to as the Gallatin House Stage Stop, so Gwen thought the talk of committees seemed silly.

She had lived in cities both large and small—had known the rowdiness and brawling of mining towns and the busyness of noisy St. Louis and Denver—and her little stage stop suited her just fine. There wasn't anything she needed that she couldn't get . . . eventually. The key to living in the Montana Territory was to have a great deal of patience.

Gwen figured things would go on much as they always had. George Gallatin had kept an open invitation for the Lassiter brothers to join them for meals whenever they liked, and Gwen certainly wouldn't change that. The boys kept the Gallatin horses well cared for, not to mention everyday tasks such as sharpening knives, mending tools and horse halters, and the like. It was a sort of barter that kept everyone happy, since the brothers had no womenfolk to take care of them.

Beth especially seemed to enjoy the attention given her by Simon and Nick. Gwen felt confident that her sister would one day marry one or the other of the men, but at present she wouldn't even court them. At twenty-two, Beth had high ideals of what marriage and romance should look like, and it apparently didn't resemble sweaty blacksmiths. Never mind that both men sported thick heads of coal black hair and brown eyes that could melt a girl's heart. They were civil, too—took a regular bath on Saturday night and always used their napkins at the table.

Gwen smiled even now as they sat across from her, doing their best to eat breakfast in an orderly fashion that wouldn't result in spilling or breaking something.

"We heard there was gonna be a railroad survey party come through this way," Simon said after finishing the last of his coffee.

Gwen brought the pot to refill his cup, but he waved her off. "Are they thinking the railroad will go through our area?"

"It's possible," Simon replied. "With this being a well-established crossroads and the road from Bozeman being traveled more and more, I think they see the potential. We know the lines are gonna be laid through Bozeman and Butte. Seems only natural they'd come through this way, or somewhere nearby."

Nick laughed. "My brother's a regular genius of deduction."

Gwen smiled, but it was Beth who asked, "Do you suppose the railroad will change everything here?"

"It's likely to change some things," Nick admitted.

"They won't need the stage if the train is here," Lacy commented.

"Of course they will," Simon countered. "Not everyone can afford the train, and besides that, the train doesn't go everywhere. It can only follow its tracks, and those lines are pretty limited. The stage will always be needed. It might be slower and rougher, but once the railroad is in place, the prices to ride will drop."

"So our pay might drop, as well," Gwen said rather absentmindedly.

"Nah," Simon said, shaking his head. "The lower prices will increase the number of folks travelin'. You might well have to add on to the Gallatin House again."

Gwen smiled. "Pa used to say that, too. He said one day this area would be settled with folks close enough to throw a stick at. He had plans to build out to the north side."

"Well, I think it would be good if you could get the place built in such a way that you wouldn't actually have strangers sleeping in the main house at night. I know you were plenty safe when your pa was alive," Nick said with a sidelong glance at Beth, "but now it's more dangerous."

"We can't send everyone to the addition," Gwen replied. "There are only four rooms there, and that hardly takes care of everyone when the stage shows up full. Besides, we always let the drivers stay in the house. They have a regular room upstairs."

Simon put in his thoughts on the matter. "Nick's right, though. You ought to consider doing things differently."

"Look, Pa thought of those kinds of things. We have a locked door on our hallway. No one can get down that way when we lock up for the night. We will be fine." Gwen got up and began to clear away the dishes and added, "We Gallatin girls are very resourceful. Lacy's become quite a crackshot with the rifle, Beth wields an oversized skillet like it was nothing heavier than a book, and I have my irons to assist me." She smiled. "You boys need to stop worrying about us and just remember to never sneak over for a midnight snack."

Lacy was blessedly preoccupied, otherwise Gwen knew she would have weighed in on the topic and given both men a piece of her mind. She didn't like anyone suggesting they were weak or incapable. Just to make sure her youngest sister held her tongue, Gwen thought up a chore.

"Lacy, would you please go to the kitchen and bring more biscuits?"

Lacy looked up and seemed to only partially shake the cobwebs from her thoughts. "What? Oh, sure. I'll do it now." She got up and left the room, her expression looking rather perplexed, as if she wondered what in the world they would do with biscuits.

"We need to be careful what we say. Lacy is feeling very defensive about our position," Gwen said in a whisper. "Suggesting that we can't take care of ourselves will only set her on her ear."

"Sorry, Gwen. I didn't think," Nick said, nodding. "I'll be more careful from now on."

To Gwen's surprise, a knock sounded on the front door, and Rafe Reynolds waltzed in like he owned the place. The scruffy-looking form stood about six foot and boasted more muscle than most men. Gwen supposed it was from hours of lifting, but she couldn't be sure. Clean-shaven and hair trimmed, she thought Rafe might be rather attractive, but his personality was definitely in need of more genteel training.

"I see you're all nice and cozy. Three gals for two guys. Now I'm here, and that evens things out."

Just then Lacy returned. She scowled and dropped the bread platter down with a resounding clatter. Biscuits danced off the plate and onto the table. "Why are you here?"

Nick and Simon frowned. Gwen knew Rafe's appearance could not bode well for the peaceful breakfast.

"And at this hour," Beth added in a snide manner. "In the four years since we moved here, I've never seen you up and around before noon."

Rafe gave her a wicked smile and winked. "I didn't know you cared. If I'd known you were watching for me, I would have made the effort."

Beth blushed furiously, and Gwen could see the comment agitated the Lassiter brothers. "Enough of that, Mr. Reynolds. What is it you need?"

"I came to make you a good offer."

Gwen frowned and looked at her sisters. "What kind of offer?" *Please don't let him suggest marriage. He's got to know I would never accept him as a husband.*

"You've got nothing we could possibly want," Lacy said, her eyes narrowing.

"I figured, what with your pa gone to his glory," Rafe began, "that you ladies would be considering what to do about the place."

Of course, Gwen thought. *He wants to buy the stage stop.* "No, I'm sorry. We haven't been thinking of that at all."

"Well, you should. You gals won't have a man around the place to do the heavy work. You won't last long that way."

"If need be, Nick and I will help the ladies," Simon stated firmly.

Lacy smacked her hands down on the table. Gwen was rather embarrassed by the fact that Lacy was wearing pants instead of a split skirt but quickly realized that was the least of their concerns with regard to their sister. Lacy blamed Rafe as much as anyone for the death of their father, and Gwen was certain he was about to hear that very thought for himself.

"We're more than capable of taking care of ourselves," Lacy said, glaring hard at the saloon owner. "We certainly don't need the help of the very man who is partly to blame for our father's death. And even if we were thinking about selling out, it wouldn't be to the likes of you. We're good Christian women, and we would never help to better your kind of business."

"You're such a good Christian woman that you're wearing britches instead of dresses," Rafe said with a laugh. He pushed back thick brown hair and held up his hands. "But don't think I mind watchin' your shapely little be-hind sashay up and down the road. 'Course, it's starting to attract Cubby, as well, and I'm afraid he's going to be hard-pressed to know what to do about such stimulation. S'pose I could send him back to visit the girls, but—"

"Mr. Reynolds!" Gwen exclaimed as Simon and Nick got to their feet.

"Rafe, that's more than enough," Simon said. "The ladies aren't used to that coarse kind of talk. Take yourself out of here."

At forty, Rafe wasn't a man to be taking orders from another man. Especially a younger man. But with Nick standing alongside his brother, Gwen saw the decision in Reynolds' expression. He would leave.

"I apologize, ladies, if I've offended. I do hope, however, you'll be considerin' my offer." He gave a mock tipping, as if he wore a hat, then made his exit in four long strides.

Gwen looked at Lacy and shook her head. "*Now* do you understand what I've been saying all along?"

"I won't have that scum running my life. Besides, I wear a

skirt when I go to Bozeman." She lifted her chin rather defiantly and added, "I work too hard to wear a dress all the time. If I were some frail little wife who did nothing but lounge around all day and entertain, then I'd wear a ball gown." She stalked off toward the back door. "I'll be cutting wood in an ever-so-ladylike manner, if anyone needs me."

The back door opened and slammed before Gwen could respond. She began to gather the dishes once again, and this time Beth joined her.

"Boy, she can sure work up a full head of steam Johnny-quick," Nick said, shaking his head. "I wouldn't want to even suggest someone making her his wife, unless he was ready for war."

Simon and Beth laughed, and Gwen couldn't help but smile. "Let's not talk about Lacy. She's struggling with Pa's death. She's hurting, but she hides her feelings away so she doesn't appear weak. In her mind, weakness equates itself to vulnerability... and then more pain." Everyone seemed to understand and took Gwen's gentle rebuke in stride.

"We'll be over for lunch today, since the stage won't be in until supper," Simon told Gwen.

"That will be fine. We're having leftovers from the funeral dinner. I hope that will be acceptable."

"It's food and I don't have to fix it," Simon declared with a grin. "What man could ask for anything more?"

Beth watched Nick and Simon walk across the backyard toward Rafe's. They wouldn't stop for a drink—at least not yet. She knew they both sampled something stronger than coffee on occasion. It was probably the biggest reason she'd flatly refused Nick's advances. She didn't want a husband who would spend his nights with drinking pals instead of staying in with her.

Of course, Gwen said that her head was full of all sorts of romantic notions, and she was probably right. Beth loved to read gothic romance novels late at night after everyone had gone to bed. She dreamed of being rescued and swept away by a larger-than-life hero, of sharing a passionate love that would last the ages.

She sighed and began to wash the breakfast dishes. *Someday things will be different. Someday I'll find the man of my dreams, and we will fall in love.* Beth closed her eyes and tried to draw a picture of the man in her mind.

"I see you're daydreaming again," Gwen said as she brought the last of the dishes in from the table.

"Dreams are free and hurt no one," Beth replied.

"What rubbish. Dreams can cost you plenty. Look what it did to Pa." Gwen set the dishes down on the counter beside where Beth worked. "Has he been there all this time?"

Beth looked up. "Who?"

"Major. He's been moping these last few days, and I just wondered if he'd been here by the stove all this time."

"He's waiting for Pa to take his morning walk, I would guess," Beth replied.

Gwen nodded. "Poor dog. He sleeps at the foot of the bed for a while each night, then gets up and paces back and forth, like he's expecting Pa to come walking through the door. The clicking of his nails on the wood floor is enough to drive me mad."

"Maybe we should just tie him up on the porch for a few nights."

Gwen nodded. "Maybe. We'll see if he doesn't settle down soon."

But as the days went by, Major only seemed more reclusive

and despondent. He stopped sleeping in Gwen's room and took to pacing throughout the house all night, looking for his friend. During the day he could often be found at the cemetery, faithfully keeping vigil over his master's grave. Gwen tried everything she could to bribe and coax him back to his old cheerful self, but she finally gave up. Obviously pets needed to mourn in their own time and way.

Their cat continued to tend to his priorities, regularly bringing offerings of rats, mice, and the occasional gopher and depositing them on the porch steps. Gwen tried not to get too upset with him—after all, he did appear to mean them as gifts—but she couldn't have rotting animal corpses on the porch when the stage arrived.

"Calvin," she chided as he brought in yet another catch. "Perhaps you should take some time to rest and reflect." The cat looked up at her as if considering the idea, gave a single yowling comment, then took himself off to his favorite porch chair for a nap. Apparently her suggestion was acceptable.

Gwen finished sweeping the porch, then retrieved the dead mouse and delivered it around to the back of the house. This was her routine, and Calvin would know where to find the snack later. She was just about to make her way back to the front when Dave Shepard came out of the saloon and gave her a wave.

"How are you doing, Gwen?"

"Not too bad, Dave. Thanks for asking." The lack of formalities bespoke of their similar age and that they'd known each other since the Gallatins settled into the area four years previously.

"Lacy calm down yet?" he asked casually.

"No." Gwen forced a smile. "I have a feeling she'll keep at this until Sheriff Cummings does something about it."

"I don't suppose my talking to her will help."

She gave a laugh. "No, I don't suppose that would help at all. Lacy sees you as the enemy. You're not doing your job, as far as she's concerned."

Dave pushed back his felt hat and nodded. "I know she feels that way, but I'm afraid she's going to bite off more than she can chew. Those boys who were at the saloon that night were a rough bunch. They'll protect their own, and Lacy is just going to put herself in danger if she keeps at it."

"I'll talk to her again, Dave, but I'm not promising it will do any good."

"Well, at least it's worth a try."

Gwen wasn't convinced, but she said nothing more on that subject. Instead, she walked to the porch and asked after Dave's family.

Dave leaned against the support post and shrugged. "Ma's working herself to death. She's so lonely since my sisters went back East, she can hardly see straight. She's been sewing and cookin' up a storm for the ranch hands—for me and Pa, too. I'm sure that as soon as there are vegetables to can, she'll be busy at that."

"It can't be easy for her to be without female companionship," Gwen admitted. "I plan to make a trip out to the ranch for butter and eggs day after tomorrow. You might tell her. It could give her something to look forward to."

Dave nodded. "Wish you'd convince Lacy to go along. I think Ma could do wonders for her."

Gwen shook her head. "Lacy's just struggling with life. She's never been the same after losing our mother, and frankly, Pa wanted a boy so much, he encouraged Lacy to be a bit more masculine."

Laughing, Dave pushed off from the support. "There's

nothing masculine about her, and that's the trouble. If she looked more like a man, she wouldn't garner the stares she gets now. When she was just a kid of fifteen or so, it wasn't such a big deal, but in case you haven't noticed, she's filled out quite a bit."

"Apparently *you've* noticed," Gwen countered.

"Who can help but notice? Like I said, she's gonna get herself in trouble if she's not careful."

Gwen remembered Rafe's comments days earlier. Here was yet another man talking about her little sister's figure. She supposed it was time to put her foot down about Lacy's wild ways.

"I'll talk to her, Dave. I'll try to encourage her to come with me to your ma's, too. Maybe she can say something to Lacy."

"I'll tell Ma to expect you."

CHAPTER THREE

The rains of May brought a brilliance of green to the country-side, creating a radiant, ethereal glow. The mountains were a pale shade of lavender, with snowy white tops that gave definition to nooks and crannies. The valley floor was dotted with farms of freshly turned dirt and trees that, though small, were budding out to add their own glorious color to the scheme of life.

Gwen thought this the finest time of year. It was still cool—even cold at night—yet warm enough to bring flowers to bloom and trees to leaf. Gwen tried her best to rally a garden out of the dirt not far from the hot springs. It was the bane of her existence each year, as the ground seemed most inhospitable, but every spring, Gwen once again would strive to create something from seemingly nothing. If only the growing period were longer, she was certain they could have a veritable feast.

The Gallatin House property was set up in such a manner that the house stood at the bottom of a large horseshoe-shaped layout. The chicken coop and hot springs house were up the left side of the U, while the outhouses—one for men and one for women—and the storage shed were on the opposite side. The yard in the middle was utilized for the visitors with a nice arrangement of homemade chairs and small tables. Many a night, Gwen took her comfort here watching the starry skies overhead or the soft glow of amber and pink twilight reflected on the mountains.

"Gwen, there's a freighter coming in," Lacy called from the back door.

Stretching to relieve her sore back, Gwen waved. "I'm coming. Hopefully it's Joe bringing us a nice supply of flour and sugar."

"Not to mention coffee and tea," Lacy added. "We're very nearly out, and I figured I'd have to go to Bozeman for more."

Gwen had nearly reached the house when she spied Lacy's rather snug-fitting pants. "Lacy, I need to say something, but I don't wish to start a fight."

Her sister frowned and put her hands on her hips. "What did I do wrong this time? I scrubbed the kitchen just like you showed me."

"It's not that. I don't know why you'd even say such a thing. I can't remember the last time I gave you grief about something as serious as what I need to say today."

"Then you'd better just let it out and get it over with," Lacy said, crossing her arms.

"You have to stop wearing britches." Gwen squared her

shoulders and met Lacy's defiant gaze. "The men are starting to talk. They are noticing your . . . well . . . how shall I say . . . womanly attributes?"

Lacy laughed. "They'd notice them whether I was buried in layers of petticoats or walking naked down the street. They notice you and Beth, as well. They're men, and they're looking for wives or companions. Of course they notice. We're some of the only single women in a two-hundred-mile radius."

"But the pants are much too form-fitting. Look at you—there isn't an inch of you that isn't clearly defined. It wasn't so bad when you were a little girl and your form was straight up and down. Now you have curves and . . . well . . . curves." She sighed. "I worry that you'll attract inappropriate attention, and people will think less of you—or of me for letting you go about that way." Gwen knew that while Lacy wouldn't care about her own reputation, she wouldn't want Gwen or Beth hurt.

Opening her mouth to retort, Lacy closed it again and let her arms go limp. She looked rather defeated, and Gwen felt sorry for her. Her sister was still such a child in so many ways.

"The split skirts are fine. They at least give more fullness. I wouldn't ask you to give them up," Gwen hurried to add.

"I suppose I can stop wearing the pants, but when winter gets here, I may go back to them. I'll at least put them under my skirts. They're warmer than petticoats."

"That would be acceptable," Gwen said with a smile. "Thank you, Lacy. I know how hard everything has been for you."

"It's been hard for you, too, and I don't aim to make your life even more troublesome," Lacy countered. "I heard you talking to Major the other night. You told him you blamed yourself for Pa's death. You've mentioned this before, but I never thought much of it. But you think you're cursed, don't you?"

Gwen hadn't expected this line of questioning, but nodded.

"I can't help it. Everyone I love has died, except for you and Beth. I'm tempted to leave before something happens to either of you."

"Oh no. You aren't running off and leaving us," Lacy said, shaking her head vehemently. "We're in this together. You aren't a curse, in spite of what you believe. That's just nonsense. Now come on. The freighter will be looking for a meal, and if it's Joe, he'll be looking for a big meal. I'll get the coffee on the table."

Gwen nodded and followed Lacy back into the house. She washed her hands at the washbasin and dried them thoroughly, then hung up her apron.

"Freighter has a passenger," Beth announced as Gwen walked toward the door. "He's the dashing type—bluest eyes I've ever seen. Looks all duded up—probably another eastern city man, come to find his fortune in gold and gemstones. He brought his own horse and saddle. Nick just took them away."

Smiling, Gwen walked out onto the porch with her sisters as the man walked casually from behind the freight wagon. Joe waved from his seat.

"I see you girls are still as pretty as a summer day," he called. "I've been dreamin' of some of your great apple pie. I hope I'm not going to be disappointed." He jumped down from his side of the wagon and dusted himself off. "I'm gonna talk to Rafe for a minute—he's got quite a few crates here. Then I'll be back for lunch."

"Sounds good, Joe," Gwen replied before turning her attention on the stranger. She sized him up as somewhat of a dandy. "Good afternoon. Would you like to clean up a bit and then have some lunch?"

The man's blue eyes stared a hole in her as he glanced from

one sister to the next. "What I would like," he said, narrowing his gaze, "is to know which one of you hussies married my brother, then killed him off."

∽

Rafe was starting his day with a double bourbon when Joe walked through the front door. The glass was midway to his lips when Joe bellowed out his name.

"I'm right here, Joe," Rafe said, putting a hand to his head. "You don't need to yell. My head already feels like it's about to rupture."

"Didn't see you sittin' there in the dark. Sorry about that." Joe made his way to Rafe's table. "I have a dozen or so crates for you. Thought maybe I could get that boy of yours to unload them while I eat lunch. I'm on a tight schedule today and can't waste any time."

Rafe nodded. "Cubby's in the back. I'll let him know."

"Good enough. Tell him they're the crates at the back of the wagon. You got my money?"

"Don't I always? Drink?" Rafe questioned, holding up his glass.

"It's a little early for me, Rafe." Joe shook his head. "I'd never make it to Old Town if I started drinking now."

"Suit yourself," Rafe said, downing the drink. He got to his feet and yawned. "So what's new in the world?" He went to the bar and grabbed the cashbox. Counting out the money due Joe, he added, "Any Injun problems?"

Joe grinned. "Not betwixt here and Salt Lake. Had a few grizzlies givin' folks problems down Ennis way. There's some floodin' on the Madison—the Gallatin, too—but I don't reckon it to be too much of a problem here. Had a letter from my sister down in Fort Worth. Guess they've been havin' a rough time of it with twisters and bad storms. Hail laid down their crops three different times."

Rafe yawned again. "Cubby!" he called out, forgetting about his head. He put one hand to his temple while handing Joe the cash with the other.

"Yeah, Pa?" The boy came from the back room, broom in hand.

"Go unload the freight wagon. Joe will show you what belongs to us."

The boy put aside the broom and nodded. Joe smiled at Rafe. "Pleasure doin' business with you. I'm sure to see you on my way back. Save some of the good stuff for me."

Rafe nodded. "Do me a favor and see if you can't get those Gallatin girls to sell me their place while you're sharin' lunch with them."

Joe and Cubby both turned at this. "Sell to you?" Joe asked. "I can't imagine those girls selling out for any reason, least of all to you."

"Everybody's got their price."

"Yeah, well, I doubt the girls can be moved that easily. It's like I was tellin' that young feller who rode up with me—those girls might have lost their pa, but they ain't lost their minds. The roadhouse serves them well. I can't see them leavin' now."

Rafe narrowed his gaze and fixed the old man with a hard stare. "What young feller are you talking about?"

"That city dude who asked me to ride him to the Gallatin House. He's over there right now gettin' ready for his lunch. That's where I wanna be, too, so enough with the questions. Like I told you, I'm in a hurry."

Rafe let them go. He knew Joe could be quite cantankerous if pushed. He needed to know, however, who it was that had come to see the girls. Maybe it was a lawyer sort, or worse still, some distant male relative who'd actually inherited the property.

He frowned and decided it couldn't hurt to make a visit to the Gallatin House. He could feign the need to order a pie or two. The girls didn't care for his company, but they'd tolerate his commerce. Maybe he'd even beg to stay for lunch. It wasn't beneath him to invite himself in, if it served his purpose.

⬚

"I can't believe your rude, outlandish nerve," Lacy said as she stepped in front of Gwen. "Who in the world are you to come here and suggest any of us are hussies?"

The man removed his hat and fixed Lacy with a hard stare. He seemed completely void of emotion—except perhaps anger or indignation. Yes, that was it. The man seemed downright offended.

"One of you certainly is that or worse," the man countered.

Gwen watched as Joe and Cubby went to the back of the wagon. Joe seemed to be pointing out what belonged to Cubby's father. She wondered for a moment if Joe had any idea who this man was and why he'd insisted on coming to Gallatin House.

"My brother was Harvey Bishop. I was told he married a Gwen Gallatin and then died shortly afterwards. I want to know which one of you is that woman."

"Well, people in hell want . . ."

"Lacy! Curb your tongue," Gwen rebuked.

"Well, he should curb his. He's no gentleman."

The man stood his ground. "Which one of you married my brother?"

Beth stepped up to declare, "I hardly think it's any of your business. Harvey told us he was an orphan, so for all we know, you, sir, are a liar. If not, then Harvey couldn't have cared much for you or your interference in his life, or he would have mentioned you."

Gwen was touched by her sister's protective nature. She kept looking at the man to detect some resemblance—some memory of Harvey in the man's stern expression—but there was nothing. This serious stranger was nothing like the man she'd married.

"I think you should go next door if you're looking for a room," Beth said, crossing her arms. "You're acting like an animal, and that's where they bed down."

"Beth!" Gwen exclaimed and stepped forward to put her hand on Beth's shoulder.

"Well, he is. He's being ridiculous. How dare he accuse you . . ." She put her hand over her mouth.

Gwen watched the stranger assess her even more closely. "So I take it you are the woman I'm looking for," he said, his voice void of emotion.

Gwen nodded. "I am Gwendolyn Gallatin, and yes, I was married to Harvey Bishop. But my sister is right. Harvey told us he had no living family."

"Well, he lied," the man replied. "Not surprising, but that's beside the point. We have some business to deal with. Just the two of us."

"You'll deal with all of us or none of us," Lacy stated firmly. She stepped between Gwen and the stranger, and Beth did likewise.

"That's right," Beth said. "We would hardly allow our sister to be subjected to such a rude and vulgar man by herself.

Why, you might take some kind of liberty with her, for all we know."

The man smiled at this, and Gwen felt her knees go weak at the way his features took on an amused—almost mischievous—look.

"Is there a problem, girls?" Joe interjected. "You look like a pack of mama bears defendin' their cub. What's got you hidin' behind your sisters, Miss Gwen?"

"This man, that's what," Lacy said. "He's causing a conflagration of emotions inside of me."

Joe frowned and rubbed his chin. "That don't sound good, Miss Lacy."

"This man claims to be the brother of my sister's deceased husband," Beth added. "He's mean-tempered and . . . well . . . he's just plain mean."

"Stranger, I didn't reckon you to be a problem for these ladies, or I'd never have brought you to them."

"I don't intend to be a problem for them," the man replied. "On my mother's behalf, I've come here on business."

"Harvey's mother is still alive?" Gwen questioned. She felt a growing confusion. Harvey had told her his mother was dead. He had regaled her with sweet stories of his mother's kindness and the joy he'd known before she'd passed away. She bit her lip and forced her eyes to meet those of the stranger.

"Our mother is very much alive, I assure you." This time the man's tone had softened. He seemed to understand that Gwen was just as confused as he was.

"Can we discuss this further over some grub, ladies? I have a schedule to keep, and I'm fallin' behind." Joe raised his eyebrows in a hopeful gesture.

"Come on in," Gwen said, moving to the door. "We'll have

food on the table in two minutes. Beth, Lacy—come help me. Joe, show our guest to the table."

"Sure thing, Miss Gwen."

The girls headed into the kitchen while Joe and the stranger could be heard talking in the dining room.

"What in the world do you suppose he's after?" Lacy asked in a whisper. The dining room and kitchen were open to each other in one great room, and Gwen knew Lacy didn't intend to be overheard.

"I have no idea. I'm just as stunned as you two," Gwen said as she sliced pieces of ham for sandwiches. "I suppose, however, we shall soon find out. Mr. Bishop hardly seems the type to be refused. Beth, please stir the stew and make sure it's warm enough." Beth nodded and immediately went to work.

"You aren't going to let him stay here, are you?" Lacy asked in disbelief.

"I suppose we really haven't a choice. He's come all this way," Gwen said. She positioned the ham on a plate and then began to slice cheese from a large wedge.

"But he obviously hates us—especially you," Beth said, testing the stew. "He would make a perfect villain in one of my books. He's got beady eyes."

"I thought you said he was dashing, with the bluest eyes you'd ever seen," Gwen said, amusement in her tone. She drew a deep breath. "His eyes are quite beautiful and very blue." She cut two more pieces of ham, then put aside the knife. "You mustn't be too hard on him. He obviously loved Harvey a great deal, so we have that in common. We simply have to convince him that I am neither a gold digger nor a killer." She smiled at her sisters but inwardly felt as if the impossibility of her statement was a weight around her neck. How did one go about convincing a man unknown to them that he could trust them and believe their every word?

Beth and Lacy delivered the food to the table while Gwen brought the coffeepot. She poured Joe a cup and watched him take a large gulp before setting the mug back down.

"Good as usual, Miss Gwen."

"Thanks, Joe." She topped off his cup, then moved to the other man. "Mr. Bishop, would you care for coffee?"

He looked at the table rather than meet her gaze. "Coffee is fine."

Gwen poured him a cup, then motioned for Beth to bring the cream and sugar. It was a routine they were all quite familiar with. Meanwhile, Joe began to pile his plate with food.

"Ain't no one got better grub than you girls."

"I didn't realize you'd be coming through, Joe. I can fix something else if this isn't enough. I do have pie, as well."

"No need to fix anything else, Miss Gwen. There ain't time. I've gotta push on. Just pack me up a couple of pieces of that pie, and I'll eat them on the road." He looked at the other man and back to the girls. "I just wanna know one thing."

Gwen looked at the older man. "And what would that be?"

"You lettin' this man stay, or do I take him with me?"

Gwen looked at Harvey's brother as the man raised his eyes to hers. Something told Gwen that this man wouldn't be forced to go with anyone. He wasn't a city dandy to be pushed around. She could see in his eyes that he was a man of decision and determination.

"He can stay, Joe. He has business here, just as he's said. Maybe stop back by for him on your way through."

"What kind of business, if I might ask?" Rafe questioned, standing just inside the dining room.

45

Gwen frowned. "What can I do for you, Mr. Reynolds?"

"I was hoping to buy a pie or two. You got any for sale?"

"I'll have some this evening. Right now I'm down to my last one. Come back around five."

Rafe nodded and looked at Bishop. "So what is it that brings you to town, stranger?"

"I hardly see that as any concern to you."

"Well, sure it is. You're a customer, and customers are always my business," Rafe said with a big grin. "My saloon is just next door. If you're staying here, you'll want to know that, because these little ladies don't serve spirits. They're temptress women."

"Although I'm sure these women can be tempting, do you actually mean *temperance* women?" Bishop asked.

Beth was snorting a giggle under her breath. Rafe was not happy to be corrected but held his temper. "What I mean is they don't agree with alcohol of any kind."

"That suits me quite well, for I myself am a temperance man," Bishop replied. He looked at Joe and added, "I have my horse. You needn't worry about coming back for me, now that I am familiar with the trail to Salt Lake." His expression seemed to darken as he muttered, *"Hoc volo, sic iubeo; sit pro ratione voluntas."*

"And what is that supposed to mean?" Lacy questioned.

"It's been my experience that men who have to hide behind foreign words do so because they have nothing of import to say," Beth said, sticking her nose in the air as if greatly offended.

The man smiled. "It's Latin and means, 'This is what I want, such are my orders: my desire is reason enough.' " He fixed his gaze on Gwen. "In other words, I'll leave when I have what I came for."

To Gwen, his statement sounded more like a threat than

mere comment. *What have you come for?* She couldn't imagine that she could offer him anything that would satisfy or justify a trip of this great length. Still, something deep within told her that everything in her life was about to change yet again. The curse was working its tiresome strategies against her. There was nothing to do but endure and hope for a painless conclusion. Unfortunately, Mr. Bishop didn't look like the painless type.

CHAPTER FOUR

"I hate the fact that Rafe has brought in prostitutes," Beth said, stretching to look out the kitchen window. She knew even though there was still plenty of light, it wouldn't be long before the cowboys started whooping it up at the saloon. Several had already arrived and were no doubt starting their night of entertainment.

"The alcohol was bad enough, but now this," Gwen replied as she pulled two perfectly roasted chickens from the oven. "I wonder if Mr. Bishop likes chicken. I never thought to ask."

"I think you've done more than enough by allowing him to rent a room," Lacy interjected as she stomped across the kitchen on her way out the back. "I think you should have sent him elsewhere."

"Look, I don't want him here any more than you do," Gwen

replied. She put the chicken aside and checked the vegetables that were simmering on the stove. Beth watched her sister's meticulous attention to detail as she mixed in just a pinch of this and that. "I figure," Gwen continued, "it's best to allow him to be here, state his business, and then see him on his way. Otherwise, he might think we have something to hide."

Lacy frowned as she picked up two water buckets. Beth was quite certain that none of this set well with her younger sister. "Yes, but he doesn't want to talk with all of us present, which makes me think *he's* the one with something to hide. He's remained in his room all afternoon. I'm certain he'll seek you out this evening."

Gwen put her spoon aside. "Then perhaps you and Beth should make yourselves scarce. I might as well talk to him and send him on his way."

Beth frowned. "How can we even be sure he *is* Harvey's brother? He looks nothing like him."

"He acts nothing like him, either. Harvey was always so sweet," Lacy added.

"Why should he lie about that?" Gwen asked. "It's not like Harvey had any wealth or hit it rich in the mines. Perhaps Mr. Bishop thinks that he did come into a fortune, but we can easily show him otherwise. And if he doesn't believe us, we can point him to Virginia City and Norris. They can certainly vouch for the fact that Pa and Harvey never made much more in gold than saw us through from day to day. If Pa hadn't sold his claim, we wouldn't have even had the money to get started here. It's not like we're living a life of ease."

"I doubt that means anything to Mr. Bishop. He's obviously after something here. We just need to find out what that might be," Beth reasoned. She checked the two dried apple pies and noted they were cool. "Should I take these over to Rafe?"

Gwen shook her head. "Let him come for them. I've seen several rough-looking characters make their way over there already. No sense putting ourselves in danger. If he happens to forget, we can always get Simon or Nick to take them."

Beth nodded and went back to tending her biscuit dough. "I'll get these in the oven if the chicken is done."

"It is. Go right ahead. Lacy, please get the water, then see that the table is set. Don't forget that Jerry and Patience Shepard are joining us for supper."

"I hope that doesn't mean Deputy Shepard is coming, as well," Lacy said with obvious contempt in her tone.

"I don't know if he is or not, but you might as well set an extra place just in case he does."

Muttering, Lacy took herself out the back door while Beth straightened after placing the biscuits in the oven. She looked at her older sister and couldn't help but feel a sense of protection. Gwen had seen them through so many bad situations and had tried her best to be a mother to Beth and Lacy, even though she wasn't that much older than either of her siblings. Beth loved her for trying, though, and would have given her life to protect Gwen.

It seemed strange that it was just the three of them now. Pa had always been there for them, even if his wild dreams had taken them all over the country. Gwen was always encouraging Beth, who really only wanted to settle down in one place and stop all the travel.

Someday, we'll stop moving, Gwen had once assured Beth. *One day, we'll have a real home.* And while the Gallatin House wasn't exactly a real home, it was the closest Beth had known since her mother died, and she didn't want to leave.

"Maybe Mr. Bishop thinks Harvey owned part of this establishment," Gwen said rather absentmindedly. She was now endeavoring to make coffee and had just put in twice as much as needed when Beth managed to stop her.

"Why don't you let me see to this," she more stated than questioned. "I know Pa said not to make the coffee too weak, but this strength would even cause Pa to reconsider his declaration."

Gwen only then seemed to notice what she'd done. "Oh no! I'm sorry. It's just . . . well . . . that man has me so flustered."

"I know," Beth replied sympathetically. "Do you have any idea what he might be looking for?"

"None at all. You know how it was when Harvey came to us. He had that battered-up suitcase with his only change of clothes and little else. If Mr. Bishop thinks he had something of value, he's much mistaken."

"Could he maybe just need information?"

Gwen met Beth's eyes. "There's precious little of that, as well. After all, if what Mr. Bishop is telling us is true, then Harvey fabricated a great deal. Any information I could offer would be tainted by that."

A knock sounded on the front door and was soon followed by a woman's voice calling out in greeting.

"It's Mrs. Shepard," Beth declared. "You go ahead. I'll take care of everything here. Lacy will be back in just a shake, and we'll finish off the table."

As Gwen exited the room, Lacy came through carrying heavy buckets of steaming water. "I'm going to have Nick look at those cart wheels. They're getting looser all the time. I think I spilled more water than I managed to get back with."

"Just pour it in the sink. The hot water will soak the pans nicely while we have our supper." Beth placed the two roasted chickens on platters, then poured the drippings into a large cast-iron skillet and began to make gravy.

"I was thinking of having a soak out there later," Lacy said as she managed the buckets. "Want to join me?"

"I don't think it'd be a good time to do it. You know there are a lot of rowdies over at Rafe's."

"We can lock the gate. Pa built a high enough fence that no one is going to get much of a look. And if they do, we have our swimming clothes."

"I know, but it's still a risk. It's always harder to keep the hot springs private when the saloon is busy. Let's wait for a nice evening when there aren't so many strangers around. For now, we really need the table set. The Shepards just got here a few minutes ago."

"Oh goodness, I completely forgot about the table." Lacy finished pouring the water in the sink before hurrying to the cupboard for the dishes.

"Look what Patience has brought us," Gwen said as she entered the kitchen with the woman close on her heels.

"Butter and more cream!" Beth declared as she spied the items in her sister's arms.

Patience, an attractive woman in her mid-forties, smiled. "I knew you could use it. I'd rather sell it to you than take it elsewhere. At least here I know it will be used for proper meals. I'd hate to tell you what Dave said he caught them doing with it at the saloon."

Beth's eyes widened as thoughts of her dime novels came to mind. Had she ever read about butter and cream being illicitly used?

"No, I think it best we not know," Gwen commented as she put the items away. "We need more ice," she said as she closed the icebox door. "I miss the times when we can just store it outside."

"Yes, but then you'd have to cut more wood and worry

about keeping the house warm enough for guests," Patience reminded.

Beth thought Patience Shepard one of the few women she'd most like to pattern herself after. It was said that the mother of three had come from a wealthy eastern family who all but shunned her when she married beneath her social standing. Over the years, however, her parents had apparently seen fit to forgive her enough to take in Patience's two youngest children— daughters who longed for civilization and finishing school. It had been hard for Mrs. Shepard to lose both her daughters at once, but they had made such a fuss, there seemed no other option. Even their father decided it would be in everyone's best interest. The girls left for finishing school the previous fall and only recently sent a letter home indicating their intention to remain with their grandparents.

Beth poured the bubbling gravy into a gravy boat. "Have you heard anything from the girls?" She looked up to catch Patience's frown and wished she'd refrained from bringing up the reminder of their absence.

"No. I expect a letter from my parents most anytime. They'll tell me all the reasons why the girls should stay, and I'll have little say in the matter. I suppose it's their revenge for my leaving the way I did."

Gwen put her arm around the older woman's shoulders. "That's nonsense. What parent would seek revenge on their child?"

Patience drew a deep breath. "Mine would. They were so bitter at my marrying Jerry and moving west. They didn't approve when he was an accountant, but then when he turned rancher, that completely put us at odds. He might as well have announced that he was setting up a brothel."

"He's such a sweet man," Beth said. "So gentle in spirit,

and smart, too. He runs that ranch in better order than ten men with twice his experience."

This made Patience smile. "Some days he makes enough mess for ten men. Between him, Dave, and the hands, I have more than enough to do, but I miss my girls."

"Speaking of Dave," Gwen said, glancing toward the dining room, "will he be joining us?"

"No. He told me he'd be busy."

"Table's set," Lacy announced. "You want me to put some of the food out?"

"Yes," Gwen replied. "Go ahead."

Beth was already pulling the biscuits from the oven. "Don't forget the mashed potatoes in the warming bin," she called after Lacy.

Hank Bishop sat down to the table of strangers and nodded toward the only other man at the table. He extended his hand. "Hank Bishop," he told the man.

"Jerry Shepard. Glad to meet you, Hank." They shook hands. "Where are you from?"

"Back East," Hank replied.

"I might have guessed. Patience and I were once from Springfield, Massachusetts."

"I know the area," Hank admitted. He offered nothing more. He knew they expected him to mention where he'd come from, but at this time he saw no need to.

"Jerry, would you offer the blessing?" Gwen asked.

They all bowed their heads as the man began to pray. Hank watched them in fascination. He hadn't prayed in years—not since he'd been a young teen. He marveled at the casual way the woman referred to the older man. Seemed everyone out here just called each other by their given names.

"Amen."

A murmuring of *amen*s followed. Did they somehow suppose that it blessed the food even more if they added their approval to the prayer?

"Hank, this is my wife, Patience. Our son, Dave, is one of the sheriff deputies in the area, and we have two daughters who are living in Springfield with their grandparents."

Hank nodded. "Pleased to meet you, ma'am." Again, he could tell by the look of expectation on the faces around him that they waited for him to be more forthcoming with his background. And again, he disappointed them.

"And are you also in the business of the law, Mr. Shepard?"

"Call me Jerry. Everyone does. No time for formalities out here. We're all far too dependent on each other to stand on social dictates. But in answer to your question, no. I ranch and raise a few head of dairy cows. Patience also has a nice number of chickens. In fact, we raised the birds that grace the table tonight. Sure smells good, Gwen."

"Thanks. You might as well carve," she instructed.

Jerry quickly went to work while Patience took a turn at asking Hank questions. "So what brings you to these parts, Hank?"

He clenched his jaw momentarily—a bad habit he had when trying to analyze a situation's importance. "I had some family business." He smiled ever so slightly and changed the subject. "I must say, this part of the country is quite beautiful. I took the train to Salt Lake City. I didn't think much of the passing territories west of the Mississippi, but this valley has tremendous merit. What crops do they grow here?"

Patience smiled. Hank surmised she didn't even realize she'd been refocused on a different line of conversation.

"Wheat and barley, mostly," Patience replied.

"But not corn," Jerry added. "There just isn't good enough land or enough time to grow decent corn. Potatoes do quite well, however."

"Yes. They grow very well in my garden."

"I wish I could say the same," Gwen declared. "I've tried for two years. I must not have your green thumb or talent for tilling."

"Perhaps the mineral content in the ground create an inhospitable base for such things."

"The mineral content?" Lacy asked, staring hard at Hank. "What has that got to do with it?"

Hank shrugged. "With the hot springs here, I thought perhaps the ground might have a higher concentration of minerals, such as sodiums and sulfates. Such materials can often aid or interfere with the growth patterns in a variety of vegetation. I propose that it might very well be the mineral content in the soil that impedes your sister's efforts rather than some failing in her ability."

"Oh," Lacy said, clearly not expecting the depth of his answer.

"Are we too late for supper?" Nick asked as he and Simon snuck in from the kitchen.

Gwen laughed and took the matter in good nature. "Not at all. Lacy, please get another place setting. Since Dave isn't joining us, we just need one more."

Hank noted the ease in which she handled the matter. His own mother had held many a dinner party, and the care and meticulous effort that went into each event always took more time and staging than the party itself. Apparently in the West, things were done on a more casual basis.

Simon and Nick each took a seat while Lacy retrieved

another setting. "You boys want coffee?" she asked as she positioned a plate and silverware in front of Simon.

"Of course," they replied in unison.

"I nearly forgot about the coffee," Beth said, getting up rather quickly. "I'll get it."

"Mr. Bishop is the brother of Harvey," Gwen stated suddenly. She smiled only a moment in Hank's direction, but her gaze never quite reached him. "He is here on behalf of their mother."

"I thought Harvey said he was an orphan without living family," Patience replied.

"I thought so, too," Gwen answered. She passed her plate to Jerry, who added a generous portion of chicken before handing it back.

"Hank, you want white meat or dark?" Jerry asked.

"Either is fine." Hank wasn't used to such simple fare, to be honest. Chicken was a staple of lower society. He found himself longing for a succulent pheasant or roasted rack of lamb. Chicken had never appealed all that much. Generally, it was too scrawny and dry to suit his taste.

Beth poured a round of coffee for everyone, then excused herself to put on another pot. Gwen passed Hank the bowl of mashed potatoes, but her eyes did not lift to meet his. He took the bowl and spooned himself a portion. He was used to servants doing such menial tasks, but he supposed this was yet another way things were done in the West.

The meal continued with an odd assortment of conversations that involved Harvey and the love people in the community held for him, as well as the now-departed Mr. Gallatin.

"Harvey was such a dear," Patience began. "He once helped me gather my best laying hens when they managed to get out of their pen. I'm still not sure what or who managed to break down the gate, but Harvey even fixed that."

Hank tried to imagine his brother chasing down chickens. The thought amused him, but he didn't let on.

"Then there was the time he came and helped with roundup," Jerry added. "He was clumsy with a branding iron at first, but he soon got the hang of it."

Hank marveled at the stories. It was as if they were speaking about a complete stranger. Harvey had been such a fragile young man when he'd left home. Sickly in his youth, their mother had done much to protect him from the harsher aspects of life. Of course, their stepfather hadn't thought much of this. Frankly, neither had Hank. He often thought Harvey was merely playing a game for sympathy. Yet these people admired his brother. In fact, to hear them tell it, his brother was a one-man army of ability and good deeds.

"Your brother was definitely a blessing to this community. He was so handy," Patience said, shaking her head. "Such a pity that he should have died from measles."

"Measles?" Hank asked. This was the first time he'd heard of what had caused his brother's passing.

"Yes. There was a small epidemic. The girls had already had their bouts as children," Patience said, nodding toward Gwen and her sisters. "No one really thought about it. Harvey said he'd been quite ill as a child, and we all figured he'd had his time of it, as well. But that wasn't to be."

"Such a loss." Jerry met Hank's gaze. "Your brother is sorely missed."

Hank said nothing and turned his attention instead to the food, finding it incredibly delicious. *Perhaps it's just that I've been on the road too long.* Since Cheyenne, the meals had been less than desirable and seldom palatable. No doubt that was the reason that, within minutes, he was asking for seconds.

He looked up and found Gwen watching him with an expression that seemed caught somewhere between amazement and curiosity. It was almost as if she were trying to place him from another time and location. Perhaps he'd misjudged her. Perhaps.

Giving her a brief smile, he took his plate back from Jerry. "The meal is quite good, Mrs. Bishop."

He saw her stiffen, but she quickly looked away. "Thank you," she murmured, then fixed her attention on her plate.

Hank thought it rather odd but said nothing more. His stomach might have protested too much had he wasted time talking instead of eating.

CHAPTER FIVE

Hank got up early the next day and began his investigation of the Gallatin House. He started with the outbuildings. Looking around a small storage shed, he found nothing among its contents that suggested Harvey had once owned it. Knowing his brother as he did, Hank had figured Harvey would have found a way to live a life of ease. Instead, he'd come to the Wild West and worked hard enough to earn the merit of his neighbors. Maybe he didn't know Harvey as well as he'd thought.

The idea troubled Hank. He had been the big brother—the one to help guide Harvey into manhood. He'd also been the one to defend Harvey when their stepfather had gotten too ill-tempered. After Harvey had run away—taking several family treasures with him, as well as a stack of stock certificates that were worth an enormous amount of money—Hank no longer thought Martin Bishop all that hard on his brother. Apparently Harvey needed more guidance than Hank had realized.

The dark, musty shed offered little light by which to explore, but the place was kept in neat order and made Hank's exploration easier. There were several old crates, a barrel that looked to hold old clothes hardly better than rags, and a small hatbox hidden behind several pieces of old furniture and odds and ends. Hank thought perhaps this was where he might find his brother's things, but instead, his search revealed a stack of dime novels.

He smiled to himself, wondering if it was the feisty Lacy Gallatin or the more romantic Beth who'd hidden them here. There was little that led him to believe it might have been Gwen who had carefully concealed such a habit.

Leaving the shed, he went to explore the hot springs. A small covered area offered some shelter from prying eyes, but most of the wooden pool was open to the skies. A nice wooden fence had also been secured around the pool, and he smiled to see that someone had even chinked between the planks to make a solid wall of privacy. Hank promised himself he would later explore the comforts of the steaming springs. The very thought of soaking his sore muscles gave Hank something to look forward to.

Moving from the hot springs area across the yard to the chicken coop and the outhouses, Hank turned up nothing of interest. Disappointed, he made his way inside and found all three girls bustling around the kitchen. Avoiding contact, he hurried back upstairs, thinking it might be the perfect opportunity to look around. There he located a small, unlocked storage area that ran alongside the stairs.

He had barely made it into the enclosed passage,

however, when Hank found himself caught red-handed in his snooping.

"What are you doing here?" He turned and found Beth, hands on hips. "This is not a public area."

Thinking quickly, Hank lied. "I got turned around. I thought it was my room. Obviously I was mistaken."

Beth frowned. "Obviously. This is a storage room. We keep linens and supplies here, but little else." She took up a stack of clean tablecloths. "If you're quite finished, you can do me a favor and close the door behind us."

Hank nodded and followed her out. He could see by the look on her face that she didn't believe him, but Beth Gallatin seemed too polite to call him an out-and-out liar.

"Your room is over there," Beth said, pointing. She offered nothing more, however, and quietly made her way downstairs.

Figuring it was best to at least make a pretense of wanting to be there, Hank entered the room and closed the door behind him. He stared at the room for a moment, wondering if there was anything he'd missed. There were two small beds, and he'd already stripped them and turned the mattresses on each one. Remaking the beds as orderly as the Gallatin sisters were capable of doing proved to be much harder.

After about fifteen minutes, Hank decided enough time had passed. He made his way downstairs to find Lacy about to head up.

"I was just coming to find you. Breakfast is on the table."

"Thank you," he said, smoothing his vest. He noted a dark smudge on his white shirt and frowned. "I wonder, Miss Gallatin, do you or your sisters take in the laundry of guests here at Gallatin House?"

Lacy cast a glance over her shoulder, her long, cinnamon

hair flying in wild disarray as she did. "Yes, but there is also a Chinese laundry over in Bozeman."

He smiled. "I'm certain I needn't travel that far away for clean shirts."

"Suit yourself." Lacy made her way to the far end of the table and joined her sisters.

"Good morning, Mr. Bishop," Gwen said as Hank took his seat. "I hope we haven't disturbed you from something more important."

"Not at all."

The girls lowered their heads, and Beth offered a brief thanks for their provision and welfare. She also added a comment that nearly made Hank laugh out loud.

"And please, Lord, help Mr. Bishop to find what it is he's looking for so that he can hurry home to the ones who love him."

Obviously no one here could claim that feeling. When Gwen and Lacy offered hearty *amen*s to the prayer, he could only presume they were all in agreement. They hoped he would leave soon.

But why? If there were nothing to hide, surely they wouldn't mind a paying customer staying on indefinitely. He watched them closely as they shared platters of ham and eggs before finally handing them over to him.

"Would you care for biscuits, Mr. Bishop?"

He met Gwen's expectant expression and nodded. "I would, thank you. I find your biscuits to be quite light, not at all the throwing pieces that I endured on the trip west."

Gwen actually smiled at this. "I can well imagine. It's hard to keep supplies and ingredients in the middle of nowhere."

"Yet you manage it quite well."

"This is hardly the middle of nowhere, Mr. Bishop," Beth

protested. "We are a stage crossroads. We see more than our share of people. A stage is, in fact, due to spend the night here. You'll see just how busy we can be. This stage is the regular one to Butte. Quite a few passengers will be heading west to find their fortunes."

"I see. Forgive me for implying you were less than the center of civilization."

Beth's cheeks flushed as she looked at her plate, but it was Gwen who rose to her defense. "No one is suggesting such a thing, Mr. Bishop. My sisters and I, however, know exactly what it is like to be located in an area without even these meager amenities. Life in the territories can often be quite isolated."

"I can well believe it, and I apologize if I offended." He buttered a biscuit and spread a liberal amount of jam on it before taking a bite. It fairly melted in his mouth. Hank had never had anything quite so good in all of his life.

"My sister tells me you were looking for something earlier," Gwen stated as if bringing up something of little import. "Perhaps if you were to tell me what it is you are searching for, we could be of help."

Hank considered her words for a moment. "And why would you be willing to help me?"

"Why not?"

He could see that Gwen's expression suggested sincerity, but he was still not convinced of her innocence. Hank took up his coffee cup and considered his response for a moment.

"I know that none of you trust me. I suppose I cannot blame you, as you have no reason to believe I am who I say. I can tell you about Harvey and his life prior to coming here, but that still would offer little to convince you. However, my brother was far from destitute when he left home. He took with him several items that belonged to our mother and stepfather. For years we had no idea where he had gone, and it wasn't until paying a private investigator a hefty sum that I managed to track him this far."

"Obviously he didn't want to be found," Lacy commented. "He was an adult—a grown man."

"A grown man who robbed from his family," Hank stated firmly.

"I just find that impossible to believe, Mr. Bishop." Gwen crossed her arms. "Harvey was such a decent soul. He loved people, and he gave of himself like no one I've ever known. He was—"

"Yes, yes, practically perfect," Hank interjected. "So I've heard."

Gwen seemed taken aback by his harsh statement. Hank hadn't really meant to upset her, but it was obvious she remembered his brother as nearly angelic—a habit often associated with loved ones of the dead.

"You really are a very rude man," Beth declared without warning. She narrowed her blue-green eyes. "We may live in a less-than-civilized land, but we still expect our guests to conduct themselves in an appropriate manner."

"I apologize again, Miss Gallatin," Hank said, putting down his coffee cup. "Perhaps now you might understand why I wish to speak with Mrs. Bishop privately."

"She's not Mrs. Bishop," Lacy countered.

"That's enough, Lacy." Gwen got to her feet. "Mr. Bishop, I am quite happy to speak to you privately, but I have nothing to say to you. Harvey came to us with very little. Certainly nothing of riches. Perhaps he once did, as you accuse, but I assure you by the time he made it to our company, he was as poor as a man could ever be."

"Why do I get the feeling that you are all conspiring to

hide the truth?" Hank leaned back in his chair and crossed his arms. "I can see the contempt in your expressions, as well as the guarded air in your conversation. I am an educated man—Harvard, to be exact. I know very well when I'm being avoided and ignored and feel that in this situation you are guilty of both."

"Avoided? Ignored?" Beth questioned. "You've hardly been out of your room—except to sneak around—since coming here. If you feel avoided or ignored, that is entirely your own doing."

"Well, I am here now, yet I feel all three of you are playing a game with me." He narrowed his blue eyes. "I believe that my brother came here with the articles he stole and most likely gifted them to your sister or sold them to lavish her with attention."

Gwen laughed out loud. It was a bitter laugh that held no humor. "Yes, you can see that I am quite lavished."

"You could be hiding the articles in question." Hank watched her closely. "The fact is, my brother could have showed up appearing to be quite wealthy, and this appealed to you enough to force him into marriage."

Lacy slapped her hands on the table. "You are out of line, mister."

Gwen's mouth had dropped open, and her eyes filled with tears. She looked at Hank in such an expression of disbelief that he immediately knew he'd misjudged her. No one was that good of an actress.

"I loved your brother," she began.

"If he really was your brother," Beth muttered. Gwen looked at Beth as if to silence her. "Well, he has no proof."

"That doesn't matter now." Gwen returned her tear-filled

gaze to Hank. "I loved Harvey with all of my heart. He knew that. I really don't care whether you believe it."

Hank found himself regretting his strong words. He watched Gwen hurry from the room, caught the angry stares of her sisters and knew that he might very well be asked to leave.

"Perhaps," he said, trying hard to mask his own frustration, "I was a bit overbearing."

"Perhaps?" Lacy replied.

"And you were rude. You certainly are no gentleman," Beth stated rather dramatically.

Though Hank would like to have finished his breakfast, he thought perhaps it would be best if he left. "I am sorry, ladies. I do have a tendency to . . ."

"Put your foot in your mouth?" Lacy questioned.

He met her eyes and nodded. "I suppose that suffices as well as anything. I do apologize."

"Talk's cheap, mister." Lacy got to her feet and shoved her chair under the table. "You've hurt our sister's feelings. Gwen never did anything to harm you or cause you grief, and the sooner you realize that, the better. I never once saw your brother with more than a nickel to his name, but if you intend to learn anything more from Gwen, you're going to have to change your methods."

"And your manners," Beth said, getting to her feet, as well. "If you intend to remain here at Gallatin House, you will definitely learn to keep your very rude comments to yourself."

That evening with a house full of stage travelers, all male, Beth and Lacy did their best to handle the work load. Gwen wasn't herself, and after pouring hot coffee on herself and nearly dumping a full pie on one of the men, Beth suggested she go lie down for a brief rest. To her surprise, Gwen did exactly that. Beth had never seen her sister so upset or frazzled. Mr. Bishop's accusations had completely unhinged Gwen's usually competent nature and easygoing spirit.

Beth couldn't help but watch Mr. Bishop as he partook of the evening meal. He didn't seem in the leastwise upset with himself or what had happened. He ate as much as ever, complimented their ability in the kitchen, and shared general conversation with the men from the stage. He appeared a carefree individual, enjoying a leisure trip.

After most of the men had taken themselves from supper to Rafe's Saloon, Beth began clearing the table. She had fretted and stewed over what should be done with Mr. Bishop throughout the evening. Standing in the kitchen watching him, she could see him focus on the coffee cup in his hand. He had his back to her so she couldn't see his face, but she imagined the stern expression and fixed thoughts. No doubt he was plotting against her sister.

"Oh, what I wouldn't give to be a man sometimes," she muttered.

Lacy had just returned with hot water for the dishes. "What did you say?"

Beth reached out to help her with the buckets. "I just wish sometimes I were a man. I would challenge that Mr. Bishop to a fight. I'd knock him out cold and then he'd be out of the way—at least for a few hours."

"So knock him out in another way," Lacy said with a wicked grin.

"What are you talking about?"

Lacy put down her bucket and went to the far pantry cupboard. She moved a wooden box in place and stepped atop it to reach the highest shelf. Rummaging around the canned goods there, she finally pulled out a couple of bottles. "Remember these?"

"That case of laudanum Pa bought," Beth said in a hushed whisper. She gave a hurried, sidelong glance to see if Mr. Bishop had heard her, but he appeared lost in his own thoughts.

Lacy grinned and stepped off the box. Pressing close to her sister, she whispered, "Pa said a few spoonfuls of this would settle a man into the arms of Orpheus."

"Morpheus," Beth corrected softly. "Orpheus charmed wild beasts with his music. Morpheus made people sleep and dream."

"Well, we want to charm a wild beast *and* make him sleep."

Beth laughed. "That we do." She took the bottle and poured a liberal dose into a fresh cup. "If a couple of teaspoons is good, a couple more ought to be great."

"Just don't kill him," Lacy whispered. "I don't want to have to explain that to Dave Shepard and the sheriff. They'd never understand."

Beth nodded. "No, I suppose they wouldn't." She put the cup down on the counter. "Mr. Bishop," she called as she moved into the dining room. "I have a bit of coffee left over if you'd care to finish it."

At first it looked like he wouldn't go for it, but after a moment Hank nodded and handed her his cup. "It is good coffee. Thank you."

Beth smiled sweetly even though she felt like tearing the man's eyes out. "You like two sugars, right?"

"Yes, and cream, please."

"Of course."

She hurried into the kitchen and switched out the cup.

Pouring the coffee to join the laudanum, she quickly added the sugar and cream. "There. It's perfect." She exchanged a glance with Lacy and smiled. "Mother's milk, as Pa used to say."

Beth made her way to where Hank Bishop sat. "Would you care for some more pie to go along with this?"

"No, I'm quite satisfied with this," Hank said, taking the coffee. He took a long sip and smiled. "Thank you."

Beth smiled again and removed the remaining dishes from the table. "Just let me know if you need anything else."

Half an hour later, Lacy wasn't so sure it had been a good idea to drug Mr. Bishop. "He must weigh two hundred pounds."

"It just seems that way," Beth said as they wrestled Bishop's sleeping form up the back staircase.

Thump! Thump! As Lacy pulled Hank up the steps, his backside smacked against the stairs while Beth fought to control his legs.

"He's gonna wonder what hit him," Lacy said, gasping for breath.

"Let him wonder. Maybe he'll . . . think twice . . ." Beth strained for air, "before insulting . . . our sister again."

"What if Gwen catches us?"

"I suppose we'll just try to explain."

They heard raucous singing coming from the main staircase as they managed to drag Hank into his room. They'd barely closed the door before several men stumbled up the stairs and made their way to their own rooms.

Beth leaned hard against the door just in case any of them mistook Bishop's room for their own. In a few minutes, however, it quieted in the hall, and she felt certain the crisis had been averted.

"Come on, let's get him into bed."

"I can't lift him into bed," Lacy protested. "Let's just get him a pillow and a blanket and let him sleep on the floor."

"That won't be very comfortable," Beth said.

"It's the best we can do. Come on." Lacy pulled a pillow off the bed and motioned Beth to take the covers. "He's gonna wonder what happened to him anyway. Might as well not get ourselves injured in the process. I'm gonna need to soak in the springs tonight, for sure."

They quickly tended Hank, tucking him in rather like a mother might a small child. Beth frowned and took up the lamp Lacy had positioned on the nightstand before they'd retrieved Hank's sleeping form.

"Let's get out of here," Beth said, opening the door, "before someone finds us and wonders what we're up to."

"Someone is already wondering what you're up to," Gwen said.

CHAPTER SIX

Hank awoke slowly, as if from a deep, clouded dream. His mouth tasted awful and had a cottony dryness to it that made him long for a tall, cold drink of water. Yawning, he sat up and winced at the pain in his back. Looking around him, Hank's confusion only mounted.

"Why am I on the floor?"

He looked at the bed and then to where he sat. Could he have fallen out of bed? That seemed highly unlikely. Especially given the fact that his pillow had accompanied him and landed under his head. Further investigation revealed that Hank was fully clothed. He even wore his boots.

Struggling to his feet, Hank eased back onto the mattress of the bed and stared up at the ceiling for several minutes. Why couldn't he remember? He rubbed his closed eyes and tried to force his thoughts to clear.

He was at the Gallatin House. He'd wanted to talk with Gwen last night, but she'd been offended by something he'd said. What was it? He shook his head and yawned again.

A quick glance at his watch told him it was still early. He could hear activity going on in the hall and remembered that a stage had come in last night. He knew there were at least half a dozen men traveling and vaguely remembered them at the supper table. He recalled the men getting up from the table and heading to the saloon.

"But I stayed to talk to Harvey's wife." He opened his eyes and tucked his hands under his head. Clasping his fingers together, he stared thoughtfully at the butter-colored ceiling.

The wafting aroma of fresh coffee prompted his thoughts. He had been drinking coffee. There was pie, too. He remembered because the girls had offered him seconds. He'd passed on the dessert but had nursed several cups of coffee as he waited for Gwen to return to the room. She never came. At least, not that he could remember.

Hank sat up, moaning softly as pain spread across his back. What in the world had caused him to be so sore and stiff? He rubbed his muscles as best he could and got to his feet. His clothes were hopelessly wrinkled, but there was little to be done about it. He hadn't had time to get his other things washed. This had been his last clean shirt. He'd heard the girls offer to do laundry for one of the stage travelers, so he supposed he could pay them to take on his clothes, as well. As for now, there was nothing he could do but go downstairs as he was. The coffee was beckoning him, along with the hope that it would wake him up and clear his mind.

The stairs seemed particularly challenging as Hank made his way to join the others. Every step seemed to jar him. Perhaps he was coming down with something.

"We're headin' out in ten minutes, whether you've had your breakfast or not," the stage driver bellowed from the bottom of the stairs.

Hank looked at the man, narrowing his eyes. "I'm afraid I'm not one of your passengers, but if any remain upstairs they most certainly could have heard that declaration."

The driver grunted and stomped off toward the front door. "Good to see you again, girls," he called out. "I'll be back through in a few days."

"Nice to see you too, Ralph. We'll be expecting you," Gwen called from the large, open sitting room.

Hank immediately fixed his gaze upon her. She wore a brown woolen skirt and a starched yellow blouse. The color served to draw out the blond highlights in her hair. She had attempted to pull her hair back, but uncooperative curls managed to slip out here and there, softening the severity of the look. Her smile faded as she turned to face Hank's scrutiny.

"Good morning, Mr. Bishop. Breakfast is on the table. You're late."

"I apologize. For my tardiness, as well as my harsh words of yesterday." He watched her for any reaction, but she seemed void of emotion. She stared at him for several seconds, then nodded and started for the dining room.

"Wait. Please." He crossed the room, trying his best to disguise the pain he felt. Gwen immediately noticed it, however.

"What's wrong? Did you sleep crooked—get a crick in your neck?"

"I'm afraid what ails me is much lower." He grinned and

rubbed his lower back with both hands. "I'm not exactly sure what happened."

He thought she seemed to pale a bit, but Gwen looked away so quickly he couldn't be sure. "We have some rubbing liniment if you need it," she said in a barely audible voice, then added, "but a soak in the hot springs would probably suit you better. We have fresh towels on the back porch."

"That sounds quite inviting. Thank you."

Several men came rushing from the dining room. "Thanks, Miss Gallatin. The food was delicious," one said as he fought to button his coat. "Wish we could stay a spell. I haven't seen gals so pretty since leavin' Colorado."

Gwen laughed. "I doubt Ralph would allow for the delay, but thank you for the compliment."

The others mumbled their thanks as they headed for the door. Hank moved aside to let two other men pass as they stumbled from the stairs and dragged toward the door.

"Gentlemen, I packed a little breakfast for you, since you slept too late to join us," Gwen announced. "The food is already on the stage."

The bleary-eyed men nodded and murmured thanks. Within moments, the house quieted considerably. Gwen stepped to the open doorway and out onto the porch. Hank, meanwhile, made his way to the breakfast table.

Beth and Lacy were already hard at work cleaning up the mess left behind. Beth smiled. "Coffee?"

It was like a bolt of lightning had struck. Hank remembered the young woman offering him coffee the night before. He remembered, too, that he had grown quite sleepy drinking the concoction. She must have drugged him! That's why he couldn't remember. That was also why he'd woken up on the floor.

He looked at her for a moment as she held up the pot. "I don't know," he said, toying with the cup on the table. "Seems like your coffee gives me a backache."

Beth's eyes widened innocently. "I've never heard anyone complain about my coffee before."

"Perhaps they've never had your special blend," Hank said. He held her gaze and shook his head.

"Maybe the wild Montana Territory is just too much for you to handle, Mr. Bishop," Beth suggested. "Maybe you should try to catch the stage before they pull out."

"Maybe it's not the territory but its women who are most dangerous," Hank countered.

"What's he going on about?" Lacy asked as she came into the room with a large tray. She began gathering up dirty dishes and looked as innocent as her sister.

Hank wasn't fooled. Someone had put something in his coffee last night. He was certain of it. They most likely had to haul him up the stairs—and probably dropped him several times on the way. No doubt that would account for his sore backside.

"Mr. Bishop's travels are catching up with him," Beth told her sister. "I was just suggesting maybe he should head on home and leave Montana behind him."

"As I said before, I'll leave when I have what I came for. Not until." He folded his hands together and eyed Beth quite seriously. "Should I have any more trouble from the coffee, it will be your backside that hurts. Not mine."

Beth lowered the pot, while Lacy gasped. "How dare you?" Beth looked at her sister and then back to Hank. "You are a very crude man."

"And you, Miss Gallatin, are a very dangerous young woman. Drugging people is not a safe thing to try, unless you are well acquainted with what you are doing. I'm hoping that is not the case. I'd like to keep you from further embarrassment and difficulty. I won't press charges against you this time, but should there be a second time, I won't hesitate to mete out my own brand of justice."

"What is this all about?" Gwen asked from the doorway.

"He's threatening Beth," Lacy said, hands on hips. Her blue eyes blazed in anger.

Hank finally allowed his gaze to leave Beth's face as he met Gwen's stunned expression. "I don't know who all had a hand in last night's adventures, but I was simply warning that it had better not happen again."

Gwen's expression suggested she clearly knew what he was talking about. "Beth, Lacy, go take care of the dishes and clean the kitchen."

Beth picked up the coffeepot and started to leave, but Hank held out his cup. "I'm going to trust that this pot hasn't been tampered with."

Beth poured him a cup. "I'm surprised you have the gumption to risk such a thing."

He smiled. The spunky young woman amused him. All of the Gallatin girls were full of spit and sass, as his mother would say. Hank was certain it had served them well in the harsh and isolated territory.

Gwen went into the kitchen while Beth and Lacy finished gathering things. She returned just as her sisters headed off to see to their work.

"I hope this stayed warm," she said, putting a plate of eggs and bacon, fried potatoes, and beans in front of him. "I have biscuits and gravy, as well." She left to retrieve the promised food as Hank began to dig in to the potatoes.

Hank thought long and hard about the girls and how he

could best handle the situation with them. He was desperate to get information. He had to find the things that belonged to him—to his mother—and do it soon. His mother would suffer greatly if she couldn't manage her affairs and regain her reputation. Reinstating her financial status would easily do that. The stocks Harvey had stolen were worth more money than he could have ever imagined. Their value had only increased as the years had gone by, and if he hadn't squandered them or used them for kindling, they would offer a tidy sum, with which their mother could spend her final days in ease.

Gwen put the gravy and biscuits in front of Hank. "Can I get you anything else?"

"No, this is fine. Very nice, thank you."

She eyed him curiously for a moment. It seemed she wanted to say something, but instead, she turned and went to work wiping down the other tables.

Watching her, Hank thought her quite a beautiful woman despite her simplicity. Or maybe because of it. The women he'd known and escorted in Boston were definitely cut from a different cloth. They would never have lowered themselves to do menial chores like cleaning a table. Not one of them would even consider working at a business such as a stage stop. Yet this woman and her sisters seemed more than happy to keep their house, care for strangers, and be independent of masculine assistance.

Such women, Hank thought, would never be intimidated into revealing information. They were much too self-sufficient. These women had faced worse adversaries. No, to get what he wanted from them, Hank would need to handle things in a completely different manner. He might even have to go so far as to woo one of them. But which one?

He considered the matter as he ate. There was Lacy Gallatin. She was a beauty with hair the color of cinnamon. Her manners suggested a certain shyness—even uneasiness—in dealing with people. The right man might be able to work such a woman to his advantage, but Hank worried that it would take too much time. The feisty tomboy was much too unpredictable. She gave the impression that she listened to no one and did just as she pleased. That wouldn't serve his purpose.

Beth was next in line. She made quite a feminine contrast next to her younger sister. Where Lacy was boots and grit, Beth was lace and flowers. There was something about her that suggested long walks with parasols and elegant teas. Hank could easily see her in a formal sitting room, gloved hands, hat perfectly placed on her head. But she'd already proven herself to be dangerous.

Hank was certain she was the mastermind behind his ill-fated cup of coffee. Beth might appear as soft as satin, but behind that façade, he could well imagine a wily creature capable of outmaneuvering her adversaries with crafty thought and planning.

That left Gwen. Hank saw her straighten and allowed himself to study her. His gaze was apparently intense enough to bring her attention back to him.

"Did you need something?"

Hank pushed back his plate and shook his head. "Not with regards to breakfast." A thought came to him. "I wondered if you might be willing to show me where my brother is buried."

Gwen's expression softened. "Of course. I'm sorry I didn't think of it. You must surely want to pay your respects. Let me put this away," she said, waving the cloth in her hand. "When I'm finished, I'll show you the way."

"Take your time."

Hank watched her bustle around. He couldn't hear her words as she spoke to her sisters, but he knew it had to do with his request as they glanced his way. Gwen would be the one to appeal to, despite her also having been his brother's wife. Her nature was gentle and kind. She was easily moved to be helpful, and her emotions could also be used to his advantage.

"If you're ready," Gwen said, approaching, "I'll just get my shawl and bonnet. It's not a far walk."

Hank got to his feet. "I'll wait for you on the porch."

He went outside and immediately noticed the large dog on the top step. The animal's coat glistened golden in the sunlight, and his expression seemed quite mournful. Hank had always loved dogs. He remembered begging his mother to allow them to have a pet.

"What's the matter, fella?" he asked, sitting down beside the animal.

The dog lifted his head momentarily and received Hank's greeting. Taking this as a friendly sign, Hank smiled. He reached out and began petting the dog with long strokes.

"That's Major Worthington," Gwen said from behind. "The Major hasn't been himself, I'm afraid, since Father died. It's only been a short time, and he continues to mourn him something fierce."

Hank looked into the animal's baleful eyes. Yes, it did appear he was sad. "It's hard to lose the ones we love," Hank murmured, not really knowing why. He got to his feet and faced Gwen. "I'm sorry about your father. What happened?"

Gwen made her way down the steps and headed for the road that ran in front of Gallatin House. "There was a shooting," she said.

Hank quickened his pace to keep up with her and was surprised to find Major Worthington at his side doing likewise. "A shooting?"

He saw the pain in Gwen's expression. "A bunch of cowboys were celebrating outside the saloon. They began to fire off their weapons, and without warning, a bullet hit my father."

"What was he doing in the midst of such rowdies?"

Gwen frowned. "It was my fault. I sent him to have the Lassiters sharpen some knives. He wouldn't have been out there otherwise."

"That hardly makes it your fault," Hank replied. "It was an accident."

"I suppose."

She left the main road for a smaller side road that barely could qualify as a path in Hank's estimation. She pointed ahead. "The cemetery is just up there. See where the trees are? It's not far from the river. My father is buried next to Harvey."

"It sounds like they were good friends," Hank said, remembering earlier conversations.

Gwen nodded. "He was like a son to Pa. My father thought him the most remarkable of young men." She paused and drew a deep breath. "I thought so, too."

"If you'll hold her," Nick instructed Lacy, "I'll tend this gash."

One of their prized brood mares had taken a fall and managed to puncture her side. The cut on her hindquarter was quite deep and couldn't be ignored.

"I've got her," Lacy called from in front of the nervous animal.

Nick went to work while Lacy spoke in a soothing tone to the mare. "That's a good girl. Easy now."

"I hope this doesn't bring on her foal," Nick said, shaking his head. "She's not due for another month." The minutes seemed to drag by as he worked. The horse was patient, but Nick knew she wouldn't tolerate his actions for long.

Lacy was encouraging. "I think she'll be fine. The fall itself could easily have killed her baby or caused the mare to go into labor. The fact that it hasn't happened is a good sign. Look how well she's already recovered." She pulled the mare's head close and stroked her rhythmically. Nick admired Lacy's way with animals.

"Yeah, I guess you're right. The baby is still active, so if we can just get her through this, we ought to be fine."

"That's a good girl," Lacy crooned.

Nick put ointment on the wound, but the mare wanted no part of it. She tried to sidestep Nick's ministering, then pressed forward, as if she could somehow escape the stall.

"Whoa. Whoa," Lacy called.

The animal would not be calmed, however. She pushed hard against Lacy, then backed against Nick. The action caused Nick to lose his footing, and he slammed up against the stall, the air rushing from his lungs. Without warning, the mare bucked up, trying her best to rear at Lacy, then slammed back down and kicked out behind her at Nick.

"Agh!" Nick cried out, then hit the ground before Lacy could still the mare. He writhed in pain and grabbed his left thigh. His entire leg felt as though it were instantly on fire.

"What's going on?" Beth asked as she entered the stable. "I could hear you yelling halfway across the road."

"Beth! Come quickly! Nick's been hurt," Lacy called.

Before he knew it, Beth was at his side. "I was just coming to find Lacy when I heard you hollering." She reached for his leg. "Is it broken?"

Nick pulled back. "No, but it hurts like the dickens."

"Let me see it."

Nick looked up and met her blue-green eyes. He felt his breath catch. "No. Don't touch it."

Beth laughed. "I've treated more injuries than you can shake a stick at. Just relax."

"I'm all right," Nick said, struggling to get to his feet. He didn't feel all right, but he wasn't about to tell her that. Beth Gallatin had stirred feelings inside him for some time. "I'll manage by myself."

It was clear to both Gallatin girls that he wasn't doing as well as he declared, however. He couldn't even put weight on the leg without it buckling under him. White-hot pain seared up his side with each attempt.

Beth quickly positioned herself next to Nick and wrapped her arm around his waist. "Lean on me. I'll help you get to the house, then I can look at the wound."

"Oh no, you won't," Nick said, flushing red. He could just imagine Beth's warm hands touching his bare leg.

Lacy started to laugh. "Beth, this isn't our brother or Pa. You can't be expecting Nick to just drop his pants so you can tend him."

Now it was Beth's turn to blush. "Sorry, Nick. I hadn't really . . . well . . . I wasn't thinking."

He trembled slightly, feeling a powerful sense of something he couldn't even put to words. Her nearness was too much. Nick longed to hold her—to return her embrace—but he feared what might come of it.

"What's all the yelling about?" Simon asked. He'd been working in the blacksmith shop and sweat poured from his head and neck, despite the coolness of the day.

"Nick took a blow to the leg," Lacy said. "Beth was trying to march him back to the house to tend his injury. We were just discussing the inappropriateness of such action."

Simon laughed and went to relieve Beth of her load and Nick of his suffering. "I'll manage this. Lacy, can you finish seeing to the mare?"

"Sure I can."

"Just put some salve on the injury and give her some feed. Keep her there in the stall," Nick commanded.

"I know what to do," Lacy called after them.

Nick looked up at his brother with gratitude. "Sure glad you came along. Those Gallatin girls don't give propriety a single thought when they've got a notion to do something."

Simon tightened his grip on Nick and chuckled. "Maybe not, but they sure are pretty. In case you haven't noticed."

Nick moaned and he wasn't sure if it was more from the leg or Simon's statement. "I've noticed," he said woefully. "I've noticed."

Lacy finished with the mare and left her calmly munching on fresh hay. The tack room was messy, so she figured to help Nick by straightening it. She put away some of the extra harnesses, then lifted a discarded saddle blanket to hang over the railing. She noted the fancy saddle that sat perched atop a wooden saddle rack. Lacy was certain this didn't belong to one of the Lassiter boys.

Just then she remembered that Hank had brought his own horse and saddle. No doubt a piece of this expense and quality belonged to him.

"It must be his—there's hardly any wear on it," she said with a smile. Running her hand over the cantle, Lacy noted something had been carved under the back housing on the skirt. There, tooled into the leather, were the initials *A. R.*

"Who is A. R., Mr. Bishop?" she quietly asked.

CHAPTER SEVEN

Hank thought the cemetery a perfect place for confession. Pines shrouded the graves from the intensity of the sun, leaving shadows to dance on the tombstones whenever the tree boughs waved in the gentle breeze.

"I've always liked to come here," Gwen said. She gazed across the dozen or so graves. "There's a peace here—a serenity that comforts me."

"I was thinking much the same. It seems like a place of reflection."

They said nothing more until Gwen stopped in front of the graves of her father and Hank's brother. The freshly mounded dirt reminded Hank yet again that this woman was still mourning a very new loss.

"It must be hard for you and your sisters, now that your father is gone."

"In many ways, it is harder than anything I've known, Mr. Bishop."

"Three women alone can hardly be a safe situation."

Gwen looked at him oddly. "We're as safe here as anywhere else."

"So you plan to stay?"

"For the time, Mr. Bishop, we do. We figure we have all summer to make up our minds as to what we want to do. Winter will mean a great deal more work, so we have to take that into consideration. However, I . . . well . . . never mind." She looked away and let out a deep breath.

Hank wanted to question her more but thought perhaps it was time for him to offer a little explanation of his own. After all, if she thought he was confiding in her, it might give Gwen the sense of their being friends rather than enemies.

"I'm sorry Harvey never told you about his family. I'm sorry he felt the need to run away and forget about us."

"He ran away? That just doesn't sound like Harvey."

"Listening to your friends speak of my brother the other night, I could scarcely believe they were discussing Harvey, either."

"Maybe it wasn't Harvey."

Hank looked at her hard. "What do you mean?"

"I don't know. Maybe the man who told me his name was Harvey Bishop was, in fact, someone else. Maybe he took your brother's name to hide his true identity. Men seem to do things like that all the time in the West. Or maybe his name was also Harvey Bishop, yet he wasn't related to you at all."

Hank felt sickened by the thought. Surely he hadn't come

all this way following the wrong man. There had to be some way to figure it all out.

"Let's suppose the man I knew really was your brother," Gwen said, looking back at the grave. "Perhaps you could describe him, and I could tell you if he looked as you remembered."

"I suppose it's a decent place to start." Hank thought for a moment. "Harvey was eighteen when he left home. That would have been the winter of 1873."

Gwen nodded. "The age would fit. He was nineteen when my father found him in November of 1874."

Hank nodded. "His birthday was in November. The tenth."

"Yes!" She looked encouraged by this news.

"Harvey didn't look much like me," Hank admitted. "He had darker hair and his eyes were more of a green than blue."

Gwen's voice was barely audible. "Yes. That sounds like him."

"Our family was four in number. Our mother, myself, Harvey, and our stepfather."

Gwen shook her head. "Harvey told me he was an orphan. He said his father had died when he was only six."

"Well, that's true enough. Our father was wrongly accused and hanged by a lynch mob." Gwen gasped and put her hand to her mouth. Hank continued. "He was an alcoholic and womanizer, but he wasn't a horse thief. When the mob learned the truth, they were very sorry, but of course it was too late to save my father."

"How awful."

"It was. Especially for our mother. She was left with two boys who could hardly help her earn a living. I was twelve and did what I could. I went to work for a man who owned a newspaper. My mother took on sewing and laundry for a time. Eventually we moved in with a widowed churchwoman who had a large boardinghouse. My mother worked for her until she met my stepfather."

"And what of Harvey?"

Hank shrugged. "He was sickly. Mother wanted him to get an education, but he could hardly be at school a week without coming down with something. Mother wanted us both to excel at our learning, so I did what I could to work around my school hours. I was blessed to have a good schoolmaster who cared that I should receive an education. Later, my stepfather was just as supportive. He hired a tutor for Harvey and made certain that I went on to college."

"That was quite fortunate for you. What happened to Harvey? Did he go to college also?"

"No. He played us for fools." He saw the shocked expression on Gwen's face and immediately regretted his words. Nevertheless, he didn't offer an apology but went on with an explanation.

"Harvey always managed to garner sympathy from the household staff, as well as our mother. She smothered him with an overprotectiveness that nearly crippled him. I must say, Harvey did have his share of sickness as a young boy, but as he grew older I could often see that he was simply playing a role."

"He did mention having been sick a lot as a boy," Gwen said, moving to lean against the trunk of a tree. "That's why we figured he'd already had the measles."

"I couldn't say. I know I had them before Harvey was born." Hank shook off the memory. "Anyway, Harvey didn't like our stepfather much. He required a great deal of us, and my brother fought against his authority. Harvey grew bitter about the demands, as well as the fact that much of the attention was taken away from him. Especially our mother's attention. She had pampered and spoiled him a great deal, and now our new father had the audacity to expect Harvey to act like a responsible young man."

"See, that is where our thoughts on Harvey differ greatly," Gwen replied. "The Harvey I knew was always quite helpful. He would lend a hand before even being asked."

"Maybe in the time before you met he learned his lesson about selfishness and seeking his own way."

"But why wouldn't he have returned home then, Mr. Bishop?"

Hank's eyes narrowed. "Because he stole valuable property from our stepfather."

"And you think he brought it here?"

Her tone suggested his idea ridiculous, but Hank wouldn't give up that easily. If she was hiding the things Harvey took, she would do whatever necessary to send Hank in a different direction.

"He must have."

Gwen pushed off the tree and paced a bit. Hank watched her as she considered his words. "When my father found Harvey, he was half dead from pneumonia. He had very little, save a beat-up old suitcase that held his only change of clothes. He hadn't had a decent meal in months—at least, it didn't appear that way to us. He was skin and bones and we thought him a goner, to be sure."

"And where is this suitcase now?" Hank was hopeful that she would tell him it was nearby. He was even more hopeful that inside he would find the missing stock certificates Harvey had taken.

"In my room. Why?"

"Might I see it?" Hank asked.

Gwen shook her head. "Not until I'm convinced of your purpose. What is it exactly that you're looking for?"

"My brother stole several expensive pieces of jewelry, as well as a stack of stock certificates that, at the time, were valued a fair amount but now happen to be worth a vast fortune."

"I can assure you, Mr. Bishop, Harvey had nothing of the sort on him when he came to us. Certainly I would have known if he were carrying around jewelry. I'm back to believing that perhaps the man I knew wasn't your brother at all, but a different Harvey Bishop."

"With the same birth date and history of childhood sickness?"

"I don't know. Often in life there are strange things that happen to cause there to be an appearance of certainty, when in fact there is no solid evidence."

Hank could see that Gwen had become quite upset. She walked away from him, and for a moment, Hank thought perhaps she would head back to the house and leave him there. All at once, however, she paused in one of the sunnier spots. The glints of light on her hair drew out the golden essence, and for a moment, Hank was mesmerized by her appearance.

"Harvey told me a great deal about his childhood, about his memories before his family died. He never mentioned having a brother at all. He only spoke of his mother and father, and of a good friend who lived nearby. I'm convinced now that the man I knew and loved couldn't possibly be the brother you seek. There would have been no reason for him to keep such things from me."

For a moment, Hank was nearly convinced himself. Harvey would never have denied their relationship. They were very close ... had seen each other through bad times. Hank had even taken Harvey's punishments on many occasions, just because he felt sorry for his little brother. Maybe he had followed the wrong trail. Maybe the man Gwen had married had killed his brother and taken his name. It was possible.... Yet listening to Gwen describe her husband and remembering everything the others had said about him, that man hardly sounded like a cold-blooded killer.

Hank thought of Gwen's comment about Harvey having a friend. Harvey had very few friends. His poor health kept him inside most of the time.

"You say he spoke of a good friend?" Hank crossed the space to stand directly in front of Gwen. "And did that friend have a name?"

Gwen nodded. "Of course he did."

"And what was it?"

She studied him for a moment and shook her head. "If you were truly his brother, you would already know it. Why not tell me?"

"Because I know of no such friend."

She nodded again and shrugged. "Then I believe you must be mistaken."

Beth stopped Lacy and pointed in the direction of the cemetery. "Look at that. Mr. Bishop won't even leave Gwen alone long enough to visit Father's grave."

Lacy followed her sister's gaze. "I think it's time we took matters into our own hands. I thought maybe he'd get the idea after we drugged his coffee, but he's a hard case."

"Well, we can be just as hard," Beth said, forming a plan

in her mind. "I think from now on we should do what we can to encourage Mr. Bishop to return back East."

This thought was uppermost on her mind the next morning as she dished up oatmeal for breakfast. Looking at the bowls she'd prepared for her sisters, Beth couldn't help but smile.

"There's no time like the present," she murmured, putting down the sugar and reaching for the salt. She portioned out salt on one of the bowls of cereal, then went to the cold cellar for the buttermilk.

"This ought to be interesting," she said as she stirred the concoction together. She put the oatmeal on a tray and carried it with the other bowls to the dining room, where her sisters and Mr. Bishop awaited.

Careful to remember which bowl had been altered, Beth served everyone, then took her seat at the table.

"Would you care to offer grace?" Gwen asked.

Beth looked surprised but nodded. "Lord, for that which we are about to receive, we thank thee. Amen."

She looked up rather sheepishly and then quickly devoted her attention to her breakfast. Mr. Bishop reached for his toasted bread first. He quickly slathered jam on top and then took a bite. Beth waited nervously, wondering when he would try the cereal.

"Did you hear what I asked you?"

Beth looked up to realize Gwen's question was directed at her. "No. I'm sorry. I was just thinking . . . well . . . about breakfast." She smiled and avoided looking at Hank. "What did you say?"

"Mr. Bishop needs some clothes washed. Would you have time to do that?"

Beth realized yet another opportunity to cause grief for

the stranger. "Why, of course. I'd be happy to help. Tomorrow is wash day, and I could do it then."

"I have half a dozen white shirts. I'm very particular about them," Hank said as he reached for his spoon. "I like them to be washed thoroughly and starched lightly. Can you do that?"

He sounded as though he were addressing an eight-year-old. Beth held her temper, however. "Of course. I've been taking care of such things since I was quite young."

Mr. Bishop met her smile and nodded. He dipped into the oatmeal and spooned a large amount into his mouth. The cereal had scarcely entered, however, before he was spitting the concoction out again.

Gwen was notably taken aback. She stared at the man as he grabbed for his coffee and then took a long, steady drink.

"Whatever is wrong, Mr. Bishop?" Lacy asked.

Gwen actually got to her feet. "Yes, are you quite all right?"

"Is it too hot?" Beth asked.

"I'm fine," the man replied, grimacing slightly. He put down his coffee cup and looked at Beth. "What in the world do you call this?"

"Oatmeal, Mr. Bishop. It's the way we eat it here. Do you not care for it?"

He looked as if he were trying to size up the situation and determine whether she had played him for a fool. Beth continued to look quite innocent. At least she hoped that was the appearance she gave.

"*Malo in consilio feminae vincunt viros,*" he muttered.

"Does that mean you prefer something else?"

Hank pushed back the bowl and shook his head. "No. I'll just eat the toast. Thank you."

Gwen thought Hank had acted quite strange throughout the day. First, there had been his reaction to the oatmeal; after that, he gingerly sampled each thing given him to eat. It was almost as if he were afraid of what he would find.

Throughout supper, he continued in this manner, with the girls doing their best to pretend that nothing was amiss. Gwen couldn't quite figure him out. He'd been in a bad mood since she'd refused to give him the name of Harvey's childhood friend. She'd convinced herself that Hank Bishop was not her dead husband's brother, but rather a misguided soul bent on a mission that she could not help him accomplish.

She'd even looked in the suitcase Harvey had left. There weren't any papers or stock certificates as Mr. Bishop had hoped. She felt rather relieved in this discovery. The stories the man told were so far removed from anything she remembered of her beloved that Gwen felt certain there was more than one Harvey Bishop in the world.

When supper concluded, Beth and Lacy began cleaning up while Gwen went into the front room to check the fire. She put enough wood on to last throughout the evening. It would die down in the night, but hopefully they would all be warm enough under their covers. She knew that she and her sisters would be fine, but perhaps Mr. Bishop was used to warmer surroundings.

Gwen watched as Hank made his way for the stairs. Surprisingly enough, the Major was at his side. Gwen approached with a smile. "Would you like for me to light a fire in your stove?"

"No. I'll be fine, thank you." His curt reply was not what she had expected. He had been so much more civil when they'd spoken in the cemetery. She supposed her attitude had put him in this state.

"Tell me, Mr. Bishop, are you cross with me?"

He paused on the steps and looked at her sternly. "Why would you ask such a thing?"

"Well, you did not seem very . . . well . . . happy at supper. In fact, you were rather preoccupied."

"I did not wish to repeat my ordeal at breakfast. Apparently you Montanans enjoy a variety of flavors that the rest of the world would rather avoid."

She thought his comment odd but thought perhaps it better to change the subject. "Tell me something, Mr. Bishop. This morning you spoke in that Latin tongue again. What was it you said?"

"Malo in consilio feminae vincunt viros."

Gwen frowned. "And what exactly does it mean?"

He raised a brow and gave her a look that sent a shiver down her spine. "Women surpass men at scheming evil."

"Excuse me?" Gwen shook her head. "What in the world would prompt you to say that?"

"Perhaps you should ask your sister." With that he was gone, the Major faithfully climbing the stairs at his side.

Gwen walked into the kitchen still shaking her head. "Mr. Bishop just said the most unusual thing."

Beth looked up from drying a plate. "And that surprises you? As far as I'm concerned, he's been saying all sorts of strange things."

"I asked him about that Latin phrase he quoted this morning.

I wondered what it meant," Gwen began. "He just now interpreted it for me. 'Women surpass men at scheming evil.' Then he told me I should ask you or Lacy if I wanted to know why he said that. What do you suppose he means by that? Neither one of you speak Latin."

Beth immediately looked guilty and cast a quick glance at Lacy. "I'm afraid it was my fault. I made his oatmeal less than palatable. I figure if we make him miserable enough, he'll leave. He'll give up this wild chase of his and let us go back to our peaceful lives."

"Oh, Beth, you didn't. You shouldn't torment people— especially not someone who already seems to hold so much against us."

"But he's not what he seems," Lacy said, glancing around suspiciously before motioning her sisters closer. "I saw something very strange in the Lassiters' barn."

"What?" Gwen asked, her mind already in a whir.

"Mr. Bishop's saddle."

Gwen shook her head. "What was so strange about it?"

"There are initials carved into the leather."

Gwen pulled back and rolled her eyes. "A lot of people do that. I'm sure Mr. Bishop felt it identified his belongings."

"Well, it might," Lacy said rather smugly, "if his initials were A. R. instead of H. B."

"What?"

"It's true," Lacy told Gwen. She looked at Beth, who seemed just as surprised. "I'm wondering if maybe he stole the saddle."

Gwen regained her senses. "Goodness, but you always jump to the worst conclusions. Maybe he just bought a used saddle. That happens all the time, and probably more than we realize back East, where people are doing less and less riding and more carriage driving."

"Where did you hear that?" Beth asked.

"Patience Shepard. She's told me all sorts of stories about when she lived back East."

"Well, I don't know about that," Lacy said, sounding rather disappointed that Gwen offered a reasonable explanation. "I'm thinking that A. R. might very well be Hank's real initials. And if they are, then he certainly can't be Harvey's brother."

CHAPTER EIGHT

"That takes care of everything but Mr. Bishop's shirts," Beth told Lacy as they hung up the last of their personal laundry. "I guess I might as well see to that."

"He deserves to have to wash his own shirts," Lacy replied. She hoisted a basket and headed back toward the large caldron.

"I'll admit that much is true," Beth said. "But still, I promised to take care of them."

"That doesn't necessarily mean you have to do it in the same manner he suggested. After all, we're just silly girls. We might not have understood exactly what he wanted."

Beth smiled. She glanced up to spy Rafe's girls working behind the saloon to care for their own laundry. Beth's first thoughts were of sympathy, even pity. She couldn't begin to imagine what type of ordeals had brought these women to such an end.

"Look," she whispered to Lacy.

Lacy's gaze followed and she nodded. "I feel sorry for them and angry at them, all at the same time. Does that sound crazy?"

"No, I feel the same way," Beth admitted. "I can't help but wonder if they understand that they're living in sin. Surely they must. I've wanted to talk to them, but we hardly ever see them. I think Rafe keeps them locked up. See how pale they are?"

She considered the three women. Marie was in her late twenties and had been a prostitute since she was a young girl. Hardened by years of dangerous living, the dark-eyed woman kept to herself, scrubbing what looked to be a blouse and saying nothing to the other two.

In contrast, the younger women were chatting freely. Ellie, a petite blonde, had been in the business for only a short time, Beth had learned. She was a young widow whose husband had been gored to death by a bull. With no other family or friends to help her, Ellie eventually found herself forced into working at saloons in order to keep herself fed.

Regina was the youngest, at seventeen. Rafe boasted that he'd won her in a poker game in Denver. Apparently, her father hadn't counted on Rafe's four of a kind. Regina was like a timid rabbit. She stuck close to Ellie and seemed shy of strangers.

"I wish there were a way to help them," Beth murmured.

Her sister plopped the basket down beside the washtub. "I don't know what we could ever do. I heard it said that they each owe Rafe a bunch of money. They can't leave until they pay it off."

"Well, it sounds like slavery to me, and Mr. Lincoln, God rest his soul, put an end to that abomination. I can't believe it's legal for Rafe to simply own these women because of their previous debts."

"I don't like it any more than you do," Lacy replied, "but I don't know what we can do about it. I suppose we could help them run away."

Beth considered the thought for a moment. "Rafe would only hunt them down. There has to be another way. I'm going to go talk with them."

"Suit yourself. I'm going to go check on the Lassiters' mare." Lacy headed off toward the front of the house.

"See how Nick's feeling, too," Beth called. She deposited some extra clothespins in the basket and drew a deep breath.

Walking with determination, Beth crossed the distance between Gallatin House and Rafe's Saloon. She was grateful that it was still early. Perhaps Rafe and his assistant would still be sleeping off their late night.

"Hello," Beth called and gave a little wave.

Marie looked up but said nothing. Ellie and Regina waved back rather hesitantly. "How are you . . . ladies . . . ah . . . doing?" Beth stammered.

Ellie looked at Marie and then shrugged. "I guess we're doing fine."

"I see it's washday for you, as well." Beth could think of nothing else to say. She stopped as she drew within five feet of Regina.

The girl seemed very pale, and dark smudges seemed permanently marked beneath her sad eyes. Beth noted her skinny—even sickly looking—form and wondered if Rafe allowed them enough to eat.

"What are you doing here?" Marie asked, coming to join them. She sounded hostile and crossed her arms against her low-cut chemise.

Beth was rather startled at the way the woman's breasts swelled against the fabric. She wore only this and a shortened skirt that revealed the calves of her legs. Did she not realize how much of herself she was exposing? Perhaps since she was just among women she didn't care, but Beth found it offensive and looked away quickly.

"I just thought it might be nice to talk to you," Beth replied.

"Maybe we could have a tea party, too." Marie's sarcasm seemed to give Beth strength.

"I was just thinking of that," she said, smiling. "Frankly, I was wondering if Rafe gave you all enough to eat."

Marie seemed momentarily taken aback by Beth's boldness. Then a grin spread across her face. "Are you here to do your Christian good deed—bring food to those who are hungry?"

"Well, if you are hungry, I can bring you some food."

"We eat enough," Marie answered. She looked at the other two as if defying them to challenge her statement. Ellie and Regina simply looked to the ground and avoided Beth's face.

"I know you haven't been here long," Beth said, trying to think of something else to talk about. "Winters are hard here. It gets pretty cold." She looked at the poorly constructed rooms that had been added to the back of Rafe's Saloon and then back at their scanty, lightweight clothes.

"I've been cold before," Marie said. Her eyes seemed like hard bits of coal as she narrowed her gaze. "What are you really trying to say?"

Beth gave up the pretense of social etiquette. "I just wondered if you have stoves in your rooms. I hope Rafe has provided you with plenty of blankets and . . . well . . . clothes."

Marie laughed harshly. "Rafe expects us to keep warm other ways, and clothes definitely have no part in it."

Ellie shifted uncomfortably. "It's nice of you to ask, though."

Beth shook her head. "I'm not asking just to be nice. I can't abide what you're being forced to do. It's a sin, you know."

Marie stepped closer. "You think we don't know what society thinks of us? I've heard enough people preach at me, I could start my own church."

"If you know it's wrong, why don't you just . . . leave?" Beth asked.

Marie made a face and mocked her. "Just leave."

Ellie stepped forward. "We don't have a choice, Miss Gallatin."

"Call me, Beth, and of course you have a choice."

Ellie shook her head. "I have no one to help me—no money of my own. My husband died, and he was the only family I had. He didn't leave me a cent."

Beth frowned and looked at each of the women. "I suppose that may be the case for each of you, but it's still wrong. God never intended for you to do the things you're doing."

"And what would you suggest, Miss Prim-and-Proper?" Marie asked.

Beth tried to think of a good solution, but answers weren't coming to mind. "Well, I don't know exactly."

"That's the trouble with you Christian do-gooders. You're always willing to judge and tell everybody what they're doing is a sin, but you offer nothing else. You can't help us—so why don't you go back to your safe little house and pretend you did your best to change the ills of the world."

"Marie, don't be so mean," Ellie interceded. "She's just being nice."

"But nice doesn't change a thing. She thinks she's better than us, because she doesn't have to stoop to our way of living."

Marie looked at Beth and for just a moment seemed to drop her guard. "She doesn't understand how hard it is or how we've tried to find our way out."

Beth was humbled by the woman's comment. "I'm sorry. You're right."

Marie shook her head. "For all the good it does."

"I think admitting one's mistake is important," Beth said quietly. "I know very little of what you've endured... I suppose I have made it all sound rather simplistic."

"But not because you were trying to be thoughtless," Ellie said, smiling. "You just didn't know."

"And since you don't know anything about it," Marie said in a tone that froze Beth to the bone, "you really should keep your nose out of it."

Beth nodded. "I suppose you're right. I can't change your situation, but you should know that if you need something, you can come to us. My sisters and I will help in any way we can."

"You already help by bringing us clients," Marie said, laughing. "You keep doing your part, and we'll do ours." She walked back to her laundry without another word.

Beth tried to think of something she could do to show her goodwill. She wondered if they would like a cake, then scoffed at her own idea. A cake? What in the world would a cake do to benefit these poor women?

"I heard you got one of those hot springs baths," Regina said in a barely audible voice.

Her words immediately put an idea in Beth's head. "Yes, we do. Would you three like to take a soak?" Even Marie perked up at this and made her way back to Ellie and Regina. "It's quite pleasant," Beth continued. "I have towels, and you could stay as long as you like. We won't have a stage in until late."

"You sure your sisters won't care?" Ellie asked.

"I know they'd be pleased."

"Let's go right now while Rafe and Wyman are still sleeping," Marie suggested. She looked at Beth and narrowed her eyes. "That is, if it's all right with you."

"It's fine. I'll fetch some towels for you." Beth smiled and headed to the back porch as the young women darted across the yard to the fencing that surrounded the hot springs pool. She felt a sense of accomplishment, even if it was just to offer these women some simple comforts.

Picking up three thick towels, Beth walked back to the hot springs and wondered what other ideas she and her sisters might come up with to better the lives of these soiled doves.

At the pool gate, she heard the women inside. They were happy. Ellie was commenting on how it was the first hot bath she'd had since leaving Missouri. Marie said she'd never seen anything like it. Regina was saying something that Beth couldn't quite make out.

"I brought the towels," Beth said, closing the gate behind her.

The pool had been constructed from a wooden frame built by her father and Harvey. It was about ten-by-ten and was situated with piping that brought the hot water into the pool at a constant rate. On the north side there was a drainage area where the water could trickle over the pool edge and run into a stream that emptied into the nearby river.

Somewhere along the way, her father had added a few benches, as well as a ledge on which folks could put their towels and other things they wished to keep dry. It was here that Beth placed the towels. She turned to the women and let out a shriek.

"What's wrong?" Ellie asked. She stood and turned as if something were creeping up from behind them.

"I . . . uh . . . well, you're . . ." Beth's words faded. They were stark-naked. Each of the women had left their clothes on the benches. She didn't want to add to her own embarrassment or insensitivity, so she forced a smile. "Nothing's wrong. Nothing at all. The towels are here."

She glanced down at Ellie, who was just turning back to face her. Beth noted a crisscrossing of reddish purple bruises across the woman's back. Someone had obviously beaten her with a belt or strop. Beth cringed inwardly and bit her tongue to keep from asking what had happened.

Ellie smiled up. "This is wonderful, Miss Gallatin. Thank you."

Beth nodded and glanced to Marie, who was floating quite shamelessly without thought to who might gaze upon her unclothed body. "I'm glad you like it. I have to get back to my laundry now. Oh, but please do just call me Beth. No need for us to be formal."

She hurried back to her washing and tried to put the scene from her mind. She'd read stories in the past of public bathhouses. In Roman times, it was especially popular, but she found it rather shocking nevertheless.

Picking up one of Mr. Bishop's white shirts, Beth could hear his instructions once again. He acted as though she hadn't the first clue about laundry. "Well . . . maybe I am rather careless," she murmured. She glanced at the pile of shirts and then smiled. "Accidents happen. Who can say what might happen to Mr. Bishop's precious shirts?"

"I can see you're still hard at work," Gwen said as she came from the direction of the chicken coop. "The hens are laying well, finally. We have plenty of eggs now, and I believe I'll make a pound cake."

"Sounds wonderful. We've not had one for some time." Beth pushed the white shirts into the boiling water.

A shriek of laughter came from the direction of the pool, causing Gwen to start. "What was that?"

"Oh, I invited Rafe's girls to soak in the pool. I hope that's all right. They . . . well . . . we were talking, and I felt so sorry for them. I just wanted to do something nice."

Gwen smiled. "I think that's wonderful. Of course it's all right."

"I can't imagine being stuck in a place like they are," Beth said softly. She stirred the shirts and sighed. "It seems so hard—so unfair. We have it so much better than they do."

A thoughtful expression crossed her older sister's face. "It's true. We should definitely count our blessings. Our future is not nearly as bleak as theirs."

"But our future could be," Beth replied. She put aside the laundry paddle and looked at Gwen. "Do you ever think about that? I mean, if Pa hadn't left us this place, we could be just as bad off."

"I know." Gwen placed the basket of eggs on the ground. She stretched as she straightened and shook her head. "Do you ever think about a different life?"

"I think about it," Beth admitted. "All I've ever really wanted was to stay in one place. Pa dragged us all over the earth, it seemed. Sometimes when we'd be somewhere for a couple of years, I'd get hopeful that we'd never move again. Then he'd up and decide we were heading for some other part of the country."

Gwen nodded sympathetically. "I know. We left many good friends behind."

"It's true. If I could ever have hated Pa for anything, it would have been that," Beth admitted. Then she immediately realized her words and added, "Of course, I couldn't have hated him."

"Of course not, but it was a hard life at times."

"Not as hard as what those girls have to face," Beth admitted. Feeling a sense of relief in her father's inability to move them to yet another location left Beth awash in guilt.

"Do you believe that we're doing the right thing?" Gwen asked.

Beth looked at her older sister and cocked her head to one side. "What is this really about?"

Shrugging, Gwen reached once again for her basket. "I don't know. I just worry that maybe we should sell the place and move on."

"Sell to Rafe?"

"He seems to be the only one interested."

Beth couldn't believe her sister was even considering such a thing. "Well, I'll never sell my share to Rafe. Besides, like I said, I'm glad to be in one place for a while. I, for one, do not intend to move again for a good long while."

"But you and Lacy might suffer for something that was completely my fault."

"What was your fault?"

"Pa getting killed. If I hadn't sent him out there—"

"He'd have gone anyway. He always liked to go talk with the Lassiter boys. If you hadn't given him a reason to go, he would have come up with his own." Beth walked to her sister and touched Gwen's arm. "You aren't cursed. You have to forget all about that nonsense. It's not true. It doesn't exist."

"But plenty of people were cursed in the Bible. There are a lot of examples of it. You can't just say that curses don't exist."

"Maybe they exist, but I don't think they apply to you," Beth said. She could only pray that Gwen would let go of the past and the things she'd been told. "I think when you belong to Jesus, you don't have to worry about curses. I'm not sure, but I'm thinking the Bible probably says as much."

"Could be. But, Beth, if you ever feel that I'm a danger to you, I won't be offended if you ask me to go."

Beth shook her head and hugged Gwen close. "That will never happen. We are family."

"Thank you. I love you so dearly," Gwen said as they pulled apart.

"I know you do. I love you, as well. Now I must get back to work. I have Mr. Bishop's shirts to finish."

Gwen frowned. "I'm sorry you have that extra work. Would you like me to take it over?"

"No, I'm perfectly content to wash his shirts for pay." Beth smiled. "I just hope he's satisfied with the results."

Laughing, Gwen made her way up the steps. "I'm sure he'll be amazed at your abilities. Well, I'd best see to getting lunch on and finishing with the baking. The stage will pull in about six, unless they've met with trouble." Gwen disappeared into the house, while Beth went to the back porch and rummaged around in their laundry supplies. Finding what she was looking for, a wicked grin spread across her face.

"You're so right, Gwen. He will be amazed at my abilities."

CHAPTER NINE

~

Hank rode his black gelding out across the field and marveled at the territory around him. Mountains seemed to encircle him, yet there was openness to this valley that yielded vast fields of farm and grazing land. Cattle dotted the landscape; many were new mothers with calves at their side. He had asked about the herds, not having any understanding or knowledge of such animals. To him, beef was something served on a plate. Joe, the stage driver who'd brought him to Gallatin House, laughed at his ignorance but tolerated his questions. It was through Joe that Hank learned there were different breeds for beef and milk. Joe also explained a bit of the territory's history. For the life of him, Hank couldn't remember ever hearing much about the place before the private investigator had learned of Harvey's journey here.

Now that he was here, Hank was rather taken aback by what he found. Nothing in his travels had gripped him like Montana. He wasn't sure why, but something here spoke to his soul. It was really the only thing that had spoken to him in years. Most of his decisions and reactions had been driven by pain or anger, but this territory promised a measure of peace and refinement.

It wasn't that Hank couldn't recognize the difficulty of living in such an isolated territory, nor that he figured life here to be easy, by any means. But there was a feeling—a sort of personality to the land. He couldn't explain it, but he felt a sense of belonging here.

"That's foolishness. I have a business and home in Boston. I don't belong here," he said aloud. The horse snorted, as if disagreeing, but Hank ignored him. What could the beast possibly know?

The gelding seemed to follow his own path along the river, pausing now and then as if to give Hank an opportunity to direct him. Hank had only owned the black since coming west. He'd purchased the animal in Corrine after departing the train. The thought had been to ride to Gallatin House, but seeing the terrain, he knew it would be an arduous journey for a novice to take alone, especially since he'd spent more of his time in the city and knew little of life on the trail.

A rabbit darted out from brush along the river and paused momentarily as he sized up Hank and his mount. The horse danced nervously at the interruption but quickly settled down. The rabbit's nose wriggled as he sniffed at the unfamiliar scents, then just as quickly he dove back into the heavy vegetation and was gone. Overhead, geese made their way north, honking in such a way that it almost sounded like a bark. The skies and earth were alive with activity.

"A fellow could get used to this place," he said.

Hank glanced at his pocket watch and saw that it was nearing lunchtime. The girls were always quite prompt with their meals, and he didn't want to be late. Of course, given the oatmeal incident, Hank couldn't say he was all that excited about any meal that Beth Gallatin had a hand in making. His stomach growled loudly, as if to protest his thoughts, however. He would simply have to be careful about what he ate. Maneuvering the black back in the direction of the roadhouse, Hank couldn't help but think of the situation and his mission there.

He didn't want to believe the sisters were trying to hide the truth from him. And he didn't really feel that Gwen meant to deceive him, but there was still a secretive nature about all three girls that left him feeling like the only one who didn't get the joke.

Major Worthington came bounding out to greet him. He had tried to follow Hank earlier, but Beth called him back and leashed him to the porch. Apparently she'd seen fit to set him free, for now the dog was at his side.

"Hello there, Major. Good to have you along. Sorry your mistress wouldn't allow you to join me earlier."

The dog trotted along with an occasional upward glance. He seemed to understand that Hank had no choice in the previous decision. Across the way, Hank spied Gwen out in the garden. She attacked the ground as if trying to kill something, yet he could see she was merely attempting to till the soil. Having never planted or worked land himself, Hank was really in no position to criticize, but it looked to him like she was going about it all wrong.

Hank brought the horse to within twenty feet, and Gwen still didn't acknowledge him. She appeared lost in her thoughts, and he almost hated to interrupt her. Major had no such concerns, however, and went up to his mistress.

"Well, hello," she said, pausing from her work. Her whole face seemed to light up with delight at the sight of the golden brown dog. "Are you feeling less forlorn?"

Hank dismounted and approached with the black close behind. "I hope you don't mind the intrusion." He didn't wait for an answer. "What are you planting?"

A worried expression overtook Gwen's previous look of delight. "We grow a hearty crop of rock in this area," she replied.

Hank noted the pile of rounded stones and nodded. "Looks tiresome."

"It is. I did manage to put in some potatoes earlier," she said, looking back at the square of earth. "There's so little time to grow things. When we lived in Missouri, it wasn't hard at all. We had long, mild springs and hot summers. Day after day, we canned fruits and vegetables until I was able to do it in my sleep. Up here, however, it seems the snow is scarcely off the peaks before winter starts up again. I've seen snow fall in every month on the calendar."

"You're jesting, right?" He could hardly believe she was speaking the truth.

Gwen smiled. "Sorry, no. One year it actually snowed on the Fourth of July."

Hank shook his head. "That's hard to imagine." He took a step closer, knowing that he had to somehow begin to put her at ease and gain her confidence—or he might never find the missing stocks and jewelry. "It seems I'm always apologizing to you, and now I find I need to do it once again."

Gwen looked at him and shrugged. "Whatever for?"

"The way I spoke to you the other day. The way I've acted

since coming here." He smiled and hoped that his expression would prove his sincerity. "It really isn't in my nature to be so harsh."

"You've suffered a shock in the loss of your brother. That's never easy to deal with. You never told me when you found out about his death."

"It actually wasn't until I got to Corrine. A private investigator had been able to locate him. I asked around and finally met up with the freight driver. It just so happened he knew my brother—or of him. When he talked about his having married and then dying shortly afterward, I . . . well . . . I found myself in a state of shock. I never expected that he would be dead." It was the truth, and Hank couldn't disguise the sadness in his voice.

Gwen looked away. "I don't think any of us ever really anticipates the death of a loved one."

"No. I don't suppose so."

"The loss is so painful in its own right, but it also leaves such a ripple of other issues—loneliness, fearfulness, confusion, and an emptiness that goes on and on."

Hank was taken aback by her words. That was exactly how he'd felt after his grandfather's death. Hank's grandfather had been a good man who had filled the gaps left by an often-absent father. The void Hank had experienced upon the death of his grandfather had been difficult to bear. When his own father had died a year later, it hadn't hurt nearly as much as losing that old man.

"I always thought I'd see Harvey again," Hank finally murmured. "I still can't quite bring myself to believe he's gone."

Gwen turned and met his eyes. "I'm so sorry." She stretched her shoulders. "It's nearly lunchtime. I imagine the girls have things just about ready."

She started to walk toward the house, and Hank followed along. "Is it true," he began, "that Harvey would have died if your father hadn't taken him in? Or was that just an exaggeration for dramatic effect?"

"We have no time for games up here—not when it comes to life and death," Gwen replied. "Harvey was very sick when my father found him. He didn't have a cent to his name, and my father paid for the doctor and medicine to treat his pneumonia."

"He had no money?" Hank found that so hard to believe.

"None. I suppose if he did take the things you believe him to have stolen, he must have sold them in the year before coming to us." She turned and stopped. "I assure you, Mr. Bishop, Harvey came to us with very little."

Hank still wasn't convinced. There was something about the entire matter that just didn't make sense. The company from which the stocks had been issued had no record of their being sold. A sale or transfer would have been recorded. Someone had to have those stocks, even if the jewelry was long gone.

"Gwen!" Lacy called as she bounded across the yard. Her long hair flew out behind her in waves of dark red. She looked more like a girl than a woman. Only her height suggested otherwise. Well, that and the slight curve to her figure here and there. Harvey thought there was something rather wild and untamed about the young woman, and from the look on her face, she was about to unleash it on them.

"You look madder than a wet hen," Gwen commented. "What's wrong?"

"It's that lazy Dave Shepard," she declared, her hands going to her hips. "He's not doing a thing to find Pa's killer. I've just half a mind to ride over to the sheriff's and confront him about the entire matter."

"Lacy, you can't do that. I need you here. There's too much work to do. We have many stages and freighters due through, and I'll need your help. Even now we need that new cord of wood chopped."

The younger woman pushed her hair back and blew out a long breath. Her expression told Hank she had barely heard her sister's words. "Someone has got to do something. The longer we wait, the better chance it is that the killer will get away. If he's one of those Texas cowhands, he'll be heading south for the winter by September, and then what will we do?"

Gwen spoke with a great deal of patience. "Lacy, God has it under control. You do trust Him to make things right, don't you? If there is a truly guilty party, the Lord will reveal it."

"But of course there's a guilty party! Pa's dead, isn't he?"

With a sigh, Gwen put her arm around Lacy and began to walk toward the house. Hank followed behind, watching as Gwen spoke in words too soft to hear. She cared a great deal for her family—that much was clear. The thought made Hank ache inside as he remembered that Harvey had never even mentioned him to Gwen. How could he have forgotten his brother? Did he truly care so little for Hank that the memories weren't worth sharing?

"Well, if Deputy Shepard and Sheriff Cummings don't plan to interrogate any suspects," Lacy declared, pushing away from Gwen, "then I'll just do it myself." She closed the distance to the house and disappeared.

Gwen stood watching her and shook her head. "Believe me when I say I know what it is to have a troublesome sibling, Mr. Bishop."

Hank smiled, but she never looked back at him.

Later that night, Hank returned to his room. He had hoped for a quiet evening of reading, but when the stage rolled in and ten men crawled out from every possible place on the conveyance, it was clear that such ideas were merely dreams.

He left the hall door open long enough to light the lamp by his bed. The golden light shone in an almost eerie manner, and had Hank believed in ghosts, he might actually have found himself spooked. Sitting on the bed, he pulled off his boots and tossed them to one side, and that's when he spied his white shirts.

Only they weren't white anymore.

They were red. Blood red. Red like the side of a barn.

"Beth." He muttered the name almost like a curse.

CHAPTER TEN

"She did what?" Gwen asked. She was mortified at the thought that Hank was telling the truth. Surely this was a joke.

"As you can see, Beth dyed my shirts red," Hank announced the next morning at the breakfast table. He stood at one end, arms crossed and a scowl on his face that left little doubt that his answer was genuine. In fact, his face was nearly the same shade as his shirt.

Gwen looked to her sister, who sat innocently at the opposite end of the table. "Is this true?"

"It happened. I guess red dye got into the water with the shirts," Beth said, shrugging. "It was too late to do anything about it afterwards. Besides, I think the red looks quite nice."

"I wanted white shirts. I like my shirts white," Hank said, his stern gaze never leaving the young woman's face.

"Well, white is nice, but out here red will hold up better," Beth said. "White will show every stain."

"I don't care!" Hank roared and took a step toward Beth.

Gwen hurried to put herself between Hank and Beth. Just then Lacy came in carrying a stack of pancakes.

"What's all the hollering about?"

"Mr. Bishop is unhappy with the way I do laundry," Beth said.

Lacy shrugged and put the plate on the table. "Let him wash his own shirts next time."

Gwen put out her hand as if the motion could shut her sister's mouth. "Enough is enough. Mr. Bishop," she said, turning to face him, "if you bring me the shirts, I'll bleach them back. I'm sorry that Beth was careless. I assure you it won't happen again."

"Thank you. I suppose I will have to continue wearing this one, as I have no other shirts available to me. My remaining white shirt is quite dirty."

"That's all right. After we get the others bleached back to white, you can trade me out and I'll take care of the rest."

Hank seemed appeased and walked back to the place where he generally sat at the table. He said nothing more, but Gwen got the feeling the matter was far from resolved. Why did things have to be so difficult where this man was concerned? And why, why couldn't her sisters just leave him alone? Couldn't they see that their agitating him did no good?

"We have a stage coming through for lunch, then nothing this evening," Gwen announced. "Since I'll be working on Mr. Bishop's shirts, I would appreciate it if you two would prepare everything for the meal."

"Of course," Beth said sweetly. "I'd be happy to."

Lacy nodded. "Me too."

Neither would look at Hank. Gwen didn't feel much like looking at him, either. She was embarrassed by what had happened. She did agree with Beth, however. The shirt looked quite nice. Red seemed to suit Mr. Bishop's sandy brown hair and complexion. Not that he would care about such things. The man clearly had no interest in Gwen's opinion.

She ate her breakfast in silence, then dismissed herself to tend to Hank's wash. Four hours later, with only minutes before the stage was due in, Gwen was fit to be tied.

"Can't you just bleach them again?" Lacy asked as Gwen held up the now-pink shirt.

"No. I've already bleached them three times."

Hank chose that moment to come investigate the matter for himself. He took one glance at the shirt in Gwen's hands and shook his head. "Don't tell me that's mine."

"All right," Gwen said, putting the shirt into the basket. "I won't tell you."

He grimaced. "Pink? My shirts are now pink?"

"I'm sorry, Mr. Bishop. I've done what I could. The color is just not bleaching out."

"Can't you try again?"

Lacy interceded. "She can't. She's already bleached them three times. If she keeps it up, it will eat the material clean through."

"And I'm afraid the bulk of the color was bleached out with the first try. The last two have resulted in very little change."

"I can't wear pink shirts." Hank's blue eyes pierced Gwen with a stare that gave her a shiver.

"I have an idea," Lacy said. "Why don't we dye them again? This time use blue. Surely you can't object to blue."

Hank looked at the girl as if she'd lost her mind, but Gwen

noticed that his features softened just a bit. She took this as an encouraging sign.

"We could dye them blue," she told him. "I'm certain it would cover the pink completely. Then if you like, I can have Lacy ride to Bozeman and buy you new shirts. At our expense, of course."

Hank shook his head. "That won't be necessary. I can buy my own shirts." He looked at the basket of pink and nodded. "Dye them blue."

Hank had endured all he was going to take. If the Gallatin girls wanted to make his life miserable, he could play that game. He could easily mete out just as much trouble as they could.

With the ladies busy making last-minute lunch preparations, Hank went forward with his plan. There was a routine the girls followed with every stage and meal. He knew it by heart, as he had been with them long enough now to observe it on many occasions. With that in mind, Hank knew exactly how best to get back at Lacy and Beth Gallatin. They'd think twice before dyeing any more of his things.

The stage arrived with three men and the driver Hank recognized as Ralph. The girls laughed at the stories and exploits Ralph shared, all while efficiently seeing to the luncheon meal.

"I thought that mama skunk was sure to get me," Ralph said, digging into the pie crust that covered the creamed chicken and vegetables.

"I'm glad she didn't," Gwen said, bringing a bowl of applesauce to the table.

"You sure are pretty, ma'am, if you don't mind my sayin' so," one of the strangers began. "I don't think I've seen anyone quite as pretty as you in the whole territory."

"Then you haven't met my sisters," Gwen said, motioning to where Lacy and Beth were offering coffee and freshly sliced bread.

"Oh, they're fine to be sure, ma'am, but I like your looks. You got a charm about you that appeals to me. And you look sturdy. Are you married?"

Hank frowned as the man reached out to put a hand on Gwen's back. She sidestepped him, but the man wasn't easily deterred.

"Why don't you come on over here and sit by me. We can get better acquainted."

"I have work to do," Gwen countered.

"It'd be nicer if you ladies would join us," another of the passengers said with a broad grin. He was hardly more than a boy, Hank thought, but apparently he was grown up enough to find Gwen and her sisters quite appealing.

"You gentlemen would do well to learn some manners. These ladies are not saloon girls," Hank said, checking his temper.

"We meant no harm, mister. You their brother?" the third passenger asked. He had collar-length dark hair that had been parted down the middle and combed back. His suit was covered in dust and grime, but he acted as though he'd just stepped from the tailor's shop as he reached up to grab his lapels. "We're lookin' for wives."

"Well, you needn't look here," Hank said.

"Mr. Bishop isn't our brother," Lacy said, giving the man a most alluring smile.

Hank wondered if she had any idea the effect such a look could have on a man. She seemed completely oblivious to having done anything wrong. Perhaps she really didn't understand.

"But he's right," Gwen added. "We aren't looking for

husbands. We're just running the stage stop and feeding weary men such as yourselves."

"Men who'd better get to eating if they know what's good for 'em," Ralph declared. "Stage pulls out in ten minutes, whether you're done or not."

This motivated the men to do less talking and more eating. When lunch concluded with thick slices of apple pie, Ralph nodded in approval, grabbed his piece in hand, and headed for the door. "I'm gonna see that the horses have been switched out. You've got three minutes, gentlemen."

The men wolfed down their food while the girls offered more coffee with which to wash it down. Hank felt a sense of relief when the last of the pack headed out the front door. Already the girls were working to clear the dirty dishes left behind.

Hank toyed with his food. It was delicious, but the scene had left him rather unnerved. He'd watched the passengers, most of whom were men, flirt with the Gallatin women before, but this time he felt rather protective of them.

"I'm going to get water," Lacy announced.

Hank had nearly forgotten what he'd done earlier to get back at Lacy, but her comment brought it all back.

"Bring extra hot water up," Gwen announced. "I'm going to dye Mr. Bishop's shirts blue."

Lacy nodded and grabbed several buckets in the kitchen. "I left the cart down by the springs. I'll make a couple of trips."

"I suppose I should get to work wiping up," Beth said. "Do you want pie?" she asked Hank.

"No," he said, trying to sound as pleasant as possible. Miss Beth was in for her own dye job. Hank could hardly wait to see the mess she created. "If you don't mind, I'm just going to sit here and finish my coffee."

"That's just fine, Mr. Bishop," she said in a sugary voice. "I'll just start at the other end of the table."

Gwen got up. "I'm going to see what can be done about your shirts, Mr. Bishop. Hopefully, they'll be done by evening." She left quickly, without waiting for him to respond. Hank knew Gwen wasn't responsible for the shirts—of that he was certain. Where Beth and Lacy were pranksters, Gwen was far too serious. She knew the value of free time and would never have caused herself more work. She was too sensible for that.

Beth returned to wipe the table. She took up the wet cloth that Hank had seen her reach for a dozen times before. The girls kept a small tub on a table between the dining and kitchen areas. The rag was always wet and ready to wipe up spills or clean away messes after meals. Hank was counting on routine to keep Beth from noticing that he'd poured an adequate amount of black ink into the center of the folded cloth.

The rag hit the table and Beth began scrubbing for all she was worth. Within seconds, the problem was quite evident. She shrieked and pulled back as black ink stained the wood of the table.

"What in the world!" She held up the cloth and then looked back at the mess.

Hank wanted to laugh out loud and make some snide comment about her getting her just desserts, but instead, he drank back the last of his coffee and put down his cup.

"What's wrong?" Gwen asked, racing into the room. "I heard you scream from outside."

"Look. Just look at this mess."

Gwen cast a glance to the table, then to Hank and finally back to Beth. "Looks like we may have to dye more than the shirts."

Beth looked at the table and then fixed her stare on Hank.

He smiled and got to his feet. "You and accidents seem to be old companions, Miss Gallatin. At least it looks better than red."

Beth looked at him for a moment, then realization seemed to dawn. She frowned and squared her shoulders. Storming off to the kitchen, Beth muttered something under her breath. Hank couldn't help but chuckle, but then his gaze locked with Gwen.

"I suppose she had it coming, but you do realize . . ."

A scream from outside sent a look of panic across Gwen's face. Hank watched as she ran for a rifle situated near the stove. He followed after her as she ran for the backyard. Beth was already out the door. She'd grabbed up a shovel from the back porch and preceded Hank and Gwen down the stairs.

"What happened?" Gwen asked, lowering the rifle. "I thought maybe a bear had attacked."

"It would have been easier to deal with," Lacy said, picking herself up from the dirt. "The wheels on the cart just came off and sent the water flying and me with it." She dusted her backside, then tried to wipe off the water from the front of her blouse and skirt. It resulted in muddy handprints up and down the front of Lacy's outfit.

"Oh bother."

Gwen looked at the cart and the buckets of spilled water. Hank couldn't be certain, but he thought a slight smile touched the corners of her downturned face.

"Well, those wheels have been loose for some time," she said. "I guess now we have no choice but to get the Lassiters to fix them."

"You ladies seem quite prone to problems," Hank said.

"Yes, especially when we have help," Beth replied. She looked at Lacy and back to Hank before bending to retrieve a bucket. "Come on, Lacy. I'll help you bring up the water."

Hank watched Lacy's eyes narrow as she took him in. She seemed to understand quite clearly what had happened. The truth of it put fire into her gaze, but she said nothing.

When the girls had picked up the empty buckets and headed off to the hot springs, Hank turned to Gwen. "You were saying?"

She shook her head. "I don't know what you mean."

"Just before we came rushing out here, you started to say something. You told me you guessed Beth had it coming, but I needed to realize something. I just wondered what it was you were talking about."

Gwen blew out a hard breath. "I started to warn you. I started to tell you that you needed to realize the girls would see this as a declaration of war. Now it's only worse. I don't envy you, Mr. Bishop. My sisters can be quite the pests when they want to be."

He laughed. "I have dealt with entire factories of unpleasant workers, as well as businessmen who sought only to destroy what I had created. I think I can handle your sisters."

"Yeah," Gwen said, shaking her head and giving him a smile, "you keep telling yourself that."

CHAPTER ELEVEN

"Purple?" Hank looked at the shirts and shook his head. "Purple?"

"Well, it's really more of a lavender," Beth replied.

"No, I think it's lilac," Lacy offered.

"Maybe a pale violet," Beth countered.

Gwen wasn't pleased that her sisters had to be a part of this bad news. "I didn't have much of the blue dye, and I guess there were just too many shirts to absorb it all. I'll get some more dye in Bozeman and try again."

Hank looked at Beth and Lacy. Gwen could see that he wondered what role they'd had to play in the situation. "I'm sorry I wasn't able to fix the problem, Mr. Bishop, but I assure you, we'll work it out."

He turned and walked away without a word. Gwen couldn't

really read him. She didn't know whether he was angry or just defeated. Major quickly joined the man, however, as if snubbing the girls for their role in the matter.

"I think they're pretty," Beth said, sashaying her shirts from one side to the other. "Like the lilacs in Bozeman."

"Stop it now. This isn't funny. That poor man has had to endure enough. Stop tormenting him."

"We didn't turn the shirts purple," Lacy said innocently.

"Maybe not, but I'm betting you know what happened to all of my blue dye. I had three new boxes before this matter came up."

Lacy shrugged and Beth smiled. "I'm sure they're simply misplaced."

"Well, I hope they find their way home soon," Gwen declared. "I'd hate to spend money on something I already have on hand."

"Oh, let him wear the purple shirts," Lacy said, laughing. "At least one of them."

"Maybe two," Beth added.

Gwen shook her head. Making her way back into the house, she tried not to be angry with her sisters. They were just looking out for her. Mr. Bishop had been unkind and harsh, and even after apologizing, they knew he still didn't believe Gwen's explanation that Harvey had come to her with nothing.

"It's time, I suppose," Gwen murmured, "that I simply put the matter to rest." She made her way upstairs, feeling a heaviness wash over her. She knew that what she was about to do would help ease Hank's concerns, but it would it only serve to stir up her own pain.

She went to her room and quickly retrieved the battered suitcase from under her bed. Hank had asked to see it and anything else that Harvey had left behind. Gwen couldn't help but run her hand over the scratched, dried leather.

"Oh, Harvey. I do miss you. You and Pa, and the way you'd make us laugh, even when life seemed hard."

Gwen pushed aside the thought and took the case with her as she made her way to Hank's room. She had thought to simply leave it on his bed and then let him know that he was free to sort through what little there was. But as she reached the door that separated the girls' hallway from the rest of the house, Gwen was surprised to find Hank coming up the stairs.

"I . . . ah . . ." She clutched the suitcase close and tried not to seem so surprised. "I thought you might want to go through this."

Hank looked at the case and then met her gaze. "Is that Harvey's?"

"Yes. Everything he left behind is here. Well, with exception to his clothes. We gave away the good ones and turned the rest into rags. But the letters he wrote me, my wedding band, his watch and Bible—they're all there in the suitcase. I swear this is all I have that belonged to him."

"Would you go through it with me?" he asked.

This surprised Gwen. She had hoped to avoid the memories. "I hardly think that's necessary."

"But I'd like for you to be with me. That way in case anything disappears or turns up harmed, you'll know it wasn't me." His eyes seemed to plead with her.

"Very well," Gwen said. "Why don't we take it downstairs."

"We could just go through it here in my room."

She shook her head. "That would hardly be appropriate."

"We can leave the door open. I'd hate for just anyone to

wander in while we're going through these things," Hank said softly. "It would seem an intrusion."

Gwen smiled. "But it's not an intrusion if you go through them?"

"I wouldn't put you through this if it weren't important."

She heard what sounded like regret in his voice. "I'm still not convinced that my husband was your brother, but I suppose this is the only way to resolve that. If you don't conclude things for yourself one way or another, I fear for your existence here at Gallatin House."

He couldn't help but chuckle. Reaching out, he took the case from her. "I can take care of myself. You needn't worry."

"But I do worry, Mr. Bishop. At this rate, I worry my sisters will burn the place down, just on the slight chance that they'll somehow inconvenience you."

This caused Hank to roar with laughter. Gwen liked the way his skin crinkled around his eyes.

"Come on. Let me see what you have here."

Hank led the way to the bedroom and placed the case on the bed. "It's in pretty bad condition, isn't it?"

"It was that way when we found Harvey. He and it both looked like they'd been through a lot." Gwen paused at the doorway momentarily, then stepped toward the bed.

"I don't recognize this valise." Hank closely inspected the leather, as if looking for something that might reveal the truth to him.

The latches unfastened, but the straps nearly tore apart as Hank released their hold. He opened the case and pushed back the cloth lining that hung in frayed disarray. Inside were the few articles Gwen had mentioned. There were several letters addressed to Gwendolyn Gallatin. They were tied with a red ribbon, and a small gold wedding band had been knotted in place on top. She easily remembered the day she'd created the bundle.

"The day after Harvey's funeral, I put them in there," she whispered as Hank picked up the bundle.

"Was this your wedding ring?"

She nodded. "It had belonged to my mother. My father saved it for me. Harvey wanted to take some of his gold earnings and get me something pretty, but I told him this ring had greater value to me."

"And the letters?"

"You can keep them here and read them later, in case there is some cryptic message that leads you to what you're looking for." Her tone was harsher than she'd intended, but she couldn't bring herself to apologize.

Hank put the letters on his nightstand and reached back into the tattered case. He pulled out Harvey's watch and held it up. "Now we have our proof."

"What do you mean?" Gwen asked.

"This watch. I gave Harvey this for his eighteenth birthday."

"No. He told me his friend gave it to him. It's even engraved," Gwen said. She couldn't bear to think that the ruthless thief Hank had described was truly her Harvey.

"It is engraved. I had it done, inside the cover." He held it up. "I don't even have to open it to be sure. I recognize it."

Gwen bit her lip and tried to breathe normally. "Very well, Mr. Bishop. What does it say?"

"*Cuisvis hominis est errare, nullius nisi insipientis in errore perseverare.* Any man is liable to err, only a fool persists in error."

Gwen felt the blood drain from her head. A dizzying wave overcame her and caused her to grip the footrail of the bed.

"Here, sit," Hank said, pulling her to the edge of the mattress.

For several minutes, Gwen couldn't speak. She was overwhelmed with the moment—with the truth. How could this be happening? How could the entire past that Harvey had shared with her be nothing more than a lie?

"I'm sorry," Hank said, kneeling beside her.

Gwen looked at him. What could she say? He'd been right about everything. Now she had to wonder if Harvey committed other deceptions, along with the stock certificates and jewelry.

"I don't . . . I don't know what to say or think right now."

He shook his head and took hold of her hand. Gwen wanted to pull away. He was the enemy. He was the one who had ruined it all. She didn't move, however. The warmth of his fingers on hers was almost mesmerizing.

"I'm glad you have your proof," she finally managed. "But I still don't know how to help you."

"I have a thought, if you'll hear me out."

Gwen nodded. What choice did she have? Mr. Bishop had already proven her husband to be a liar. She owed it to him to cooperate in any way possible.

∞

"Mr. Bishop would like for me to accompany him to Virginia City to search for the items Harvey stole," Gwen announced to her sisters.

Hank watched with great interest at their reaction. Beth shook her head, while Lacy looked at him like he'd suddenly grown a second head.

"You can't go off alone with him," Beth declared. "It wouldn't be appropriate. He could kill you in your sleep."

Hank nearly choked on his coffee at this statement but managed to swallow in the nick of time. "I beg your pardon?"

Beth shrugged. "Well, there's no telling what you might do to her if you had her alone."

This much was true, Hank realized. He was finding himself more and more drawn to Gwen and her gentle spirit. At first, it was nothing more than his hope to woo her in order to get what he'd come for. But now he wasn't so sure.

Gwen sat completely still. Her stiff, unyielding posture suggested to Hank that she was hoping to just put all of this behind them.

"I'll take one of you with me," Gwen said.

"Take Lacy, then," Hank threw out. "I wouldn't want there to be another 'accident.'" He eyed Beth with a raised brow. "I'd hate to roll off a cliff in my sleep."

Beth rolled her gaze to the ceiling and crossed her arms. "You are a very unforgiving man, Mr. Bishop."

"Lacy will come with me. Beth, you can run Gallatin House for a while. I'll ask Patience to come and help you," Gwen announced.

Her sisters turned in unison to look at her as if she'd lost her mind. Hank noted, however, that even as Beth began to protest this idea, a look crossed over Lacy's face that suggested something else had come to her mind.

"It won't take all that long," Gwen told Beth. "We'll go on horseback so we can move quickly. We'll be gone a week, maybe a few days more. You should be just fine."

"I still don't like it."

"I think she's right, Beth," Lacy said, suddenly taking her sister's side. This made Hank even more suspicious. "The sooner we do this, the sooner Mr. Bishop will leave us alone. I'll get things ready and have Simon make sure our horses are in good order." She got to her feet and left the house before anyone could say another word.

What was she up to? Hank couldn't help but wonder at her sudden enthusiasm. Gwen, too, seemed rather taken aback by her younger sister's action. She looked at the front door and then back to Beth.

"I promise we won't be gone any longer than we have to be. I'm not even sure the place where we lived in Virginia City is still standing."

Gwen stood, causing Hank to do likewise. He might be in uncivilized country, but there was no need to forget his manners. She was a lady, after all.

"Well, you might as well take him to Norris, too," Beth said, getting to her feet. "Harvey could have hidden something there, as well. Goodness, but I'll never marry. In-laws are just too much trouble." She went off in the direction of the kitchen.

Hank laughed. "She'll be some man's pleasure and curse to bear. A lady of her caliber won't stay single for long."

"Beth is no one's curse. That job, unfortunately, is mine," Gwen said as she walked from the room.

Hank stared after her for several moments. It was the second time he'd heard her reference herself in that manner. How was it that she saw herself as cursed?

❧

Gwen had finished packing for the trip and had just brought her small pack downstairs when Dave Shepard knocked on the door and poked his head in. "Howdy, Gwen."

"Come on in, Dave. What's going on?"

"I'm afraid it's your sister." He took off his hat and ran his hand back through blond hair. "Lacy is causing trouble with some of the area ranchers."

"In what way?" Gwen put her pack down and straightened.

"Yes, in what way?" Beth asked as she came in from the dining room.

Dave looked rather sheepish. "I'd just as soon talk to Gwen alone, if you don't mind."

"Well, I do," Beth said, placing her hands on her hips.

"I do, too," Lacy said, following in behind Beth.

Dave looked to Gwen. She felt sorry for him, but there was no way either of her sisters were going to leave now that he'd announced a problem with Lacy.

"Okay." He turned his back on the girls and faced Gwen. "Sheriff wants you to keep Lacy from going out to the area ranches and snooping around."

"Have you been doing this, Lacy?" Gwen asked.

"I just figure if the sheriff won't do his job, then I will," Lacy said, defending her position. "It's not my fault Dave and his boss are lazy."

"If you can't keep her home," Dave continued, "Sheriff Cummings said we'll have to arrest her for trespassing."

"Just let him try," Lacy said, coming to stand in front of the six-foot-three deputy. "It'll take more than you, Dave Shepard. You'd better bring an army if you plan to arrest me."

"I'll bring as many gentlemen as I need," Dave promised, leaning down until they were nearly nose to nose.

Gwen watched as Lacy gave him a smirk. "But if only gentlemen are allowed, you'll have to stay behind."

He pressed forward, causing Lacy to bend backward to avoid his touching her. "I'll bring hardened criminals if it means settling you down. Why can't you just be a lady like your sisters?"

"Oh!" Lacy gasped and stepped back. She was nearly at a loss for words and stormed from the room. "I'll show you!"

Dave couldn't seem to leave well enough alone. "Why don't you learn knittin' or quiltin'? That would keep you too busy to run around stickin' your nose in where it doesn't belong."

"If I were you, Dave," Gwen said softly, "I'd leave now. There's no telling what she's gone to fetch. There is a rifle in the kitchen, you know." Beth nodded and threw a glance over her shoulder.

He blanched ever so slightly. "I guess I have overstayed my welcome. Just see that she stays home, Gwen. Otherwise, I'm afraid she'll get hurt."

"She's coming with me to Virginia City and Norris," Gwen told him. She pushed him toward the door. "That ought to keep her plenty busy for at least a few days."

❧

"I heard Lacy is going with you and Gwen," Nick said.

Hank looked up from securing the last of his gear to the saddle. "You heard right."

"I don't envy you." Nick laughed and moved to finish saddling Gwen's horse. "Lacy Gallatin is pretty worked up about finding her pa's killer. I don't know how much good she'll be to you on this trip."

"At least it's not Beth going along."

Nick frowned, and Hank could see there was something in what he'd said that bothered the younger man. He checked one more time to make sure his cinch was tight enough. This whole saddling thing was new to him, and while he'd practiced every day since acquiring the animal, Hank was far from expert.

"Beth's a good woman. She's not anywhere near the trouble her sister can be." Nick straightened and pushed his dark brown hair back.

"Well, she's given me a fair amount of grief, and I'm just as glad to have her stay here. Maybe having her hands full with the extra work will keep her from pulling any pranks."

"Beth?" Nick shook his head. "I don't know that I would ever believe her capable of that. She can get her dander up—"

"Seems to me all of the Gallatin women are good at that," Hank replied. He gave Nick a smile. "I've never met women with more gumption and determination."

"I'll second that," Simon said, joining them. "The Gallatin girls are strong. They have to be to make it out here."

"And then after all their pa put them through . . . He used to really regret that."

"What did he put them through?" Hank asked.

Nick shrugged. "Oh, just things like workin' 'em hard, movin' them from place to place all the time. They never had a real home after their ma died, until Gallatin House."

"How did their mother die?" Hank found himself suddenly wanting to know everything.

"Childbirth, I think. They don't talk that much about her." Nick came to where Hank stood and nodded. "You're gettin' better. Looks tight enough to keep you going."

Hank pulled several coins from his pocket and handed them to Nick. "Thanks for your work. If I find what I'm looking for in Virginia City, I may not be back this way."

"Well, good luck to you," Nick said, taking the money.

"You're takin' all your clothes in those saddlebags?" Simon asked.

Hank looked at the bags and shook his head. "Some of my clothes have met with . . . well . . . an accident. At least, that's how Miss Beth Gallatin describes it." He moved toward the door, and Major jumped up from where he'd waited near the front of the stall. "We'll be back shortly for the horses."

Hank and Major were just crossing in front of Rafe's Saloon when the owner himself made an appearance.

"Howdy, stranger."

"Hello," Hank said, nodding.

"You've been around these parts for a spell now, but you've not come to see me."

"I've had no business with you."

Rafe frowned. "I'm Rafe. I own this here saloon and den of pleasure." He laughed. "I figure everyone has business with me."

Hank shook his head. "I'm afraid not. I've no use for your type of business."

"So what is your business, mister?"

"Just that. *My* business." Hank narrowed his gaze and stared hard at the man, as if challenging him to suggest otherwise.

"It's a small town. Just lookin' out for it and the people who live here," Rafe said. He stuck his thumbs in his waistband and rocked back on his heels. "I'm kind of the self-appointed mayor."

"I doubt anyone other than you sees it that way," Hank said with a smile. "Nevertheless, I assure you that my motives are pure, and my deeds are not to cause harm to any of . . . your people."

"Then why not share a drink and a bit of fun?"

"Because saloons are not my idea of fun."

Rafe let out a grunt. "I suppose you're one of those do-gooder Christians like the Gallatin girls. Can't abide for folks to enjoy themselves." He turned and stomped off into the saloon, leaving Hank to stare after him.

Hank shook his head. Rafe had completely misjudged the situation. Hank was neither a do-gooder, nor a Christian.

CHAPTER TWELVE

The skies were still streaked with light when Beth came to check on Nick's leg. The days were growing longer and longer, and Beth liked that she could still tend to business well into the evening.

Nick was focused on the work before him and didn't even hear Beth's approach. She thought he looked quite handsome as he deftly handled a piece of iron. She couldn't make out what he was doing exactly, but his dark hair fell over his left eye in such a way that she wished she could push it back.

"Hello."

Nick looked up mid-stroke. "What are you doing here? Kind of late, isn't it?"

"I finished my work and figured to check on you. Patience is minding the house."

Nick put his things aside and wiped his hands on his apron. "Sure glad she decided to come stay with you. I wouldn't have felt good about having you there alone."

"I'm perfectly capable of taking care of myself." She hoped her tone betrayed her irritation that he would think otherwise. "How's your leg? I came to check on your progress."

"You don't need to worry about it," he said with a grin. "I'm perfectly capable of taking care of myself."

She crossed her arms. "Sometimes, Nick Lassiter, you are a very difficult man." Turning to go, she hoped he'd call her back or maybe come after her. She wasn't really mad at him, but neither could she allow him to sass her. She deserved respect.

"Can't take your own medicine, eh?" he said, joining her on the walk back to Gallatin House.

"I was just being neighborly," Beth said, sounding more put out than she felt.

"But I can't be?" he questioned.

They walked past Rafe's, and Beth could see there was some activity going on inside. Cubby waved from the front door, where he sat polishing a spittoon.

"Evenin', Miss Beth," he called. "Howdy, Nick."

"Cubby," Nick replied and nodded.

Beth poured on the sweetness in her tone. "Hello, Cubby. How are you doing? How's your arm?"

Cubby raised his left arm and circled it around. "Much better. Thanks for the liniment. Pa said I probably just strained it carrying those barrels up from storage."

"Glad to help," Beth replied. "Glad, too, that you don't take offense like some when I ask after your injury."

This clearly confused Cubby, but he only lowered his arm

and went back to work. Beth made her way to the porch with Nick at her side.

"That was a bit uncalled for, don't you think?" Nick asked.

"I'm sure I don't know what you're talking about," Beth said in the same sweet tone.

"You know very well what I'm talking about. I didn't take offense because you asked about my leg. I just didn't want you frettin' over it. It's healing just fine. There's a large bruise, but otherwise, I'm perfectly well. Does that satisfy you?"

Beth took a seat on one of the porch benches and smiled. "I'm glad to hear that you are doing well."

He sighed and went to sit on the porch rail opposite her. "If you care so much about me, Beth Gallatin, why won't you let me court you?"

Beth hadn't been prepared for this line of questioning. Nick and Simon had each asked to court her on different occasions, but Beth had always refused them. They knew why.

"You know very well why I won't court you."

"Because I have an occasional beer?"

"That and other things."

Nick shook his head. "I just don't see that an occasional beer hurts anyone."

"An occasional whack over the head with a tree branch doesn't hurt anyone all that much, either," Beth's sarcastic tone was not lost on the man.

"It's not like I go get drunk at Rafe's. I never do that. I never have."

"You don't have to defend your actions to me, Nick Lassiter." Beth got up and moved to the porch swing. She sat down and kicked out her feet to get the swing rocking.

"You must feel guilty, since you need to so adamantly explain your actions."

Nick pushed off the rail and came to stand in front of her. "I don't feel guilty for havin' a beer. I just don't understand why that keeps you so uppity in regards to courting me."

Beth shook her head. "It isn't just the beer. You aren't a Christian."

"And what makes you say that? I don't get drunk. I don't cuss. I help people when I can and do good when I get a chance. There isn't a church around here for quite a few miles, or I would probably go every Sunday 'cause I like to hear good preachin'."

"But those things don't make you a Christian, Nick."

"Just 'cause I don't go around carryin' a Bible and prayin' all the time doesn't mean I'm not a Christian."

"Yes, but the fact that you think being good can save your soul implies to me that you don't really understand. You need to trust Jesus. Believe in Him, repent, be baptized, turn from your wicked ways, and live for God."

"And I suppose one of my wicked ways is drinkin' a beer once in a while?"

Beth shrugged and let the swing slow to a stop. "I didn't say the beer was necessarily evil, in and of itself. A beer sitting in a mug doesn't do anything wrong or right. But the effect of that beer could cause a great deal of harm once it's ingested. You've seen it, and so have I. It's most likely the reason my father was killed." Beth's voice broke with emotion she hadn't anticipated. "They were drinking that night, Nick. You know they were."

Nick sat beside her, and the porch swing suddenly seemed very small to Beth. He reached for her hand, and she looked away, not quite sure what to do. She didn't want to offend him by pulling away, but neither did she want to encourage him with false hope.

"I wish it had never happened, Beth. I also wish you wouldn't judge me so severely. I might not be doing everything you think is right, but I care about you. I'd be a good husband to you."

Her head snapped up to meet his gaze. "Husband?"

He smiled. "Well, that is what courtship is all about. I wouldn't consider it with a woman if I wasn't also thinkin' towards marriage. I'd like to make you my wife, Beth."

She drew a deep breath. "I can't . . . even think . . . about marriage to you." She got to her feet, knowing that his nearness was distracting her thoughts.

"Because I drink beer and, in your book, I'm not a Christian."

"You are helping to support Rafe and his business. Those poor women are suffering as prostitutes because you are helping Rafe to prosper."

"I've never visited any of those women. I wouldn't do that," he said, jumping to his feet. "And for you to suggest I would—"

"I didn't say that you did. It's just that by going there to drink, you are helping Rafe make a profit so that he can buy more girls."

"And you don't help him at all?"

Beth looked at him in disbelief. "Of course I don't help Rafe!"

"Who was here first? Rafe or the Gallatin stage stop?"

"We were. Why?"

"Rafe built his saloon because of the stage stop. He saw the prospects and knew that with a main road and freighters and stages going through and stopping here for meals and for the night, there would be plenty of business for him, as well."

"It's not my fault that the men leave Gallatin House and go there for . . . entertainment," Beth protested.

"But if you weren't here—if Gallatin House weren't here—then the stage wouldn't stop. If you didn't hold the contract agreement, there would be no passengers—no customers. Think about that before you go trying to pluck the speck out of my eye, Miss Gallatin."

He vaulted over the rail of the porch and stalked off across the yard to the road. Beth watched him go but did nothing to stop him. He was wrong—wrong to suggest that Gallatin House was the cause of anything associated or related to Rafe's business. But in the back of her mind, a nagging doubt needled at her conscience. Maybe she *was* the one who was wrong. Maybe if there were no Gallatin House, there would be no Rafe's Saloon.

"It's hard to get used to the sun being up for so long," Hank told Gwen.

They rode side by side, while Lacy was well up ahead, scouting out a safe place to make camp for the night.

"When we first came here, it was hard for me, as well. Winters are even worse, however, with there being so little light. The days are often bright enough, but for a much shorter time. The darkness is much harder to deal with."

"So where did you live before coming here?"

Gwen laughed. "It's probably easier to say where we *didn't* live. We moved around a lot. Pa was always trying his hand at one thing or another and never was much good at anything until we got the roadhouse."

"And what about your mother?" Hank had wanted to ask her about this since talking with the Lassiters.

"She died in childbirth when I was nine." Gwen stared straight ahead. "We lived in Texas then, and my father worked as a cowhand. We lived a fair distance from town, and when my mother went into labor, we girls were alone with her.

"She didn't think anything of it, of course. She'd given birth three times before, and she was pretty sure that, with my help, she could deliver safely again."

"But she didn't?"

Gwen shook her head and looked at Hank. "No. The baby was too big. She was in bad pain for a long time, and then she began to hemorrhage. Beth did all she could to help me, but we knew we needed Pa and a doctor. Lacy was just five, but she was the only one I could send. She could already outride Beth and me, so I helped her saddle a horse and sent her to find our father."

"Sounds like a terrible responsibility for little girls to manage."

Gwen squared her shoulders. He thought she looked as if she was trying to put distance between herself and the memory. "It was the life chosen for us. We had to be strong and do what was required of us."

"Did Lacy find your father in time to go for a doctor?" Hank asked softly, surprised by the compassion he felt for this woman. Here she was, the one keeping him from Boston and all that he knew, and yet he felt sorry for her. Something about the way she looked made him want to hold and comfort her. Those were feelings that hadn't stirred in him for some time.

Gwen didn't answer right away and by the time she did, Hank could see that Lacy was stopped up ahead. They would soon be reunited, and then he knew such confessions would end.

"She didn't find him at all. When Lacy came back, our mother was already dead. Beth was hysterical."

He studied her profile for a moment, imagining her as a child. "But not you."

She shook her head. "No. I realized there was nothing to be gained in crying about the situation. It certainly wouldn't bring her back."

"What did your father do when he came home?"

"He was devastated. He blamed himself. Lacy blamed herself, as well. She was never the same after that. None of us could convince her that it wasn't her fault, that Mama would have died even if Pa had made it back. We even had the doctor talk to her, but she wouldn't believe it. After we buried Mama, Pa moved us to Nebraska, where his widowed sister lived."

"How long did you stay there?"

"A year."

"Why only a year? Where did you go after that?"

"My aunt died, so we moved to Illinois, where my father's parents lived. They died the next year, and we moved again." She waved at her sister and seemed to shrug off the darkness of her tale at the same instant. "Looks like Lacy has found us a place to camp."

Hank wanted to ask more questions but knew it would have to wait. There was a resolve in Gwen's tone that suggested she was done with the memories and storytelling. He watched her kick her horse and hurry ahead to speak with Lacy. His black tried to pick up speed as well, but Hank held him back. He needed a moment to gather his thoughts. He needed time to extinguish the feelings that Gwen had flamed to life.

CHAPTER THIRTEEN

"You girls certainly know your way around a camp," Hank said, finishing the last of his coffee. "You cook as well here as you do at home." He moved stiffly toward the fire to retrieve another cup.

"Thank you. We've a fair amount of experience," Gwen replied.

"I'll say," Lacy added. "I honestly think we've spent more time cooking over campfires than kitchen stoves."

Laughing, Gwen nodded. "Possibly."

"I'm beginning to think there isn't much you ladies can't manage." He winced as he sat back down on the ground.

"You aren't used to riding all that much, are you?"

Hank looked up with a grin. "I hoped it didn't show."

"Your moving around like an eighty-year-old man gave it away," Lacy said rather snidely.

"It'll pass in time," Gwen added. "But you'll feel pretty bad, come morning."

"I'll manage," he said, nursing the coffee.

Gwen tried not to notice the start of a beard forming on Hank's jawline. She tried, too, not to notice how nice he looked sitting there at the camp, wearing his despised red shirt. He'd forsaken the coat earlier, but now that the sun had set, the mountain air was quite chilly, and Gwen wondered if he'd soon reclaim it.

Lacy added more wood to the fire and stoked it up. "Gwen, I need a bit of privacy. I'll be back in a few minutes." She took up a Sharp's .50-caliber rifle and headed down toward the thicker stand of trees near the river.

"Will she be safe?" Hank asked.

"She'll be fine." Gwen patted the shotgun beside her. "We know how to shoot and defend ourselves. We've learned to be prepared for just about anything over the years. After our grandparents died, we girls only had each other while Pa was off working. Once, we were living in a soddy on the Kansas prairie when a snowstorm hit while Pa was off helping some neighbors. The blizzard lasted four days, and the girls and I did just fine. Pa came as soon as he could, but he said he never worried about us even once."

"I can't even begin to imagine. Back in Boston, children are watched over quite closely. At least in the circles from which I hail."

"Things are different west of the Mississippi, my pa used to say." Gwen stretched her hands out to the fire. She'd decided at the last minute to bring her father's leather coat and was now quite glad she had. The warmth of the wool-lined piece was welcomed as the temperatures continued to drop. "You have to grow up fast out here."

They fell silent, and for several minutes Gwen stared at the flames and thought of what they were doing. She hadn't been back to Virginia City since leaving nearly five years ago. She wondered if seeing the place again would stir up uncomfortable memories. Times had been so hard there at first. Eventually, her father and Harvey had made a modest living. Norris had proven to be even better, but there had been pain along the way, as well.

She looked up and found Hank watching her intently. It was as if she were a puzzle, and he needed to figure her out. When he realized she was watching him, Hank's gaze seemed only more intimate. His expression made Gwen tremble, and she quickly looked away, rather unnerved. If she hadn't known better, she would have thought his look one of longing—even desire. His next words only served to confuse her more.

"Will you ever marry again?"

"Excuse me?" She looked back at him, and the passion in his gaze was gone.

"I just wondered if you would ever marry again. Are you over losing my brother? You seem awfully young to put aside the idea of a husband and family."

Gwen hadn't expected such a line of questioning. "I . . . well . . . no. At one time I wanted a husband and family."

"What changed your mind?"

Gwen thought about the curse upon her life. She'd seen too much loss, and she feared should she marry and have children, it would only be that much worse. Still, what could she say to Mr. Bishop? He'd never understand her situation. He was much too calculating and logical. He would call her silly and dismiss the entire matter. Gwen thought perhaps she could distract him with a different line of questioning.

"What about you? Have you ever been married?"

He shook his head. "I've been too busy trying to establish my business and, of late, look for Harvey." He paused. "I've noticed that folks refer to you as Miss Gallatin. Why don't you call yourself by the Bishop name?"

"Harvey and I were . . . well . . . we never had a chance to . . ." She let the words trail off. "It's why I took back my maiden name. Pa and I discussed it," she hurried on, embarrassed that she'd allowed the conversation to turn so intimate. Why was she rattling on in this manner?

"Pa said it might be less confusing if I went back to just being Miss Gallatin." She laughed rather nervously. "So my plan is to remain a spinster, Mr. Bishop."

"No wonder you looked so stunned when I called you Mrs. Bishop." Hank looked at her for a moment, and then it was as if a light of understanding went on in his head. "I think I comprehend the situation. Harvey got sick on your wedding day."

"Yes," she said, glad to have that matter settled. She could see Lacy's shadowy form in the dim light. Gwen got to her feet, needing to distance herself from Hank and his insight into her situation.

"And you being a good Christian girl, and Harvey having taken on the same beliefs, you never . . ." He looked up, and Gwen felt her face grow hot.

"No. We never."

She took the rifle and hurried to Lacy. "I'll be back in a few minutes." She was desperate to just let the matter lie. She didn't know why it bothered her so much. A part of her had wanted Hank to understand that she'd never consummated her marriage. For reasons that were beyond her, it seemed important that he know. Maybe he would better understand her convictions—her heart.

But for the life of her she didn't know why that was so important to her.

Hank watched Lacy approach the camp. She looked at him oddly for a moment. "Did you upset her?"

"Why would you ask that? Do you always just suppose I'm going to say or do the wrong thing? Do you really think so poorly of me?"

Lacy plopped down on the ground and stared at him hard. "Yes, Mr. Bishop. I do think that poorly of you. You might as well know—I don't trust you. I don't know why Gwen ever agreed to this trip. I suppose she was hoping it would get you out of our hair that much quicker if you were satisfied that there was nothing to be found."

"She knows it's important to me and is just too kindhearted to do otherwise," Hank replied. He liked Lacy, despite her tough-as-granite exterior, knowing she cared deeply about her sister. He not only admired that, he understood it, as well.

"And you knew she'd feel that way and took advantage of her," Lacy replied.

"I suppose I did . . . a bit," Hank said thoughtfully. "But it wasn't for the purpose of causing her harm or pain. This entire trip has been made on behalf of my loved one—my mother. She desperately needs her money returned to her. My step-father had a great deal of business debt, and my mother had to sell most everything to see it paid off. Now she needs money to live on, or her future will be quite grim."

"If you care so much, why don't you take care of her?"

"That's exactly what I'm doing." Hank shifted to stretch his legs out in front of him. "I don't expect you to understand, Miss

Gallatin, but my mother grew accustomed to living a certain way—in a specific manner of comfort. I'd like to see her continue in that. I have money—at least, a reasonable amount—but most of it is tied up in my business affairs. Finding the stocks would allow me to return them to my mother, sell a few for her immediate needs, and help her start a new life."

"What is she doing all this time while you're gallivanting all over the country?"

Hank smiled. "She's living with her sister in Rhode Island."

Hearing movement in the trees, Hank was relieved to see Gwen heading back to the camp. "Your sister is quite a woman. I can't imagine many ladies being quite so brave."

"She is brave, but she's also fragile in many ways. She's much too hard on herself and way too kind toward strangers." Lacy fixed a cautious gaze on him. "I'd suggest," she continued, "that you sleep on the far side of the fire tonight. Gwen and I will sleep over here."

"And why would that be?"

Lacy shrugged. "I won't have you hurting my sister—even by accident. I'm a light sleeper and a crackshot, Mr. Bishop. I wouldn't hesitate to shoot if I thought you were harming Gwen."

"Couldn't we just go back to dyeing my shirts?" Hank asked with a grin. "I still have one that's white."

Lacy smiled. "Just be warned. I love my sister, and I won't see the likes of you hurting her."

Gwen was in hearing range now, and Hank could only hope she hadn't overheard Lacy's threat. She didn't seem to have any concerns, however, as she took her place at the fire. "It's certainly chilly tonight." She placed the rifle between her and Lacy, arranged her split wool skirt, and shivered.

"Would you like my jacket?" Hank asked. He got up to retrieve it. The ache in his backside was worse than it'd been when he'd dismounted.

"No. I'll be fine once I warm up here," she answered, sliding closer to the campfire.

Hank pulled on his coat and noted that Lacy watched his every move. It was Gwen, however, who captivated his attention. He couldn't explain the feelings he had for her. Learning that she and his brother had never been intimate somehow pleased him. But why? Why should that matter?

He eased back to the ground but said nothing. There was a concern growing in his mind that perhaps he'd allowed himself to be sidetracked by Gwen Gallatin. Perhaps his anger had served him better, for he no longer felt the same sense of drive to find the certificates as when he'd first arrived. Oh, he still wanted them—still intended to recover them—but now his mind was clouded with additional thoughts. He actually found himself wondering what it might be like to relocate to the Montana Territory. The land was ripe for new business—especially general stores. Towns were springing up everywhere, and businessmen with sound minds and plans could find success.

"I suppose I don't really have the right to ask a favor of you, Mr. Bishop, but since it seems that everything Harvey told me was a lie, I wonder if you might tell me about your childhood—and his."

It seemed a simple and reasonable enough request, but Hank hesitated. Did he really want to remember those days?

"I'll understand if you'd rather not," Gwen added.

"No, it's all right," he finally replied. "I was six when Harvey was born. Our father was seldom around long enough to do anything but cause trouble. His passion was gambling and alcohol rather than our mother. My grandfather, however, was a loving man who could not abide his son's neglect. He took it upon himself to step into the shoes abandoned by our father. In fact, my only experience sleeping out in the wilds, under the stars like this, was with him."

"In the city?" Lacy scoffed. "That hardly qualifies for the wilds."

"Lacy, don't interrupt," Gwen chided.

Hank smiled. "There are still some unspoiled and rather wild areas in the East, Miss Gallatin, I assure you. My grandfather actually took us quite a ways from the city into the western woodlands of the state. But that hardly matters now."

Hank couldn't suppress the bitterness that edged his tone. "Our grandfather died the year after my father was wrongfully hanged for a crime he didn't commit."

"Hanged?" Lacy shook her head. "That sounds like the kind of thing that would happen here."

"It actually happened in the backcountry of Virginia. The next day, they learned who really had stolen the horse, but it was too late. Vigilante justice had been served. When the men responsible learned the truth, they took up a collection for my mother. They gave her fourteen dollars. She once commented that my father had been worth more to us dead than alive. Ironic, don't you think?"

"I'm sorry, Mr. Bishop."

"My father deserved his fate. Even if he wasn't hanged for the right reason, my grandfather often said my father should have been hanged for one thing or another. My father caused such misery that my grandfather felt his death might bring some inkling of peace."

"How did your grandfather die?" Gwen asked.

"The years simply caught up with him. It was hard to lose him," Hank admitted. "He taught me much, and I will always be grateful for that. A few years later my mother remarried. Our stepfather was the complete opposite of our father. Martin Bishop believed in strong discipline and a plan for the future."

"Bishop?" Gwen asked. "But wasn't your last name already Bishop? Was he related?"

"No. He adopted us and we took his name when he married our mother. He insisted it be that way, and frankly, after the grief given in my childhood, I was glad to have a new start."

"Was he a loving father?" Gwen asked.

Hank thought about this for a moment. "In a way. He loved my mother dearly and knew that in order to reach her heart, he would have to be good to her sons. Otherwise, I'm not convinced we would have mattered. Still, he did well by us, although Harvey could never see it. Harvey was difficult at every turn. He resented our stepfather for taking a good deal of our mother's attention—attention Harvey had always enjoyed until that time."

"It's so hard to imagine Harvey that way," Gwen admitted.

Lacy finally chimed in. "Yes, my sister is right. The Harvey we knew was a loving man who—"

"It's obvious Harvey had some change of heart after leaving us," Hank interrupted.

"The change had to do with giving his life to Jesus," Gwen said softly. "Our father helped him to come to a better understanding of God when Harvey was so sick. He would pray over Harvey's feverish body every night before going to bed. Then each morning, my father would bathe Harvey and pray for him again. As Harvey recovered, he wanted to know why our father put such stock in prayer. He wanted to know how it was that Pa could trust a heavenly Father he'd never seen or touched, when earthly fathers often failed so miserably with their children."

Hank felt a band tighten around his heart. Hadn't he asked himself the same question? A growing discomfort washed over him. He wasn't sure he wanted to know the answer. Somehow, he was very certain that knowing the answer would mean making some kind of change to his already well-ordered world.

He got to his feet, unable to suppress a groan. "Guess I'm getting old." He motioned to the darkened woods. "I believe I'll take my turn."

"Better take the rifle," Gwen reminded.

"I'll be fine," he replied and kept walking despite the pain. If he turned and saw her face, Hank knew he'd beg her to give him the answer Harvey had learned. Worse still, he knew beyond a doubt that, no matter what she told him, he'd believe her.

CHAPTER FOURTEEN

Virginia City yielded nothing useful to Hank. He was still sore and stiff—still frustrated by the lack of information or answers. They didn't even have white shirts in stock that would fit his rather broad-shouldered frame. The girls took him to the shack they'd lived in with their father and Harvey. It was little more than a ten-by-ten log structure that Hank had figured to be used for storage. When Gwen had announced that five people had actually lived within its meager confines, he had a new admiration for the girls.

Folks in the area had pretty much given up on gold. There were a few old-timers still panning and working the creek beds, but the town was a mere shadow of what it once had been. Hank spoke to anyone he thought might offer him answers, yet he found nothing but additional questions.

The days slipped by, and as the trio made their way toward Norris, Hank couldn't help but notice the temperatures had dropped considerably. It was nearly June, and they had seen both uncomfortable heat and bone-numbing chill within the same twenty-four-hour period.

"It's amazing to me that it could be so hot in Virginia City and so cold here," he said as they set up camp for the night in the mountains southwest of their next destination. Lacy had chosen their route, declaring she knew a shortcut back to Norris. Hank thought it beautiful country but worried that the valley would have been a better choice for them. At least there they had a well-established road. Here, it was little better than a path.

"Those clouds suggest snow," Lacy said. "I don't like the looks of it, Gwen. Maybe we should push on."

"But you said yourself that this was a good place for shelter. This rocky overhang will keep any snow off our fire, and we have plenty of water from the stream."

"I suppose," Lacy said, looking again at the sky.

"Even if we get a storm, we have a good supply of wood and food. I'm sure we'll be just fine."

"You aren't seriously thinking it will snow that much, are you?" Hank could imagine a few flakes, but certainly nothing more dramatic.

"It's dangerous to not be prepared," Gwen told him. "Mountain weather is too unpredictable."

Lacy nodded. "Pa used to be able to tell us almost to the minute when we could expect a rain in Kansas, but not here. I'm gonna gather more wood, just in case." She took up an ax and headed off toward where several trees had fallen and were long dead.

"Should I help her?" Hank asked.

Gwen looked to where Lacy had gone, then shook her head. "There's just the one ax, and Lacy likes to work with her hands. You can always offer later, but right now I think she needs to be alone. She's been pretty moody lately. I'm not sure what's bothering her, but she's not talking about it."

Hank could well understand; he had been troubled by his own thoughts of late. He couldn't help but wonder what would happen if they found nothing in Norris. Should he simply return home without the documents? And what of Montana? He could easily bring his mother to live with him, and they could have a pleasant life together. She would want for nothing. Perhaps that was the answer.

"Is there some way in which I could assist you?" he asked, abandoning the urge to make a decision.

Gwen smiled. "You've already done enough. Sit and relax. I know you're still sore from riding. I can try to rub some of the ache from your back, if you like, after we eat. I'll have supper ready in just a few minutes."

He wasn't sure he could relax. Not around Gwen, and especially not if she touched him. Their days of travel had put them in such close contact that Hank found himself thinking about her constantly. He didn't like the idea of her remaining a spinster. If ever a woman needed a husband and children, it was Gwen Gallatin.

Settling on the ground and leaning back against the edge of the rock face, Hank tried not to watch her as she worked, but his gaze kept traveling back to her form. His thoughts continued to nag him. Why would she give up on marriage—on a husband and children? Was her love for Harvey so deep that she couldn't bear the idea of another man's touch?

She appeared surprised to find him watching her. "Is something wrong?"

"No. I was just thinking." He quickly forced his mind to put his thoughts on the outcome of the trip. "I want you to know that I was wrong."

"Wrong? About what?"

"I had you figured for a gold digger. When I learned Harvey had taken a wife, I figured you had seen the jewelry and stocks and presumed Harvey was a wealthy man. I know now that I was wrong. Obviously you loved my brother quite deeply— otherwise you wouldn't still mourn him."

Gwen's expression turned confused. "I don't still mourn him. I mean, I wish he hadn't died, but that was a long time ago. At least, it feels like it now. I know Harvey is safe in heaven, and it comforts me to know that."

"Then why remain single? If you aren't still in love with my brother and are able to let go of your sorrow over his loss, why did you say you planned to remain a spinster?"

Gwen straightened and squared her shoulders. Hank watched as she seemed to steel her emotions. "Because I'm dangerous for others, Mr. Bishop. When I love someone, bad things happen. It's just the way things are."

Lacy was making her way back with an armful of wood; otherwise, Hank might have asked Gwen exactly what she meant. Sooner or later, when they were alone, he would ask. He needed to know exactly what she meant.

⮌⮎

Gwen could scarcely draw breath. She wanted to scream, to shout out a warning to Lacy, but it was too late. The rowdy cowboys circled her little sister and pointed their revolvers at her while Gwen was frozen in place.

"We're gonna see you dead, just like your pappy," one of the men said. He grinned to reveal yellow, rotting teeth.

It seemed that invisible arms held Gwen in place. She tried to move, but her legs felt like they were made of stone.

"Lacy!" she tried to yell. Her mouth formed the words, but no sound came out.

Just then one of the cowboys fired his gun. Gwen screamed, but again nothing could be heard. She watched Lacy sink to the ground, clutching her bleeding abdomen.

"No!" Gwen moaned. "No!"

"It's all your fault," one of the cowboys declared. "If you weren't cursed, none of this would be happening. It ain't us that killed 'em." She looked across to where there were now several bodies laid out beside Lacy's. She could see her father, Harvey, Beth, and even Mr. Bishop.

"It's all my fault. I shouldn't have gone," she cried.

Someone took hold of her. Perhaps they meant to shoot her next. She used all of her strength to fight back. The arms only tightened around her.

"Wake up. Miss Gallatin, wake up."

She heard the voice, but nothing registered in her mind. She fought and then he whispered against her ear, "Gwen. You're safe. It's just a dream. Wake up."

"I shouldn't have gone," she moaned, her head flailing from side to side.

"Gwen."

She opened her eyes and found herself in Hank Bishop's arms. His face was only inches from hers, and he cradled her like a mother might a babe.

"Why are you . . . what's happened?" She suddenly went very still as the images of her dream—her nightmare—came back to mind. "Oh," she whispered.

"Are you all right? You were crying and screaming. I thought maybe Lacy would come to wake you, but she slept on." He smiled. "So much for being a light sleeper."

"What are you talking about?"

He laughed. "She told me she was a light sleeper—that I'd better mind my ways."

Gwen smiled groggily. Sleep still tried to hold her captive. "Lacy's like that."

"So I gathered."

He reached up and pushed back long strands of hair from Gwen's face. His touch against her cheek felt warm and pleasant. Gwen felt mesmerized. She couldn't draw her gaze away from those steely blue eyes.

"Do you want to tell me about it?" Hank asked, his voice soft and reassuring.

"There's really nothing to tell. It was just a bad dream."

"I get the impression it was more than that. You said something about it being your fault—about how you shouldn't have gone somewhere. Tell me about it."

Against her will, Gwen found herself confessing. "When I was nine, just three weeks before my mother's death, there was a fair in town. Pa took us, but Mama wasn't feeling up to it. She did, however, warn us about doing anything we knew was wrong. She told us not to go into any of the saloons, not to play cards or go off with strangers, and definitely not to see the fortune-teller. I was fascinated, however, when this old woman told me she could tell me my future. When you're young, that seems most impressive."

Hank smiled and nodded. "Go on. What happened?"

Gwen relived it as if it were yesterday. "I told the woman I only had a nickel. She said she'd make an exception for me, because she felt certain I needed to hear my future. I gave in.

I went into her tent and listened to her tell me I was cursed—that death had marked me to be his companion—that most everyone I loved would die, while I would live. Three weeks later my mother died, and I just knew it was my fault."

"That's nonsense. I don't believe in curses," Hank said firmly.

"There are plenty of examples of people who were cursed in the Bible," Gwen countered defensively.

"Yes, but isn't there also something about Jesus becoming a curse for us? Seems to me your faith in God would cancel out any gypsy curse."

"There's a verse like that? Are you sure? I mean, you aren't . . . you don't even . . ."

He laughed. "What? You think that just because I'm cynical about God that I don't know anything about Him? Believe me, I've looked into it. I grew up with a mother whose faith was quite strong. And my grandfather completely put his trust in God."

"But you couldn't?"

Hank shrugged and touched her cheek once again. "I wanted to. I wanted to know a father's love—the security that comes in belonging. I wish I could have your kind of faith, Gwen."

Hearing him call her by her given name caused Gwen to tremble. He was too close—too gentle and kind. Realizing that he still held her, she pulled away.

"I'm sorry. I . . . ah. . . . I'm sorry." She got to her feet and could see a faint hint of light at the edge of the mountains. It would soon be light. The air still held a taste of snow, but thankfully the ground was dry.

"I think we should wake Lacy and get going." She went to where her sister slept and reached down to shake her. To Gwen's horror, however, Lacy wasn't there. There was nothing more than her bedroll fixed to look like a person was beneath.

"She's not here!" Gwen looked around, anxious to see something that would ease her growing concern. "Her horse is gone."

"Gone?" Hank was on his feet, looking to where his black stood alongside Gwen's mount. "Where could she be?"

Lacy knew it was later than she'd planned as she hurried her horse back toward camp. Hank and Gwen would soon be waking, and it would do her little good to be found out.

Her investigation had proven fruitless. She hadn't really expected that anyone would confess to her, but she had hoped someone would at least talk to her. While in Virginia City, she learned of a cattle drive. Some of the men from the Rocking K were moving cattle south. She knew that some of their men had been at Rafe's the night her father had been killed. Learning approximately where they were, she had waited until Gwen and Hank were asleep before heading out to intercept the group.

Sneaking into camp had been easy. The night rider was asleep in the saddle, and the cattle were unconcerned with her presence. Once she was there, Lacy realized she hadn't really come with a plan. She didn't want to stampede the cattle by firing off her revolver, but she needed to get the men awake as quickly as possible if she was going to question them and get back to her own camp before dawn.

"Wake up, you bunch of no-goods," she had called out.

One man had come quickly awake and was reaching for his rifle, even as Lacy anticipated his move. "There isn't any call for weapons. I'm here peaceably."

The man had looked at her a moment, then growled in anger. "What are you doing here?"

Lacy had explained her situation, but none of the men were very cooperative. She thought they might have dragged her from her horse to give her more trouble than she wanted, until she pointed her revolver at them and announced her intention to leave.

All she wanted was some answers, but they scoffed at her and taunted her. *If only Dave Shepard would do his job, I wouldn't have to risk my life.*

She approached the camp where she'd left Gwen and Hank sound asleep. Unfortunately, that wasn't the same state she found them in now. Gritting her teeth, she urged her mare toward the other horses.

"Where have you been?" Gwen demanded. She rushed to Lacy as she dismounted. "I was terrified when I found you gone."

"I'm sorry. I just couldn't sleep. I needed to ride and clear my head. I didn't mean to worry you." She looked at her sister with a smile. "But look—I'm fine."

"You may be fine, but you're also pretty thoughtless," Hank threw in.

Lacy eyed him with contempt. "You stay out of it. You have nothing to say about my welfare or actions."

"Stop it!" Gwen declared.

Lacy wasn't used to her sister's sharp tone of voice and instantly went silent. She looked at Gwen and shook her head. "I didn't mean to worry anybody. I'm sorry. If you hadn't awakened so early, you wouldn't even have known I was gone."

"That's hardly the point," Gwen said. "I trusted you to be here. If something would have happened to you out there in the dark, we wouldn't have had any idea of it until it was too late."

Gwen's voice was laced with fear, and Lacy felt really bad for having scared her. "I won't do it again. If I can't sleep tomorrow night, I promise to wake you up and make you talk to me." She smiled. "Please forgive me."

"Of course I forgive you." Gwen pulled Lacy into her arms and hugged her tight.

Being taller than her older sister, Lacy was able to look over her shoulder to where Hank Bishop stood shaking his head. He obviously wasn't as easily convinced that nothing was wrong or that Lacy's indiscretion should be overlooked.

"Let's break camp," Gwen said. "We can eat on the trail."

"Sounds good," Lacy agreed.

Gwen went to pack up her things while Lacy tethered her horse with the others. She hadn't realized Hank Bishop had come up behind her until he spoke.

"She may buy into all of that, but I'm not so easily sold. Someone ought to turn you over their knee," Hank said in a hush.

She whirled around and met his very serious expression. "And I suppose you think you're just the man?"

He shook his head. "I wouldn't even attempt the job, Miss Gallatin. But someday, someone will. And you'll deserve it."

⚮

By the time they headed out of Norris, Hank was thoroughly discouraged. Gwen felt sorry for him. The tiny mining area where they had lived offered nothing. Even the small house her father and Harvey had put together was gone—burned to the ground during a forest fire.

She wanted to say something to encourage him, but little came to mind. Finally Gwen settled on the only thing that seemed logical.

"Mr. Bishop, I am sorry that we weren't able to locate any information about Harvey and the stock certificates. I have a thought, however. The First National Bank in Bozeman was where my father banked. It closed down last year, but the men who owned it are still in town, as far as I know. Why don't you ride over there and ask if Harvey had an account at any time? He might have kept it from me, as he apparently did everything else."

She tried not to sound bitter, but it was so hard. Even now, as the realization of who her husband had been and all of the pretense and lies he had allowed between them sank in, Gwen found her anger rising. How could Harvey have done that to her? Why would he have thought it necessary to lie?

And if he lied about all of that, had he also lied about loving her—about needing her?

"The idea does have merit, Miss Gallatin. I suppose that should be my next course of action."

She smiled. "I thought perhaps you would start calling me Gwen, like everyone else."

He looked at her a moment and nodded. "I'd like that. But only if you call me Hank."

CHAPTER FIFTEEN

"Where'd your sisters go?"

Beth looked up to see Ellie watching her with great curiosity. Beth struggled to maneuver the water cart to the house. She held a new appreciation for Lacy. Apparently she was much stronger. Beth had only hauled two loads and already she was exhausted. "They had to make a trip with Mr. Bishop to Virginia City." She brought the cart to a halt and straightened with a smile.

Ellie's eyes lit up. "I remember Virginia City. We stayed the night there when I first came here."

"It's a nice enough place," Beth admitted. "I used to live there, and the people are really good to help each other. Where'd you come from before that?"

Ellie's expression looked pained. "Cheyenne. And before that, Omaha. My husband and I grew up there."

"I heard he died," Beth said sympathetically. "I'm sure sorry."

The petite blonde nodded. "He wanted to be a rancher, but he really knew nothing about such things. He was gored by a bull. It was pretty awful, and he suffered a couple of days before he finally succumbed." Her face paled as she spoke.

"That must have been terrible for you. Do you not have other family?"

Ellie shook her head. "No. My folks are dead, and I haven't any brothers or sisters. My Billy was the only one to love me and see to my needs. We married when I was just sixteen. I'm eighteen now. Been trying to stay alive on my own for the last eight months."

Beth looked at the girl's thin, barely dressed frame. She seemed so tiny—so young. *I'm not that much older,* Beth thought. *It could have been me.* She couldn't keep from asking the question uppermost on her mind.

"How did you end up here—with Rafe?"

Ellie looked at the ground. "I was starving, and I tried to get a job. No one wanted to hire me because I was so young and inexperienced. I had few skills. I even went to the church for help, but so many folks were already on hard times for one reason or another, they couldn't."

"Surely someone could have fed you," Beth protested. "You could have stayed with someone and helped with their children."

"But I'd be another mouth to feed," Ellie said, still not looking up. "Leastwise, that's what I heard over and over. I'm ashamed to say, I started stealing food. I'd sneak into people's gardens at night and take just a bit here and there. Once, I took a loaf of bread from a windowsill as it cooled." She shook her head. "I'm not proud of what I did then. I'm not proud of what I'm doing now."

Beth was deeply moved. "But you had to do something to survive."

The girl looked up, grateful for Beth's compassion. "That's why I'm here. There didn't seem any other way. I met up with a man who was traveling. He offered to take me west with him—said there were lots of opportunities for a gal like me. I didn't know what he meant, but he offered me a steak dinner and that was all it took. I was already on the road with him when I found out what he had in mind. He wanted to take me from mining camp to mining camp and sell me out to entertain the men."

"How awful. I'm so sorry." Brutal images came to mind and Beth quickly tried to force them from her head. "Why didn't you try to get away?"

"I did, but he always came after me. Always found me and beat me afterward. I guess I just gave up trying to get away after a while."

"Rafe beats you too, doesn't he?" Beth couldn't help but remember the marks on the young woman's back.

"Sometimes. He gets worked up about one thing or another," Ellie admitted. "I try not to do anything to make him mad, but sometimes it takes just the smallest thing. Like talking to you out here."

"Howdy, Beth." Simon Lassiter said as he rounded the house. "Oh, morning, Ellie," he said, smiling.

"You know each other?" Beth asked.

"I've seen her around," Simon replied. "This is a tiny community, so it's hard not to know folks."

Ellie blushed and looked at the ground, causing Beth to wonder just how intimately Simon and Ellie knew each other. Surely Simon wasn't frequenting the makeshift brothel.

"I thought I'd check to see if you needed some wood cut." Simon looked to Beth and then to the woodpile. "Looks like it's getting down a bit. I'll chop you up some." He went and took up the ax. Meanwhile, Ellie skittered away like a frightened mouse.

Beth couldn't help herself. "How well do you know Ellie?"

Simon looked at her and grinned. "Why? Are you jealous? You know I'd marry you in a minute, Bethany Gallatin."

She caught the twinkle in his dark brown eyes. He was taller than her by a head and had strong broad shoulders from hours of labor at the blacksmith forge. He wasn't at all a bad-looking man, but Beth didn't feel anything but a sisterly affection for him.

"I wouldn't be right for you, Simon Lassiter, and you know it." She picked up a bucket of water and poured it into the washtub.

Simon turned his attention to the wood but continued to speak. "When are the girls due back?"

"I expect them most anytime. I just hope Mr. Bishop was as honorable as he seemed. I don't worry much about Lacy, but Gwen is so giving and kind, she could easily be hurt."

"I think he'll treat them right," Simon said between swings. "Nick and I both promised to hunt him down if he didn't."

Beth laughed. "I'm glad you were looking out for us."

"Like I said, I'd be happy to look out for you all the time, Beth." He turned and glanced at her.

Beth noticed, however, that his gaze quickly went beyond her to the petite Ellie, who was hanging up a few pieces of laundry on the line. She realized Simon was watching the young woman quite intently.

"I feel really sorry for her," Beth said in a low tone. She didn't want Ellie to overhear. "She's a good girl who fell into bad circumstances. Maybe you should marry her, Simon."

He looked at Beth oddly and started to swing the hammer again. "Maybe I should."

∽

Gwen looked at the skies overhead and frowned. The temperatures were brisk and the clouds heavy. The risk of snow seemed lessened by the fact that they were out of the mountains and now crossed a broad, grassy valley near the Madison River. Still, Gwen figured they would be in for a rain and that could be just as dangerous and miserable.

"The wind's coming up," Lacy said, pulling her horse up alongside Gwen. "I don't like the looks of it. I don't think we can make it home before the storm hits."

"What do you suggest?" Hank asked.

Gwen was surprised that he was willing to seek their advice. "We should definitely take cover. We aren't that far from the Shepard ranch. Why don't we just head over there? I know Patience will probably be back home by now, as we didn't have a stage due to the house for a couple of days. She'd welcome us with open arms."

Lacy frowned. "I suppose you're right. I just hope Dave is

elsewhere. I'm in no mood to hear how I ought to be wearing a dress."

Gwen noted her sister's form-fitting pants. She'd said nothing about them because of their travels, but she'd fervently hoped Lacy would change back into her split skirt before they returned home. "We'd best be at it, then. There's at least another five miles, and those clouds are rolling right in." Gwen maneuvered her horse back onto the trail and urged him to pick up the pace.

"Road seems decent enough," Hank said, making small talk.

"We'll cut away from it once we get past the river. It'll be quicker that way." She noted that Lacy was looking for the best place to cross. The horses wouldn't like it; they were already quite nervous.

"How did your father get enough money to buy the stage stop?" Hank asked out of the blue.

"This looks good," Lacy called back and started her horse into the Madison River.

"Come on," Gwen hurried to catch up.

The water was deep enough at one point that the horses had to swim for it, but they quickly managed the river and were up on the other side before things could turn bad. Gwen noted that the current was pretty fierce. No doubt the spring melt was causing the river to rise higher than usual.

She thought of Hank's question and realized he would want an answer. She hesitated—not because she had anything to hide, but because she wasn't sure he'd believe her.

Gwen tightened her grip as her horse spooked at the wind. "As for the Gallatin House purchase, my father met with some luck in Norris. As I told you, he bought a claim from an old-timer. Actually traded him food, clothes, and a little money for it. The man had found some color, but not a lot. Pa was hopeful they would strike it rich. He and Harvey started working it—Lacy panned and Beth and I did odd jobs around the area—mostly mending and laundry, some cooking, too. We put our money together no matter what, however. It was our way of helping contribute.

"Anyway, it was only a few days after the man left that Pa and Harvey found several large pieces of gold. They figured it was a fluke, but within days they'd amassed a tidy amount. They hid it away and continued to work, but the gold thinned out, and soon they were back to finding only bits here and there. By this time, Pa had made friends with many of the stage and freight drivers from his time in Norris and Virginia City. He found out about Gallatin House, which wasn't much more than a scrawny cabin. We decided to put all our money into it and build a regular stage house where folks could sleep and get meals."

"So he sold the claim in Norris?"

"Yes. There were plenty of others who wanted to try their hand at making their fortune." Gwen laughed. "It's kind of funny the way folks think they'll somehow find what everyone else has missed."

Lacy joined in at this point. "If you're honest, Gwen, you'll have to admit Pa was one of those folks."

Her sister was absolutely right. "Pa was always sure his pot of gold was under the next rainbow."

Hank smiled. "But it wasn't, eh?"

"No. Pa was not at all what I would consider lucky," Gwen declared. "He tried so hard."

"But he wasn't good at much," Lacy added. "Except talking

to people. He was a great talker, and folks loved to hear his stories. The stage drivers particularly enjoyed coming to the house. They said that out on the trail they got lonely, and Pa helped ease that feeling."

"They used to joke with Pa about hiring him to come along and just talk to them."

A few sprinkles of rain began to fall. Gwen pulled her wide-brimmed hat down lower. "We did our best to help, but there was never all that much we could do."

"We didn't want Pa to feel bad, though," Lacy said sadly. "He always felt bad enough."

"It's true," Gwen replied. "Still, I don't know why he had to struggle with it so. He knew we loved him."

"It's important to a man to provide for his loved ones," Hank said. "He probably felt like he'd failed you."

Gwen looked at him for a moment. "Is that what drives you so much to find these things for your mother?" She thought he looked uncomfortable for a moment, but then he quickly went back to his neutral expression.

"I don't want her to suffer. She worried so much after Harvey left. It nearly killed her. She mourned his absence like a death."

Gwen had never thought about it that way. She couldn't imagine a mother having a child disappear and never again hearing from him. "Does she know he's dead?"

"No. I haven't let her know. I figured information like that needs to be shared in person. When I head back, I'll go to Providence and tell her."

"That's kind of you. Let her know, too, what a good man Harvey turned out to be." Gwen couldn't keep the edge of regret from her voice. "He really was a good man—we're not just exaggerating that. I suppose he had to grow up fast when he came west."

"And nearly dying is bound to change a man," Lacy offered softly.

"I'm sure it would," Hank admitted. "I know it will mean a lot to my mother to hear these things."

Lacy surprised them both by turning to Hank. "Who's A. R.?"

He looked startled. "What?"

"A. R. You have it carved on your saddle skirt. Why?"

He looked away, and for a moment, Gwen thought perhaps he wouldn't tell them. Then he shrugged casually and looked back at them. "A. R. is me. At least, it was before my stepfather adopted me. It was also my grandfather on my father's side. I was named after him. I inherited his saddle when he died and kept it all those years. When I made this trip west, I knew I'd have to ride a horse at least some of the time, so I brought the saddle with me." He laughed. "Sounds silly, I suppose, but I felt like I had a part of him with me."

"It doesn't sound silly at all," Gwen said before Lacy could reply. "What does A. R. stand for?"

Hank looked away. His expression was clearly one of discomfort. "Aloysius Rivers."

Gwen and Lacy both started at the name. "Aloysius?" they questioned in unison.

"Hank's my nickname. My father gave it to me. He said it was less controversial than Aloysius."

"He was right," Lacy agreed. "Say, Gwen, didn't Harvey have—"

"Stop!" Gwen ignored the coming storm and stopped her horse. The other two could only do likewise, unless they wanted to leave her behind. Hank turned his horse to face her, while Lacy just looked back over her shoulder.

"What's wrong?" her sister asked.

"Nothing is wrong," Gwen said, shaking her head. "I want to be the one to tell him."

"Tell me what?" Hank shook his head even as he questioned.

She met his concerned expression and smiled. "Remember I told you Harvey had a dear friend that he told me stories about?"

"Of course."

"His name was Aloysius," Gwen said softly. The meaning was clearly not lost on Hank. Obviously Harvey hadn't wanted her to know he had a brother, but he couldn't quite leave Hank behind him.

Hank looked at her for a moment, then nodded. "I can just imagine the stories he told you."

She laughed. "There was the one about when you decided to be chimney sweeps. Oh, and the time when you snuck out of the upstairs window to go off to some mischief, and he followed you. Or the time—"

"Enough!" Hank said, raising his arm in mock horror. "I can't bear to hear any more."

The three shared a laugh, and for the first time, it seemed Hank had let his guard down completely. He seemed happy that they knew his secret—almost as if a weight had been lifted from his shoulders.

The rain began to fall in earnest, and the wind whipped down the canyon, sending the droplets toward them like icy blades.

"We're going to get drenched. The ranch is just over the

next hill," Lacy called out against the wind. "Come on!" She kicked her horse hard and flew off in a gallop.

Gwen did likewise and found Hank at her side, keeping up easily. For a man who hadn't that much experience in riding horses, he was learning fast.

CHAPTER SIXTEEN

"Goodness, but you're all soaked to the skin!" Patience Shepard declared. "Girls, I have clothes you can change into. You just come with me. Mr. Bishop, I'll be with you directly. Just stand there by the fire."

"But I'll drip all over the rug," he protested.

Patience laughed. "It won't be the first time it's been dripped on. You'll find we don't worry about such things around here."

Gwen allowed Patience to hurry them off to her bedroom. She fussed over Lacy's long, wet hair and insisted she sit by the fireplace to dry it. "You'll get sick for sure if you don't get it tended to."

"I'm made of tougher stuff," Lacy said with a laugh, "but the fire does sound good."

Gwen was quickly out of her wet jacket and blouse. She was grateful for Mrs. Shepard's tender care. It was nice to be watched over.

Patience handed Gwen a dark brown garment. "Here's a serge skirt. I have blouses in the wardrobe that will be a little bit big, but they should work until we can get your clothes dry. Just help yourself."

"If you have an iron," Gwen said, putting the skirt aside in order to change out of her own wet things, "I can always dry it out that way."

"I'll put the irons on," her hostess declared, "but in the meantime, just hang them on these hooks by the fireplace. They'll dry out pretty well, and you can iron out the rest of the dampness after you have some supper." Patience moved to the door. "I'll leave you girls to change. Just join us downstairs when you're dressed."

"Thank you so much," Gwen called after her. She turned to find Lacy struggling out of her wet pants.

"Mercy, but I'm glad I packed my split skirt," Lacy said, putting the pants aside. She reached to unfasten the ties on her saddlebags. Pulling dark blue material from inside, she smiled. "See? Nice and dry."

"Well, don it quickly. We don't need you catching your death." Gwen took up the skirt and pulled it on. "Sure glad we came here. That wind is really howling out there. I hope it doesn't snow."

"Even if it does, it'll pass quick enough. It's that time of the year." Lacy got into her split skirt and then pulled a wrinkled but dry blouse from the other side of her bag. She slipped into the calico top, then without bothering to button or tuck it in, she squatted down by the fire and began to work her fingers through her wild hair. "Hmmm, this feels wonderful."

Gwen explored the wardrobe and found a simple blue cotton blouse that had seen better days. She drew it out and quickly dressed. Joining Lacy at the fire, she sat on a small stool and watched her sister for a moment.

"Lacy, I want the truth."

Her sister looked up rather sheepishly. "I suppose I can guess what this is all about."

"Did your disappearance the other night have to do with looking for Pa's killer?"

"Yes."

Lacy didn't even try to lie, and Gwen was grateful. "Lacy, you have to stop."

"I can't. Nobody else is worried about getting to the truth."

The firelight glistened on her face. Gwen thought Lacy looked so small and vulnerable like this. She longed to protect her sister from pain and the danger she seemed so determined to claim for her own.

"You have to stop."

"I can't, Gwen. Please don't ask me to, because I can't. Pa deserves justice."

"But what would justify his death? Another killing? Seeing a man die who never intended to kill Pa in the first place?"

Lacy met Gwen's eyes. Seeing the pain in her little sister's expression, Gwen reached out. "I know it hurts. I know it's a hard thing to bear, but we have each other, and we have God. He will see this thing brought around right. God alone knows for sure what happened, and He's not going to just sit by and let the innocent suffer."

"Why not?" Lacy questioned, standing. "He's done a pretty good job of it so far. Especially with this family. We've done nothing but suffer."

"That's not true," Gwen replied.

Lacy fastened the buttons on her blouse and refused to look at Gwen. "Please just stay out of this. I can't leave it alone until I have some satisfaction. If the sheriff isn't going to take it seriously, then I have to."

"But you could end up getting killed. I couldn't bear to lose you. I've already lost so many others," Gwen said, fighting back tears. "Oh, this is all my fault."

"None of it's your fault, Gwen. It's this accursed country and the men in it. Men who don't feel they need to worry about the law—because the law isn't worried about them."

Gwen felt a stabbing pain at Lacy's choice of words. It wasn't the country that was cursed. She couldn't make her sister see the truth of it. For a moment, she couldn't think of what to say. She longed to convince Lacy to remain safe and sound at Gallatin House, but Gwen couldn't even believe for sure that they were safe there.

"This is a cruel territory that just demands too much of its people," Lacy said, tucking her blouse into the waistband of her skirt. "The isolation is enough to make even the sanest person mad. The weather would just as soon kill you as let you live, and the terrain is unforgiving."

"Then why did you agree we should stay and keep Gallatin House running?" Gwen asked in complete disbelief. She'd never heard Lacy talk like this before. She'd always presumed that, of all of them, Lacy was the one who loved Montana and the independence the primitive land afforded.

Lacy's sober expression made her age before Gwen's eyes. "I couldn't very well look for Pa's killer if we moved. Plus, I don't want to help Rafe in any way. Selling out to him would do just that."

"But if there were another buyer?"

Lacy moved to the door, mindless of her wet, tangled hair. "Then I'd say sell. I'd have more time to find the murderer if I didn't have to help out with the stage and the house." She opened the door and left Gwen to consider her words.

A million thoughts swirled inside Gwen's mind. Lacy had grown so hard and bitter. What might happen if Lacy actually found the man responsible for their father's death? Would she try to kill him herself? Would she force him into Bozeman at gunpoint? Gwen shuddered.

Lacy could hear Patience working in the kitchen and quickly exited the house. The rain had stopped temporarily, but the wind still blew with a bone-numbing chill. Making her way to the barn, Lacy knew their horses would need to be put away properly. They had only taken the time to stable them when they'd first arrived, and it wasn't fair to leave them standing in their saddles for much longer.

"Easy, there," she said as she came upon Hank's black. The horse was a fine specimen and stood at least sixteen hands. If he hadn't been gelded, he might have been good for breeding.

Lacy quickly unsaddled the horse and took off the damp blanket. Hanging both over the side of the stall, she went to look for a towel to use to dry the gelding's back. She had barely begun her search when a voice called out.

"If you're looking for your pa's killer in our barn, I can assure you he's not here."

Straightening, Lacy met the amused expression of Dave Shepard. "I'll be the judge of that," she replied with as much sarcasm as she could muster. "After all, you and the sheriff haven't been looking for him, so I have to believe that the barn hasn't been searched, either."

Dave frowned. "Why can't you leave well enough alone and

be like other women?" He went to Gwen's mount and quickly unsaddled the horse.

"I'm sure I don't know what you mean," Lacy replied innocently. She went to her own gelding and quickly freed the cinch.

"You know full well. You need to act more the part of a woman—a lady. You need to leave a man's job to a man."

"If there were any available, I'd happily do so," she said, taking a few steps toward him. Just before she reached him she veered to the right and tossed the saddle over the stall. "If you were doing your job, as I've said before, I wouldn't have to."

Dave moved to her with lightning swiftness. He took hold of her arms and held them tight. "You are playing with fire. You're stirring up folks in a way that isn't going to bode well for anybody. You have to stop it, or Sheriff Cummings is going to put you in jail."

Lacy bowed her head and sniffed. "No one cares." She did her best to beckon tears to her eyes. If Dave wanted her to act like a girl, she'd oblige him. "It's just so hard. You have no idea."

Dave loosened his grip just as she'd hoped. "I'm sorry, Lacy. Nobody wanted to see your pa die."

"It's just that there's no one to count on. We're just three women." She sniffed again and wiped her eyes. Looking up, she batted her lashes for effect. "We need a strong man to help us. We're all alone."

"You aren't alone." He reached out and gently touched her cheek. "You might not believe it, but I care a great deal about what happened. I'm doing what I can."

Lacy turned away and hugged her arms to her body. "Oh, it's just too much. I can't bear it anymore." To her surprise, Dave came up behind her and wrapped his arms around her.

Her reaction was swift and unexpected. She elbowed him hard in the ribs and brought her boot down hard on his foot.

Dave let out a yell that they could have heard in the house if not for the roar of thunder. "What was that all about?"

She smiled. "A lady doesn't allow a man such liberties. Surely you realize that. If I'm to be a sniveling little flower and act like a lady, then you, Mr. Shepard, should learn how to act like a man and not an animal."

He was clearly shocked. "Act like a man?"

She raised a brow. "That's what I said."

"I'll show you how men act," he said, reaching out to pull her into his arms without warning.

Lacy never expected him to kiss her. Worse still, she never expected to like it. He let her go with the same abruptness he'd taken her hostage. She was so shocked by the entire process, in fact, she could only stand there, looking at him rather stupidly after he released her.

He stormed from the barn, never uttering another word. Lacy forgot about towels and the horses momentarily. She touched her lips and frowned. What in the world had just happened?

Supper was a strange affair. Hank observed the easygoing manner in which Patience and Jerry Shepard entertained. They were completely unconcerned that visitors had dropped in on them from out of nowhere. Patience laughed and talked with them, all while serving copious amounts of delicious food.

"You might as well stay the night with us," Jerry said after returning from checking on the weather. "It's raining again, and there's no telling how long it will go on."

"I'd hate to be a burden," Gwen said, looking to Lacy and then to Hank.

"It's probably for the best," Hank suggested when the normally outspoken Lacy said nothing. Something wasn't quite right with the girl.

Gwen nodded. "Thank you. I suppose it would be safer to stay than try to pick our way home in the dark. We'll leave at first light."

"Well, if it's still storming in the morning, you're welcome to stay here as long as you like," Patience said with a smile. "I can't tell you how nice it is to have young ladies in the house again."

"Have you heard from the girls lately?" Gwen asked.

Hank saw the sadness cross their hostess's expression. "No, but I heard from my folks. The girls don't plan to return to Montana. Not even for a visit. They've got beaus now, and my mother seems to think things are serious. If they decide to wed, I'll probably never see it."

"Oh, but you could go back East for the wedding," Gwen suggested. "Even if they won't come to you."

"I don't know that I could," Patience answered. "I don't know if I could bear it. I suppose we'll wait and cross that bridge when the time comes."

"Well, they are young ladies," Lacy said, finally joining the conversation. "It's only right that they conduct themselves as such."

Hank saw Dave look up and eye her with contempt. "Unlike some," he muttered.

Lacy ignored him and looked instead to her sister. "I'm feeling ever so tired." She put her hand to her forehead. "If you don't mind, sister dear, I'm going to retire for the evening."

"Oh brother." Dave got to his feet. "I think I'm going to

be sick." He stomped off, nearly knocking over his chair as he went.

"I can't imagine what's wrong with him," Patience said, getting up. "I think I'd best go check on him."

Hank could only imagine. Given the orneriness of the Gallatin girls, he wouldn't have put it past the smug Lacy to have poisoned the poor man.

CHAPTER SEVENTEEN

⤫

The house was painfully quiet. Outside, the wind had calmed and the rain had ceased, but in spite of this, Gwen found it impossible to sleep. She got up and sat on the side of the bed, hoping her movement wouldn't wake Lacy. There was no sense in stirring the whole house just because she couldn't rest.

She lit a candle, hoping the dim light wouldn't be a nuisance to her sister. Lacy slept on as though dead to the world. Gwen couldn't help but wonder what was going to become of her youngest sibling. Lacy seemed to attract trouble, just by the nature of her being. She wouldn't allow people to tell her she couldn't do something.

Lacy's obvious disgust with Dave Shepard had made the evening difficult. Gwen had tried to get her to talk about it when they'd come to bed, but Lacy would only say that the day had been particularly trying and that Dave had been the bulk of the problem.

Poor Lacy. She couldn't really remember their mother, and it haunted her. From time to time, she would ask Gwen questions about her, and it almost seemed as if Lacy were desperately trying to remember something—anything—that would offer her comfort and connect her to the past.

Taking up the candle, Gwen moved to the small desk by the window. The Shepard house held a coziness that Gwen appreciated. There were homemade curtains at the window and handmade quilts on the bed. Even the rug upon which the bed stood had been braided by Patience. Mrs. Shepard had often said that her daughters wouldn't appreciate the homemade articles once they found luxury in the East. She had always known that her daughters were given to wanting more than the West could offer.

Raindrops remained on the window, causing Gwen to reach out as if to touch them. The pane of glass was cold, making her grateful to be spending the night indoors. Almost against her will, she thought of Hank Bishop. He was Harvey's beloved Aloysius. That amused her to no end. It also gave her new hope in Hank's character. Harvey had spoken of Aloysius as if the man could walk on water. He had told her that, next to her and Jesus, Aloysius had been his best and most beloved friend. For some reason, to know that it was Hank comforted Gwen a great deal.

She hugged her arms against her body. The chill of the room was enough to send her back to the comfort and warmth of the bed, but Gwen continued to wrestle with all she'd learned about Hank and her husband. If Hank spoke the truth about who he was and why he'd come, then there had to be some explanation. The stock certificates had to be somewhere. She retraced their steps, thinking of actions years earlier as they moved from Virginia City to the mining camp at Norris and then to Gallatin House. Harvey never mentioned anything about stocks or wealth. She'd never seen any pieces of jewelry and could only presume he'd used them to pay for his life prior to coming to Virginia City.

Oh, Harvey, why did you do this? Why did you put your family in this bind and cause so much grief? You were such a good man when I knew you, but obviously there was another part of your life I knew nothing about.

Gwen then thought of Hank and how he'd changed since coming to stay at Gallatin House. He had arrived with such rage and anger that she'd been afraid of him. His declarations and comments had been frightening, for they always managed to shake the foundations upon which she took comfort.

It was hard to imagine Harvey as Hank had described him, but perhaps even more troubling was Hank himself. Gwen couldn't keep from thinking about him. She remembered with great embarrassment how he'd held her the night she'd had the nightmare about Lacy—could still feel his arms around her.

Moving the candle to one side, Gwen put her head on the desk and imagined what it would be like to be in his arms again. Hank was older than Harvey, and his features were completely different. He had a serious nature that matched her own, yet he also had a humorous streak.

"He'd make a good husband," she whispered.

The idea so startled her that Gwen jumped up. "Husband?"

She heard Lacy moan and held her breath. She hadn't meant to be so loud. Turning back to the table, Gwen was just in time to see the overturned candle set fire to the curtain. For a moment, she could only stare as flames quickly climbed up the length of the window.

What have I done?

She put out her hand as if to extinguish the flames, but they were already well beyond her reach. There was nothing to be done but call for help. If she didn't hurry, the entire house would be aflame.

Smoke quickly filled the room as Gwen went to the bed to awaken her sister. "Lacy!" She groped for her sister's form and battled the stinging burn of the smoke in her eyes. "Lacy, wake up!"

"Hmmm, what?" her sister murmured and rolled over.

Gwen shook her hard and coughed. "Wake up. There's a fire. Hurry. We have to get help."

Lacy sat up and coughed against the acrid air. "What happened?"

"I'll tell you later. Come on. I'm going to get Patience and Jerry."

Gwen ran for the door and opened it. The fire seemed only to grow with this action, sucking greedily at the new draft of air. Knowing Dave was just across the hall, Gwen pounded on his door first. "Dave! There's a fire!"

Dave could be heard fumbling around and within seconds was at the door. His groggy appearance passed quickly as he seemed to take in the situation all at once. "Get my folks up. I'll get Hank."

Gwen did as he told her. She was crying by this time. "Oh, Patience," she said as the woman came to the bedroom door, "I've set fire to your house."

Lacy ran for the water pitcher almost as soon as Gwen exited the room. She knew there wasn't much chance that it would put the fire out, but she hoped it might slow things down.

She poured the water into the bowl, thinking it would afford her more coverage as she threw it. This proved to be the case, and Lacy felt confident that this had been the right thing to do. Next she grabbed the quilt and climbed onto the chair by the desk to pound out the fire.

"What are you doing?" Dave asked, coming up behind her.

"Having tea, what's it look like?" She coughed hard and continued to swing the quilt at the flames. She was making good headway, and soon the fire would be out.

"Get out of here," Dave said, grabbing her by the waist. He whirled her around off the chair and took the quilt from her. "Get out!"

Hank came into the room. "Let me help."

"I was . . . doing . . . just fine," Lacy declared between fits of coughing.

"Get her out of here," Dave said, taking over where Lacy had left off. Hank led her from the room as Jerry Shepard arrived to aid his son.

Lacy coughed all the way outside. She found Gwen sobbing in the arms of Mrs. Shepard and heard her sister's confession.

"I hadn't meant to startle. I knocked the candle over. It's all because I'm cursed."

"That's nonsense, Gwen, and you know it. It was just an accident," Patience countered.

"I could have killed us all. I could have burned the house down to the ground."

"But you didn't. Now calm yourself. See, there's Lacy,

and she's just fine. The boys will soon have the fire under control."

Gwen looked at Lacy and in a broken voice asked, "Are you . . . are you . . . all right?"

"Yes. The smoke . . . got to me . . . that's all." Lacy's struggle to speak only caused her sister to cry all the more.

Lacy felt the icy air blow through her borrowed flannel gown. It wasn't much protection against the cold. The feeling of having no air in her lungs continued to leave her weak. Her throat burned from the smoke's irritation.

"The fire is out," Hank announced from the doorway. "The place is plenty smoky, though. We should probably open everything up, despite the cooler temperatures."

"We'll get to it," Patience said. "Come along, Gwen; you can help me."

Lacy watched her sister dry her tears and follow after the woman like a small child with her mother. Hank waited for them at the door, then joined them inside.

Unwilling to head indoors, Lacy walked to a small stone wall and sat down. The cold of the rock permeated the thin gown, but she didn't care. Right now, all she wanted to do was stop the coughing. After a few minutes she started to feel better, but just when she thought the worst of it had passed, another fit would take her.

"Here, drink this."

Lacy didn't even bother to look up. It was Dave, and he'd no doubt come to give her a hard time about fighting the fire. Goodness, but men could be so silly. If she hadn't started fighting the blaze, things might have gotten much worse. Surely he could see that.

"Lacy, I have some water here. Ma said to drink it."

She straightened and looked at him for a moment. Taking

the glass in hand, she did as he'd instructed. The water felt cool and cleansing against the smoky taste in her mouth. Lacy felt better almost immediately.

"Thank you," she whispered. Her throat felt raw, so she drank again.

"Are you all right?" he asked softly. He sat down beside her and slipped something around her shoulders. Lacy quickly realized it was his coat.

"I'm fine."

"Not burned anywhere?"

She looked at him oddly. "No."

"Are you sure?"

Lacy felt her defenses rise. He always made her feel like she was a little child. Well, not always. There was the kiss . . . She shook that memory away. "I'm fine. Do you want to check for yourself?"

Dave surprised her by grinning and getting to his feet. "You sound more like your old self now. That was quick thinking up there. Thanks for saving my folks' house."

"Not exactly a ladylike thing to do," she countered.

He shrugged. "Maybe not, but exceptions can always be made for emergencies."

She nodded. "Why are you being so nice to me? I thought you hated me." She coughed a bit, took another drink, then got to her feet.

"I don't hate you, Lacy Gallatin. In fact, I find you kind of amusing, like a runt pup we used to have. He went around with the rest of the litter, but he had to try ten times harder than any of the others to get attention. You're kind of like that, too."

"A runt pup? You kiss me, then call me a runt pup?" Lacy's anger was building by the second.

He laughed out loud at this and headed back for the house.

"If it's any consolation," he called over his shoulder, "I kissed the pup, too."

"Look, I know it's late, but I want to share something with you before you head back to bed," Patience told Gwen. "You have to understand that you aren't under a curse—nor *are* you a curse."

Gwen shook her head. "I'd like to believe that, but the old fortune-teller told me I was and that death would be my companion. Look at all the loss I've suffered—all the folks who've died. She was right about death following me, so why not assume she was right about my being cursed?"

"But people die all the time. Look at all the people born."

"Not in my family."

"Gwen, God doesn't work that way."

"But there are all sorts of people in the Bible who were cursed."

"True, but they were folks without Jesus to save them from their sins. Listen to this."

Patience opened the Bible. "It says right here in the third chapter of Galatians, verse thirteen, 'Christ hath redeemed us from the curse of the law, being made a curse for us: for it is written, Cursed is every one that hangeth on a tree.' Don't you see, Gwen? Jesus became a curse for us. We can't be cursed if we are in Him."

"Hank told me there was a Bible verse that said as much," Gwen admitted. "I just don't know what to think about it. For so long now I've believed this to be my burden to bear."

"But it's not. No one stands to gain anything positive by such thinking," Patience told her. "Only Satan is served by continuing down such a path. He wants you to feel defeated and hopeless. He wants you to focus on yourself instead of on

Jesus. On the cross, Jesus took your curse and bore it in your place, while He gave you salvation."

Gwen pulled her shawl close. "Then why has there been so much death in my life? Mama and the baby she carried, my aunt, my grandparents, my husband . . . my father. They're all gone."

"They were all older or had circumstances that often take lives. I would imagine if you look at folks around you, you would see there are more similarities than not. You have had your share of sorrows and loss—there's no doubt about it. But you aren't alone, and it certainly wasn't due to some curse upon you."

"I'd like to believe that."

"Then do," Patience said with a smile. "God has freed you from such things. Don't let yourself be taken into bondage because of a lie."

"But I'm afraid. I worry about Lacy and Beth. I could have killed Lacy tonight. I could have killed you all."

"The fire could have done that, but it didn't. God was with us and watched over us every second. The fire damage was minimal, and now everyone is safely back to bed. Except for you."

Gwen shook her head. Exhaustion was claiming her strength by the minute. "You should go to bed. Morning will come soon enough."

"We should both go to bed," Patience said with a smile. "Gwen, I care deeply about you and Lacy. Beth too. You girls are like breaths of fresh spring air to me. I miss my girls so very much, but with you and your sisters nearby, I at least feel useful. Don't be deceived by the prince of lies. He wants you to doubt your value—your usefulness. He wants to steal your joy. Don't let him, Gwen."

Gwen nodded. "I'll do my best."

Later as she snuggled into bed, ignoring the scorched scent, Gwen thought of the verse Patience had shared with her. Surely it was true—it was, after all, Scripture. But how did it apply to her? Wasn't it possible for a person to still bear a curse, even if Jesus had become one on their behalf?

She tossed and turned for what seemed to be forever, and it wasn't until she opened her eyes to the hint of light in the room that Gwen even realized she'd fallen asleep. Lacy rolled over and moaned.

"Are we burning daylight?"

"Don't talk to me about burning," Gwen said, looking at the damaged wall. Black soot lined the edges of the window. "I still can't believe I set fire to the house. But to answer your question, no. It's not even really light yet."

Lacy yawned and sat up. "There's not that much damage. Patience said she'll be making new curtains, and it will give her something to do. She said she'll make Dave paint the room."

"I should be the one doing all of that. I'm the one who caused the mess to begin with." She got out of bed and reached for her clothes.

"What happened, anyway?" Lacy asked, helping Gwen to dress.

"I startled and knocked the candle over."

"But why were you even out of bed?"

Gwen shook her head. "I couldn't sleep. I kept thinking of how Harvey had lied so convincingly to me all those years. I thought of how Hank . . ." She fell silent and looked at her sister's quizzical expression. "Never mind. I really shouldn't think of him at all."

Lacy nodded in agreement. "We shouldn't think of any man. They're just trouble. One minute they're being all nice to you, and the next, they're yelling at you." She pushed back the covers and stretched. "Men are just too hard to figure out, so you might as well not even try."

Gwen had no idea what had prompted this from her sister, but she couldn't help but laugh. Lacy made a very valid point.

CHAPTER EIGHTEEN

∽

Hank hadn't meant to listen in to Patience's discussion with Gwen the night before, but he hadn't been able to help himself. He'd been on his way upstairs to bed when he heard the women talking softly in the dining room. Patience referenced a verse in the Bible. It was the very verse he mentioned to Gwen. The verse that had haunted him since his father's death.

"For it is written, Cursed is every one that hangeth on a tree."

As a child of twelve, only weeks after his father had been brutally murdered by the lynch mob, Hank had gone with his mother and brother to church. He hadn't wanted to be there. He didn't feel like being out in public knowing how everyone felt about his father—a horse thief and murderer.

He knew what people thought, what they were saying. His

father was a no-account, and he deserved to die. Hank could accept that. He'd never quite understood his father's lack of concern for his own wife and children. Hank had never figured out why gambling and prostitutes held more interest, but he figured it had to do with his own failing rather than his father's.

What Hank couldn't accept, however, were the whispers of how the Rivers boys would probably follow in their father's footsteps. There were cruel comments made by the adults. They spoke in hushed tones that were just loud enough to guarantee that Hank might overhear, yet still look accidental.

But it had been no accident when his Sunday school teacher, Mr. Weatherbee, chose that verse of the Bible from which to teach. He had been staring at Hank for half of the morning, and when it came time to teach the young men their Bible lessons, the man demanded Hank come and sit close to the front of the gathering.

"God has cursed everyone who hangs on a tree," he remembered Mr. Weatherbee saying. *"Cursed them for their sins. Do you know what this means?"* He had looked directly at Hank, as if trying to force an answer, but Hank had merely looked away. Someone else had answered the question, however.

"It means they'll never go to heaven; they're going straight to hell."

Hank had known his father was a lowlife, but to think of him going to hell, condemned for all eternity . . . well, it was just too much. So, too, was the implication that if Hank followed in his father's footsteps, he would also be condemned—cursed. He'd stormed from the room and vowed never to go to church again. And he'd pretty much kept that promise.

And those were the thoughts that had haunted him through the night. They were with him even now as he made his way downstairs. He'd slept very little and hoped there might be some strong coffee ready to help him face the day.

"I thought you might be the first one down today," Patience said as he looked into the kitchen.

Hank looked at her in surprise. "You did? Why?"

"I felt the Lord put you on my heart. I got up extra early hoping you might come along so that we could talk."

"You felt the Lord put me on your heart? What does that mean, exactly?"

Patience laughed and held up the pot as if he'd asked for coffee instead. "How about a cup?"

Hank nodded. "That was actually the very thing on my mind. I couldn't sleep last night. Too much excitement, I guess." He took the mug she offered.

"Why don't you sit down, and I'll explain what I said," she offered.

"All right." Hank followed her to a small table and chairs there in the kitchen. A part of him wanted to run from what she had to say, but an equally strong part hoped desperately for answers.

"It will be warmer here. The stove is heating up nicely." She smiled as if to disarm him, but Hank didn't find it reassuring.

Sitting, Patience folded her hands together. "I tried to just go to sleep after all that had happened last night, but your face kept coming to mind. I didn't know why, but I knew I was supposed to pray for you. Then this morning I woke up much earlier than usual. I felt wonderfully refreshed and knew that the Lord wanted me to get up and start my day. Then you came to mind again, and I just knew He would bring you to me to talk."

"How could you?" The very thought of God preplanning anything on his behalf was more than Hank could imagine.

Patience shrugged. "The Lord knew you would need to discuss whatever it is that's bothering you."

Hank nursed the coffee for a moment, then looked up. It seemed crazy to be talking to this stranger, but he couldn't for the life of him refrain.

"I heard the Bible verse you shared last night with Gwen."

Patience nodded. "Go on."

"My father was hanged. He was thought to be a horse thief and murderer, and a lynch mob strung him up. A few weeks later, they found out he wasn't the guilty party, but of course, it was too late. There was nothing they could do about their mistake. Oh, they passed the hat for my mother, but it was a poor way of apologizing."

"I'm sorry for your loss."

"It wasn't like he *couldn't* have done it," Hank said. "I mean, when we heard about it, we figured he was guilty, just like everyone else. He wasn't a good man. He was a womanizer and a gambler—and broke my mother's heart on a daily basis."

Patience took it all in, nodding and murmuring. Hank found her simple acceptance of his words to be somewhat comforting. Most ladies would never have wanted to hear such a story.

"Shortly after my father died, my Sunday school teacher made a point in class of telling me my father was cursed to hell. He used that verse."

"How awful. I do dislike when people manipulate the Bible

to fit their particular agenda," Patience said sadly. "That must have been quite hard on you. How old were you?"

"Twelve."

"Very nearly a man."

"They were definitely worried about my becoming a man—especially a man like my father. I think that old teacher thought he would scare the devil out of me and save my soul."

"But he didn't, did he?" She smiled. "He only made you want to get farther away from God."

Hank looked at her and shook his head. "How did you know that?"

"Oh, it just stands to reason, Hank."

"I felt so alone. I guess . . . I still feel that way, Mrs. Shepard."

"Jesus felt it, too. He knows exactly how you hurt."

Hank laughed. "I don't believe that. He's the Son of God. How could He truly know the feeling of being alone—of being so condemned by everyone around you, there's no place you can go where you feel wanted?"

"Because Jesus took on the sins of the world. He became an abomination to everyone, but especially to His Father in heaven."

She surprised Hank by reaching out across the table and taking hold of his hand. The motherly gesture was nearly his undoing. "You have to understand—Jesus went to the cross knowing what it meant. He knew he'd become a curse. He knew the price for His actions and yet He went willingly. The pain of being separated from God was so intense that Jesus actually cried out from the cross, asking God, 'Why hast thou forsaken me?'"

"I guess I've asked that myself," Hank admitted. He put

down the cup and looked Patience in the eyes. "I'm still asking it."

There was no condemnation in her gaze. "You don't have to ask anymore. He hasn't forsaken you. He stands ready to welcome you with open arms. You have only to ask His forgiveness and accept Jesus' sacrifice for yourself. Then you won't be alone anymore."

"I want to believe that, but all of these years . . . well . . . I've been so bitter—angry. I felt it so wrong and unfair that my mother should have to suffer the shame she endured. God seemed cruel."

"He allows things to happen that we can't understand, Hank. Jerry tells me it's because we live in a sinful world that chooses to defy God. But I have to admit, sometimes I just don't understand it at all. Jerry says that's where faith comes in. Bad things will happen. People are heartless and cruel, and there doesn't always seem to be any hope of justice. But there is. Jesus is that hope."

Hank could see that she thoroughly believed what she was saying. He wanted to believe it, too. Was that possible? He suddenly felt so tired—so alone. He was that twelve-year-old boy again, longing to feel accepted . . . to be whole. It nearly overwhelmed him. Could he really find peace in trusting God? Could it be that simple?

"I know you want to believe," Patience said, as if reading his mind. "I know you want that more than anything else."

Hank fought back the roiling emotion that threatened to overpower him. "I do want it."

"Then pray with me, Hank. Pray right here and now and make it right between you and God." She smiled. "I promise you, He won't be surprised, and He definitely won't turn away."

Hank looked at her for a moment, then glanced back at the doorway to the kitchen. "Here? Now?"

She nodded. "What better time?"

Dave Shepard stared at the ceiling of his bedroom. He knew he should get up and start his day, but for the life of him, he felt unable to even move from the bed. His mind pored over memories of the night and day before. He'd acted like a fool in the barn. When he'd seen Lacy out there working to put the horses away, he'd never intended to upset her.

He'd heard threats against her and knew that her interference with the local ranchers and their workers was not boding well for her. Dave only wanted to keep her safe. He cared about her—more than he liked to admit.

Why couldn't he like Beth instead? Beth was sweet and seemed to enjoy being a lady. Lacy was something entirely different.

He shook his head and closed his eyes. Lacy was different, all right. Beth was pleasant and appreciated his company, but Lacy hated him and thought he didn't care about her father's death. She thought he was lazy. But nothing could be further from the truth. He didn't want her to get hurt.

"Lord," he prayed, "I don't know what you have in mind for me where Lacy Gallatin is concerned, but I could sure use a little help."

He thought of the kiss he'd given her. He never should have touched her. It only served to ignite a fire in him that he knew was impossible to control on his own. Dave already found himself thinking about her every day, but now she would haunt his nights. He could only plead with God for the strength to fight his emotions.

When he'd seen her in the fire, so close to the flames, Dave had panicked. He'd taken hold of her and pulled her from the desk. The urge to hold her and ensure her safety had been overwhelming, but he'd fought it. He couldn't bear the thought of anything bad happening to her.

But I can't always be there to protect her, he thought with a heavy sigh.

Lacy Gallatin was trouble. There was no way around that. If she didn't end up getting herself killed, she might very well end up hurting someone else. Either way, it wasn't something Dave wanted to see happen.

Knowing that sleep was a lost effort, Dave opened his eyes and decided to face the day. He heard Lacy's voice in the hall and smiled. She was arguing with Gwen about something.

She's always arguing with somebody about something, he thought, throwing back the covers with a smile. *I might as well get in on it.* After all, facing Lacy and her arguments was still better than not getting to be with her at all.

Beth got a fire going in the stove. She was glad she'd laid it all out the night before. The wood caught quickly and crackled and flamed to life. It wouldn't be long now before the stove would be hot, and she could get breakfast going. The morning was cold, but nothing like the winter dawns when they'd have to unthaw the bread and water before they could even start the meal.

She couldn't help but wonder when Gwen and Lacy might

return. They should have been back the day before, but she figured the storm slowed them—maybe even stopped their progress altogether. No doubt they'd be along shortly. She hoped they'd found what Mr. Bishop was looking for. She'd be glad when he left them and returned to the East. He was a thorn in her sister's side, and she didn't appreciate the torment he'd caused them all.

Taking up a bucket, Beth traipsed down to the hot springs. The warmth of steam coming off the springs felt good. It smelled of minerals—not all that pleasant, but she'd grown accustomed to it. She shivered at the brisk chill of the morning air as she made her way back to the house. It was nearly enough to send her back for a long, hot soak in the pool. And she might very well have chosen such an early-morning respite had it not been for the pounding she heard on the front door as she came back into the kitchen.

Beth put the water aside and quickly went to see who might be arriving at Gallatin House at such an hour. She opened the door to find an entire congregation of men standing on her porch.

"Hello, ma'am," the man nearest the door announced. "I'm Adrian Murphy, and these are my men. We're with the railroad." He was tall and ruggedly handsome. Beth immediately thought of the many romances she'd read. He looked like the perfect hero.

She forced her mind back to his comment. "The railroad? There isn't a railroad around these parts."

"There will be soon," the man countered with a twinkle in his eyes and a broad grin, "if we can figure out the best route to lay track. But unless we can get a decent meal, I fear that might never happen. Some of my men are ready to mutiny unless I see them properly fed. We heard about the roadhouse and thought we'd give you a try . . . well, give *it* a try." He smiled boldly, as if he wasn't at all sorry for the blunder.

Beth laughed and felt her knees grow weak. My, but he was a charmer! "Well, I suppose we can see to that. I'd hate to stand in the way of the railroad coming through." The men chuckled at this as she stepped back. "You might as well come in and make yourselves comfortable. It will be at least a half hour before we can eat."

She watched the men as they came into the house. She counted twelve as they filed past. They took off their hats and gave her the briefest nod, some even commenting on her generosity. Oh, but she wished Gwen and Lacy were back.

"Meals are two bits apiece," she told them. "I haven't gotten the fireplace lit yet, but I'll get around to it now."

"You just go on ahead, ma'am," Adrian insisted. "We can get the fire going, and two bits for a home-cooked meal sounds like a bargain, by my account."

Beth nodded. "Very well. Thank you. I'll see to breakfast. I hope ham and potatoes will suit you. We're nearly out of beef, and I haven't yet gathered the eggs. If there are enough, I'll fix those, as well."

"Sounds like a feast," Adrian assured. "After living off beans and hardtack, I can guarantee you'll get no complaints from us." He winked and smiled at Beth, adding, "Especially when the cook is so pretty."

She felt her cheeks flush as she looked away. He certainly knew how to endear himself to a gal. Beth found herself humming all the way out to the chicken coop. It was just like one of the novels she'd read. A stranger came into town and swept the heroine off her feet with one single smile.

Beth giggled, and the hens looked at her strangely as she began to gather the eggs. "I know I'm silly," she told them, "but one can never dismiss the possibilities that true love can show up on your doorstep when you least expect it."

Several of the hens clucked at this, as if chiding her for her girlish ideals. Beth refused to be moved, however, and merely lifted her chin in defiance. "What do you know about it? You're just chickens."

CHAPTER NINETEEN

Major Worthington came bounding out to meet them as Hank, Gwen, and Lacy rode toward Gallatin House. The dog barked in greeting and wagged his tail to show his approval of their arrival.

"He's sure happy to see you," Gwen commented. She dismounted and reached up to the horn to take down a large basket of eggs. It hadn't been easy to keep them from jostling around, but she thought they'd made the journey in no worse condition than when they'd started.

Hank stepped from his black and reached down to pet Major. "How are you, boy?"

The dog barked again, and Gwen laughed. "I believe he's telling you that he's fine."

"I'll take the horses to the Lassiters," Lacy offered. She

remained atop her mount and waited for Hank and Gwen to bring her their reins.

Gwen noted noise coming from the house. "Sounds like a party going on, but I can't imagine what it is at this hour." She looked around. "There isn't a stage."

"Maybe it's just a few travelers on their own," Lacy said, glancing at the house. "I'll turn the animals over to Nick and get back here to help. Beth's probably beside herself."

"Is there something I can do?" Hank asked Gwen as Lacy led the horses away.

"I don't know. There very well might be. I suppose we'll know better after we go inside." She hurried to the front door and opened it, only to have the cat streak through.

"I guess he doesn't much like the noise," Hank suggested.

"Calvin hates for his sleep to be disrupted."

Hank chuckled. "I know the feeling. Kind of like being awakened in the night due to the house being on fire."

Gwen put her hand to her throat. "I'm already mortified by what happened. You needn't tease me."

"It was an accident," Hank said with a smile. "The Shepards know that, and the damage was minimal. Make them a nice pie, and they'll forget it ever happened."

Gwen relaxed. "I would, but Patience already makes the best pies in the county."

Inside the house, Gwen could see that Beth had her hands full. There were men everywhere. There must have been at least a dozen.

"Beth?" Gwen maneuvered through the gathering as best she could. Making her way to the kitchen, she saw Beth moving with lightning speed. "Tell me what we can do. I have a basket of eggs, if that will help."

Her sister looked up and an expression of relief passed over her face. "They all want breakfast. I've been working at it for about half an hour, but I feel like I'm not making any headway. The ham is heating in the oven and the potatoes are done, but I haven't begun to work on the eggs or any oatmeal."

"That's probably for the best—at least where the oatmeal is concerned," Hank said with a grin. "Gallatin House oatmeal leaves a great deal to be desired."

Beth shook her head. "Don't start in on that. I don't have time to so much as sass you for such comments."

Gwen nodded. "Hank, please go fetch some water and more wood. You'll find the cart at the back of the house, and the hot springs run free, just beyond the pool. Woodpile and chopping block are between the outhouses and shed."

"No problem," Hank replied. He took off his coat and tossed it on a peg by the back door.

Beth looked at Gwen quizzically. "So you're calling him Hank now?"

Gwen laughed. "We just spent a good deal of time on the trail together, and I very nearly got him killed last night after I set fire to the Shepard place."

Beth nearly dropped a bowl of biscuit dough. "What?"

"It's a long story," Gwen said, pulling on an apron. "Suffice it to say, I knocked over a candle, and Lacy's quick thinking saved the day. Look, I'll get to scrambling up some eggs. Get the ham out of the oven and get those drop biscuits in. Then slice up the ham."

Lacy arrived at that moment. The men seemed more than a little bit interested in the youngest Gallatin girl, and some even followed her partway into the kitchen.

"I haven't got time for you boys just now," Lacy told them. "Not if you want to eat."

"I can't believe we're getting breakfast with three beautiful women," one of the men declared. "I ain't seen nothin' but these miserable mutts for weeks."

The other men laughed and agreed that the girls were a wonderful change of scenery. Gwen gazed toward the ceiling. They were always getting comments from their male customers, and quite often, proposals of marriage soon followed.

Getting to the tasks at hand, the three sisters worked in perfect unison. They knew what was needed to make order out of chaos, and it wasn't long before the trestle tables were set with dishes and food.

"So I understand you men are scouting out routes for the railroad," Gwen said as she made the rounds with the coffee-pot. She spotted Hank and motioned him to sit. "You might as well join them. I know you didn't have anything to eat before we left."

A man with light brown hair spoke up. "I'm Adrian Murphy. I'm heading up this expedition for the Northern Pacific Railroad."

"I heard they went bankrupt after the panic of '73," Hank said, taking a seat at the end of the table.

Adrian extended his hand, and Hank shook it. "They did go under for a time, but with a little reorganizing and new bond sales, they've regained some ground. In fact, the stronger the economy, the stronger they've become."

Gwen poured Hank coffee while he reached for the bowl of biscuits. "I'm glad to hear it. Railroads are important to this country."

"Indeed, they are. Every community wants a railroad."

"I don't know that I do," Lacy said. She served a platter of ham slices to a man at the opposite end of the first table. "The railroad would just hurt our business."

"Nonsense," Adrian said with a flash of a smile. "The trains need hotels, same as the stage. Besides, with gals as pretty as you three, the railroad would advertise the spot just to attract customers."

Lacy laughed, and Gwen felt her cheeks grow hot as Adrian turned back to her and winked. "Are you all single?"

"That's hardly any of your business," Hank declared with a frown.

"It could be," Adrian countered. "I wouldn't be too unhappy with any one of them for a wife."

Beth nearly dropped the bowl of gravy she held. It clattered to the table, sloshing thick white liquid on the polished wood. "Sorry," she murmured.

Adrian flashed her a smile. "Never you mind that. These fellows would eat out of your hand if you'd let them."

Beth flushed and hurried from the room. Gwen shook her head. "I'll get more coffee. If you gentlemen need anything more, just ask."

"I wouldn't suggest that," Hank muttered.

She wasn't sure why he seemed so out of sorts, but she left them to their railroad talk. "They certainly are an interesting bunch," Gwen said as she joined Beth.

"That's putting it mildly. I'm sure glad you got back. Were you able to find what Mr. Bishop was looking for?"

"No." Gwen went to check on the biscuits she'd left in the oven. "But I do think I understand him a little better."

"In what way?"

"Well, I know more about his childhood and about Harvey. Remember all those stories Harvey used to tell us about his friend Aloysius?"

"Of course. They were best friends." Beth looked at her oddly. "Why?"

"Hank *is* Aloysius." Gwen pulled the biscuits from the oven.

"Truly? That's . . . well . . . unexpected, I would say."

Gwen laughed. "That's putting it mildly. I couldn't help but think over all the things Harvey had said about his friend, and now realizing it was his brother all along . . . well . . . that makes it very special. He adored Hank. That much is obvious."

"Yes, but he didn't adore his family in general. At least, not enough to be honest about them."

Gwen frowned. The nagging doubts that had surfaced in the face of Harvey's lies were more than a little troubling. "I know. There were a great many problems. I don't know why Harvey lied. I'll never know, but I am determined to let it go—to just forgive him and move forward."

Beth nodded. "It's probably for the best."

"We need more biscuits," Lacy announced, bringing the empty bowl.

"They're ready," Gwen said, pointing to the pan. "But this is the last of them."

"I'll take out more potatoes, as well." Beth reached for the large cast-iron skillet. "Hopefully they'll get their fill, or we'll have to charge them four bits apiece."

Gwen returned with a fresh pot of coffee to hear that the men were still discussing the Northern Pacific.

"Things aren't perfect," Adrian Murphy told them, "but they've improved. I think the Battle at Little Bighorn proved to the country that the railroad is important to the territory. You know, Custer and his men were assigned to guard and protect the railroad surveyors and construction crews in '75. It was a mighty big shock to hear of his death."

Hank held up his cup for Gwen to refill. "I suppose the

company must be sufficiently on its feet again, if they sent another survey team out."

"They're definitely in better shape now than four years ago," Murphy admitted. "They just put Frederick Billings, a lawyer from Vermont, at the helm. He seems to have some good ideas, according to my boss. Wants to build as much track west of the Missouri River as we can get figured out. He has teams out all over the territory."

"Sounds like an ambitious goal," Hank said.

"Ambitious ain't the half of it, mister. He'd like to build one hundred miles before winter sets in."

Gwen shook her head. "One hundred miles? I can't even fathom it. The land must be very difficult to cross, and there are still problems with the Indians from time to time. There are the renegade bands to contend with."

Adrian nodded and fixed her with an intense gaze. "There are troubles, to be sure, but the railroad is going to change your world, Miss Gallatin."

Gwen turned away, nodding. "That's exactly what I'm afraid of."

❧

Hank was glad when the men from the railroad had their fill of breakfast and began to clear out. They paid above what the girls asked, so Hank couldn't fault them for their generosity. He wasn't all that impressed with their manners, however.

"Ma'am, if you would just marry me," one man told Gwen, "I'd be the happiest fellow in the world."

"Yes, but would she be the happiest woman?" Beth teased.

The man looked thoughtful for a moment, then nodded.

"I believe she would be. I'd take mighty good care of her. I'd even buy her a new washtub."

"Well, that is a high recommendation," Beth said as she gave the man a nudge from the dining room, "but I couldn't do without my sister just yet."

"You could come along," the man offered over his shoulder. "I've got me a brother who's lookin' for a wife."

Hank couldn't believe how brazen the men were. They didn't seem to care if the girls were embarrassed by their flattery or attention. He finally took a stand.

"The Gallatin ladies have more than enough work to do in the wake of your attack on their dining room and home. I'd like to recommend you move on."

"Mr. Bishop is right," Adrian Murphy said, raising his arms. "We need to hit the trail. Let's get on over to the smithy and gather our horses."

There were moans and groans, but most of the men moved in an orderly fashion toward the porch. One man approached Gwen with his hat in hand. He looked rather sheepish as he raised his gaze from the floor.

"Ma'am . . . ah . . . I'm powerfully embarrassed to admit that I ran out of paper in the men's outhouse and tore off a piece of the newsprint from the wall. I hope you'll forgive me."

Gwen smiled sweetly at the man. "It's not a problem, I assure you. Thank you for letting me know."

Another man came up at this point. "I'm afraid I tracked mud on your rug, ma'am. I tried to clean it up, but there's a stain."

Gwen nodded and maintained her gentle nature. "It's not the first time, I assure you. Please don't give it a second thought."

"Let's move along, men," Mr. Murphy called from the door.

Once the last man was out of the house, Hank turned to find the girls hard at work. He admired the way they shared the responsibilities. It wasn't long before the mess was cleared away and the dining room was set to rights.

The girls were chatting in the kitchen, and Hank felt rather the outsider. He had liked being a part of the team earlier. It gave him a sense of belonging he'd not felt in a long time. There was something about this place—this land—that seemed to do that for him, but for the life of him, he couldn't understand why.

With nothing else to capture his time or attention, Hank decided to go for a walk. He whistled for Major and found the dog eager to join him. Hank hoped the girls wouldn't mind that he'd encouraged Major to leave the cabin. He certainly didn't want to see the animal get in trouble.

"It seems to be a fine day," he told Major. "It'd be even finer if I had the certificates I came for."

But if he found them, he'd have to leave. Hank frowned at that thought. He didn't want to leave. He'd found peace here. He'd found hope again. Mrs. Shepard had helped him to understand God better, and while Hank still had a lot of unanswered questions, he knew that his life would be forever changed because of that one event.

He thought of Gwen and knew she had changed him, as well. He'd never cared about falling in love—about having a wife and family. But now he did. Setting his heart right with God had helped him to set it right in so many other ways. He supposed that was why dealing with the railroad surveyors had made him a bit moody. They had no right to suggest marriage to a woman they didn't even know.

"I have no right, either," he muttered. "I hardly know her any better than they do."

Major took off running after a magpie, apparently bored with Hank's grumblings. Hank looked off toward the east and the range of mountains that marked the horizon. Snow capped their crowns, but the lower elevations were green and tree covered. He felt as though he'd grown to be a part of them.

But what about Boston? What about Mother in Rhode Island?

He couldn't very well leave her to fend for herself. Nor could he just walk away from his business ventures. Or could he?

He could sell out easily enough, and his mother had plans to travel with her sister. She'd be in Europe, so long as the certificates were found. And if they weren't found, Hank already knew he could sell the business and give his mother a good portion of the money and pretend he had found them. He could just start over here in Montana.

I still have to tell Mother about Harvey, he thought, shaking his head. Hearing about the death of her youngest would not be easy. So long as no one spoke the words, a chance still remained that her child was alive and well.

Hank glanced across the field to where the cemetery stood. He was surprised to see a woman walking beneath the trees. There was a familiarity to her gait, and Hank knew without a doubt it was Gwen.

Walking slowly so she could spy him and leave if she wanted, Hank made his way toward the graveyard. She didn't acknowledge him, however. Her back was turned to him, and even as he approached, she didn't seem to realize someone had joined her.

She stood staring down, not at her father's grave, as he'd seen her do on other occasions, but at Harvey's.

"Would you rather be alone?" he asked.

Gwen turned but didn't appear surprised to see him there. "No."

Hank studied her for a moment. His heart stirred with emotion. What could he say? What *should* he say? The silence hung uncomfortably between them for several minutes.

"I know you really loved him. I'm sorry I ever accused you of anything else."

Gwen shook her head. "I loved the man I knew as Harvey Bishop, but that man lied to me. He wasn't at all who he said he was. I came to realize the other night that I never really even knew him."

Hank felt sorry for her. The pain in her tone was clear. "I'm sure he loved you, Gwen."

"I like to think so, but maybe even that was just a game to him. Something to hide behind, in case the past ever tried to catch up with him."

"I don't think my brother would lie about loving you."

She turned away from the grave and faced Hank. "Why not? He lied about loving you."

"Not really. He told you of his love for Aloysius." Hank saw the hurt in her eyes as she nodded. "Gwen, time will heal your wounds. That's all I can say." He stopped and shook his head. "Well, that's not exactly true. I guess it took Jesus to help heal mine."

She looked at him. "What do you mean?"

"I had a long talk with Mrs. Shepard. She helped me to see some things straight—especially where God was concerned."

Gwen smiled. "She has a way of doing that. She helped me too, although I'm still not completely sure what it means for my life. I don't know what my future holds."

Hank didn't want to admit he'd heard the conversation Gwen had shared with Patience. Especially since he had something entirely different in mind. Stepping toward her, he reached out and touched her cheek. "I have some thoughts on what your future might include."

Her eyes widened as he lowered his lips to hers. Hank savored the feel of her as she yielded to his touch. She still smelled a bit smoky from the Shepards' fire, but that only endeared her to him all the more.

Without warning, she stiffened and pushed him away. "I need to go."

"Wait. I know you're still in mourning for Harvey, and I shouldn't have done that. Please forgive me. I'm no better than all those lovesick survey men."

Gwen looked rather confused for a moment, then shook her head. "I'm not mourning Harvey anymore." She lifted her skirts and very nearly dashed across the cemetery to cross the distance to Gallatin House.

Hank had no idea what to think. If she wasn't mourning Harvey, then why had she pulled away? Why had she submitted to his kiss one minute, then ended it the next?

Gwen raced into the house, her heart pounding from the run as well as the fear that coursed through her. She had fallen in love with Hank Bishop, and apparently he had noticed it. Otherwise, why would he have kissed her? Why did she always have to wear her heart on her sleeve?

Her eyes blurred, and her heart felt as if it might break. Hank would leave soon. With or without the certificates, his life was in Boston. Blinded by her tears, she hurried up the stairs and didn't realize Beth was there until she knocked into her at full speed.

Beth cried out and grasped for the banister as she began to fall backward. Gwen reached for her sister, but it was too late. Beth crashed against the steps and railing with sickening thuds.

Gwen screamed, but there was no one and nothing that could stop the tragedy from unfolding before her.

I've killed her. I am *cursed.*

CHAPTER TWENTY

Hank came running at the sound of Gwen's scream. He couldn't imagine what would send her into such hysterics. Major passed him quickly and bounded into the still-open front door, barking in a fitful ruckus as he went.

Reaching the porch, Hank's feet never touched the steps. He leapt onto the landing and rushed into the house. "What's wrong?"

He saw Gwen standing on the stairs, frozen in place with her hands to her mouth. At the bottom of the steps lay Beth, unconscious and bleeding from a blow to the head.

"What happened?" he asked, kneeling beside the still form.

"I . . . oh . . . I . . ." Gwen sank to the steps.

"Gwen? Are you all right? What happened to Beth? Did Mr. Bishop hurt her?"

Hank threw Lacy a scathing look. "I do wish you didn't think quite so highly of me, Miss Gallatin. Your sister obviously fell. Is that what happened, Gwen?"

She seemed to recover some of her senses and rushed to Beth's side. "I wasn't watching where I was going. I knocked her down. Oh, Beth! Beth, please wake up." She reached for Beth's body and pulled her into her arms. Rocking her back and forth, Gwen sobbed. "Please don't die. Please, Beth."

"I'll go for the doctor," Lacy said. She was out the door before Hank could approve her plan or state otherwise.

"Let's get her upstairs to bed," Hank said. "You lead the way; I'll carry her."

Gwen seemed reluctant to let him take Beth but finally yielded and got to her feet. "It's the last room on the left, once you go down our private hall." She raced ahead of him and opened the door.

Hank carefully maneuvered Beth's petite frame through the door. The bleeding wasn't so bad, he thought, but the goose egg on her forehead was growing by the minute. "Do you have any ice?"

Gwen turned at her sister's bedroom. "I think there's still a little in the cellar. There won't be much."

"Get what you can. We need to control the swelling on her head."

Gwen went first to pull down the covers on the bed. "I'll be right back with it," she told him as she raced for the door.

Hank placed Beth upon the bed and smoothed back her hair. Spying the bowl and pitcher, he took up a nearby towel and dampened it. He cleaned the blood away from the wound, happy to see that the cut was minimal. Hopefully, the blow wouldn't cause internal problems.

She moaned but didn't awaken. Hank shook his head, remembering her innocent act when he'd learned of the red dye she'd used on his shirts. When they'd returned this morning, he'd been happy to find the remaining lavender shirts were now a dark blue. They suited him much better. No doubt Beth had been responsible for this change, as well.

He smiled. The Gallatin women were certainly an unpredictable and charming bunch. He rinsed the cloth and put it on Beth's forehead. As he did so, Hank spied something sticking out from beneath her pillow. He reached for it and smiled. It was a dime novel, not unlike the ones he'd found in the shed. This one appeared to be a romance that suggested mystery and scandal.

The Lost Lady of Malburay. He chuckled and put the book back under her pillow as he heard Gwen approaching down the hall.

"Here," she said. "It isn't much, but I did my best to chop it up a bit." She handed him a knotted dish towel.

"It's plenty," he assured. Hank removed the wet towel and replaced it with the bag of ice.

Gwen sat on the opposite side of the bed and took up Beth's hand. "I can't believe I was so careless. If she dies . . . if she . . ."

"She's not going to die. Look—she's already coming around."

Beth's eyelashes fluttered and opened. She looked rather befuddled. "What's happened?"

"Oh, it's all my fault," Gwen told her. "I knocked you down the stairs in my rush to get to my room. I was so lost in my own thoughts that I didn't even see you there."

"I hurt. My back feels twisted."

"Lacy's gone for the doctor, but it will probably be a while before they get back," Gwen told her. "Just lie still and let me know if there is anything I can do for you."

"I suppose I'll just rest," Beth said, closing her eyes with a grimace. "It hurts too much to do anything else."

It was nearly time for the evening stage when the doctor finally arrived. Gwen paced back and forth downstairs as she waited for the doctor to return from examining Beth. Lacy did likewise.

"You ladies will wear a hole in the floor if you don't stop pacing," Hank said. He got up and stoked the fire in the hearth. "I'm sure she'll be fine. She didn't seem to hurt as much by the time the doctor arrived."

"But she's still injured," Gwen said, taking a seat. She gripped the arms of the chair as if to be ready to leap forward at any minute.

Hank straightened and looked at his watch. "What time is the stage due in?"

"Oh no," Gwen said, jumping up. "I forgot about the stage. I have to get supper on. They'll be here at six-thirty. What time is it?"

"Five-thirty," Hank replied. "Look, I'm happy to help. Tell me what needs to be done."

Gwen looked at Lacy and then back to Hank. "It's Saturday night. We usually have beef stew. I'll need to check and see how much meat we have. With the warm weather, it just doesn't keep." She seemed to consider the situation for a moment. "Hank, bring up the water like you did this morning, as well as more wood. Lacy, you get the stove heated up and start mixing a cake."

"I don't know how to make a cake," Lacy said, looking at her sister as if she'd lost her mind.

"The recipe is in the drawer with the others," Gwen said. "Use the one for ribbon cake. I'll bring up the butter and milk from the cellar. You'll find the rest of the ingredients in the cupboard. Just start it, and I'll come help after I get the stew on."

Hank watched them swing into action once again. He made his way out back to bring up pails of hot water for the sink. He couldn't help but smile at the feeling of usefulness. Boston held its charms, for something always stood ready to offer entertainment and excitement. But here a person often entertained himself—made his own excitement.

Next door, Rafe's Saloon was well lit and ready for business. Cubby was hauling supplies in from a shed behind the main building.

"Nice evening," Hank called as Cubby crossed the yard.

"Yeah, sure is." Cubby paused and looked at Hank. "You workin' here now?"

"Just for the time being," Hank replied. "Beth took a fall, and I figured the girls could use a hand."

"Is Miss Beth going to be all right?" he asked, the concern quite clear in his voice. He put his crate down momentarily.

Hank looked at the scrappy youth and smiled. "I think she'll be fine. You know it takes more than a tumble down the stairs to keep those Gallatin ladies down."

Cubby smiled. "They sure are fine ladies, aren't they?"

"They are indeed."

"Someday I'd like to marry a fine lady," Cubby said

wistfully. "I don't reckon none will have me, though. Pa says I'm not fit to be good company for much of anybody."

"Well, I'd hate to say your pa is wrong," Hank said, glancing at the saloon, "but I believe you're great company. I was going to ask if maybe you could show me a good place to go fishing—even join me, if you had the time. Say, tomorrow morning after the stage pulls out?"

"I know all the best places," Cubby said, his chest puffing in pride. "I'd be happy to take you with me."

"Good. Then it's a plan. I'll meet with you in the morning after all the chores are finished."

The boy nodded and picked his crate back up. "I'd best get this inside."

Hank figured he should do likewise with the water. He had just stepped inside the kitchen with two pails when he heard the doctor speaking.

"Her back is badly twisted, but I did not perceive any breaks. She has good feeling in her extremities, so I have no reason to believe she's suffered any permanent damage. Keep her in bed a couple of weeks."

"What about her head? That was a nasty blow she took."

Hank heard the fear in Gwen's voice. He put the water down and went to join the trio at the door. Lacy looked at him for moment as if to protest his intrusion but said nothing.

"She'll be fine. She's got a hard head," the doctor said and winked. "I think it's one of the best qualities about you Gallatin girls."

Hank smiled at Lacy's scowl. "I've got work to do," she said and pushed past him to the kitchen.

"I'll be heading back to Bozeman," the doctor said. "You girls come pay me next time you're in town."

"You're welcome to stay the night," Gwen told him. "The

stage is due in most any time, but we've always got room for you."

"No, I have three different cases that need attention. I'll look in on them as I make my way back." He smiled and patted Gwen's arm. "Now, try not to fret. I know you're like a mama bear with her cubs when it comes to your sisters. Bethany will be just fine."

The stage pulled in twenty minutes late and was loaded with more men than Hank had figured possible to stuff onto the conveyance. As he watched them make their way into the house, Hank also noted a large group of riders approach the saloon—clearly local cowhands. It looked like there would be a lot of activity in the area tonight.

Hank's prediction proved to be accurate. After a hearty dinner, most of the travelers made their way next door. Soon, music and laughter could be heard throughout the valley. He was just returning with another armful of firewood when he caught sight of someone slinking across the backyard. Pausing behind the outhouses, the figure seemed to assess the situation before moving inside the back of Rafe's Saloon.

It was Lacy. Hank was certain of this. *What is she up to now? If she's not careful, we'll be needing the doctor for her.*

Hank deposited the wood and brushed off his clothes. He wondered what he should do.

"Let me go, you lousy poltroon!" Lacy yelled as a big, burly man wrestled her out the back door. "I said, let me go!"

"You little minx—you know better than to come into the saloon. Unless you want Rafe putting you to work in the cribs with the rest of the women, I'd suggest you mind your manners."

He had her by the hair and seemed not in the least bit prepared when she changed directions and moved toward him.

Hank heard the man cry out as Lacy sank her teeth into his arm.

"You wildcat!" The man pulled her backward until Hank thought he might bend her over completely.

He figured enough was enough and stepped forward to see if he could intervene on behalf of the youngest Gallatin.

"Evening," he said rather casually. "Am I interrupting?"

"Yes, you are!" Lacy said, twisting in the man's grip. "I don't need you helping me."

Hank crossed his arms and eyed the man quite seriously. "I think it'd probably be best to let her go, friend. She seems all worked up about something."

"She's worked up, all right. She's mad because I won't let her stay in the bar and hound the customers about where they were the night her pa got shot."

Without warning, Lacy straightened and kicked the man hard in the groin. The man released her and doubled over, howling in pain.

"You ever lay a hand on me again, Wyman Jenkins, and I'll give you worse than that. I have a right to find out who killed my pa. I'll learn the truth sooner or later, and when I do, I hope the sheriff comes and shuts Rafe's place down. After all, he's responsible for getting the men drunk in the first place."

The man straightened and moved forward as if to strike a blow. Hank stepped between the two, however. "I wouldn't do that, mister. You'll only get her mad."

"She ever tries that kind of stunt again, I'll kill her."

"You'd better bring friends if you're going to try," Lacy called out as she came around Hank.

Hank reached out and took hold of Lacy's arm. "I think you've hurt the man enough. I'm sure Gwen is wondering where you've gotten off to. Hadn't you better head back?"

She glared at him but moved away. "Just remember what I said, Wyman."

"*You* remember, missy—show up in there again, and I'll let the boys have you." He turned and walked back to the saloon. It was obvious he was still hurting, but his pride wasn't about to let him show it.

Hank turned to go back to Gallatin House and found Lacy standing only about ten feet away. She looked plenty mad, and Hank knew she'd have words for him.

"Before you get started," he said, raising his hand as if to ward her off, "would you mind telling me what you were doing at the saloon? Your sister would have a fit if I told her."

"Gwen has a fit about a lot of things."

"Truly? She's always seemed rather easygoing to me."

Lacy put her hands on her hips. "I know her better than you do, and she has a lot to be upset about. She throws plenty of tantrums when she wants to."

"And you don't?"

"I didn't say that. I know I'm spirited. Pa used to tell me that, of all of us girls, I bore the closest resemblance to our mom in looks and attitude. He said she was spirited, and I take that as a compliment."

Hank folded his arms. "You might also take it as a warning."

Lacy stiffened. "In what way?" Her tone suggested she was offended.

"Spirited folks don't always consider the outcome of a deed before attempting it. Spirited folks sometimes rush in without heeding the danger at hand."

"So be it. Sometimes you just have to do a thing without thinking about it. Thinking about it just slows things down."

Hank chuckled. "Sometimes thinking resolves a problem without creating one."

"Go ahead and laugh at me all you want, Mr. Bishop. I'll be the one laughing when I accomplish what I set out to do."

"And what exactly were you attempting to do? Will your sister also laugh when she knows the truth of it?"

This seemed to take the wind out of Lacy's sails. Hank watched her take a deep breath and consider his question. She seemed troubled, almost as if she were about to break into tears, but he knew that was probably only due to her anger.

"I was trying to find Pa's killer," she finally said. "I want to see justice done. It's important to me."

"Why?"

"Because it is!"

"But why?" Hank asked again. "Why is it so important? It won't bring your father back to life."

She looked at Hank as if he'd lost his mind. "Why do you want to reclaim the certificates Harvey stole? They won't bring him back to life."

"That's entirely a different matter. I want to pay my mother's debts and give her peace of mind."

Lacy nodded. "It's no different for me. I want to pay back a debt and have peace of mind."

"What debt are you talking about?" Hank looked at her oddly.

She squared her shoulders and let out a heavy breath. "A debt of honor."

"How are you feeling?" Gwen asked Beth, bringing her a bowl of soup.

"Better. The laudanum helped. Sure glad the doctor suggested it. Of course, I feel rather woozy." She giggled. "Do you suppose this is what those cowboys feel like when they've imbibed too much liquor?"

"I couldn't say," Gwen replied, watching her sister run her finger along the quilt as she traced out a pattern.

"I hope I'm not a nuisance," Beth said, suddenly looking up at Gwen. "I feel rather silly and useless. The medicine is quite strong."

Gwen smiled. "There's nothing wrong with that. After all you've been through, you deserve to feel no pain. I brought you something to eat. Are you hungry?"

"No. Sleepy. I tried to read, but the words just blurred together. Remember when we gave laum . . . laudamum . . . laudanum . . . to Hank? I suppose this is how he felt. I don't feel so bad about it now." She giggled again.

Gwen worried that perhaps they'd given Beth too much medication. "And why is that?" Gwen put the soup on the nightstand beside the bed.

"Because it feels quite . . . well . . . wonderful. I feel fine, not at all like I did before. Before, I thought my back was broken. I thought my head was going to explode."

Gwen sat down beside Beth and took hold of her hand. "I'm so sorry. I can't tell you how horrible I feel. I was so afraid I had killed you."

Beth shook her head and smiled. "You were just in a hurry."

"I was upset. I should have been paying attention, but my mind was elsewhere." Gwen looked away and closed her eyes. "It's hard not to believe I'm cursed when things like this keep happening."

"You aren't cursed. That's jus' silly," Beth murmured, her

speech beginning to sound thick. She closed her eyes. "You're only human." She opened her eyes as if a sudden thought permeated the thick fog of her brain. "Why were you upset?"

Gwen looked at Beth and could see that she was fading fast. "It wasn't important. I thought it was at the time, but it wasn't." She pushed away thoughts of Hank and his kiss. How could she explain her heart to Beth when she didn't even understand it herself?

CHAPTER TWENTY-ONE

"Hank, we really appreciate the help you've offered us," Gwen said as they finished up breakfast. "Still, I know this isn't the reason you're here."

Her comment only served to remind him that time was slipping away. He'd already been gone from home over two months and hadn't been in contact with his mother for nearly six weeks.

"I figured since you needed supplies," he began, "I could go to Bozeman and bring them back for you. That way, I can ask questions about Harvey and see if anyone knows anything."

Lacy looked at him oddly for a moment. "Why are you being so helpful? You came here spewing all sorts of insults and anger—and now you want to help?"

"And as I've told your sister, I was wrong. I misjudged her."

"I'll say." Lacy unrolled her left sleeve and buttoned the cuff. She seemed to dismiss the subject as quickly as she'd brought it up. "Gwen, I'll ride over to the Shepards and get the butter and eggs. I'll have Nick ready the buckboard for Mr. Bishop, as well."

"Oh, Lacy, we'll need milk and cream." Gwen moved to the kitchen and returned with a stack of white cloths that Hank knew had once held squares of butter. "Maybe see if you can borrow Nick and Simon's wagon. And don't forget the money."

Lacy nodded. "I should be back by late afternoon. I know Patience will want me to join them for lunch."

"Take your time, Lacy. The chores are caught up, and we aren't due a stage until tomorrow. I plan to spend the day baking, catching up on mending, and seeing to Beth."

"Will you be all right here alone if I head to Bozeman?" Hank asked.

"I'm hardly alone," Gwen protested. "I have the Lassiters if I need help, and Beth is doing much better. We'll be fine."

Hank wasn't completely convinced, but he had been anxious to get to Bozeman ever since they had come up dry about the missing stocks when visiting Virginia City and Norris. He got to his feet. "Then I suppose I'd best be on my way."

"If you decide to spend the night in Bozeman, don't worry about us," Gwen said, smiling. "I assure you, we will be perfectly fine."

"I don't have any desire to do that." The truth of that statement rather startled Hank, and he wondered how Gwen would take his comment after the kiss they'd shared.

The ride to Bozeman was some fifteen miles to the east.

Hank didn't really notice the rise in altitude as the horses plodded along the trail, but he was told the landscape climbed as much as six thousand feet. The valley ahead of him was carpeted in green and gold. Wheat was a primary staple of local farmers, and every accessible spot was planted. Hank drew a deep breath and felt a sense of peace rush over him. This was a far cry from the busyness and noise of Boston, yet he knew for certain he had to return east. Yet he would also leave a part of his heart, for he'd come to love this land—and Gwen Gallatin.

He wasn't exactly sure what he should do about either issue. He'd never expected to care about any woman other than his mother. At least not enough to consider the things that were going through his mind. He could actually see himself married to Gwen. He could easily imagine living here the rest of his life and raising a family.

A family? He'd always sworn he would never sire a child. Given his own miserable upbringing, he wanted no part in causing such anguish to settle upon another person, much less his own son or daughter. He had figured to remain celibate and alone—to stop his father's cursed existence from being revisited upon future generations.

He thought of Gwen and how she had believed herself cursed. Some people just accepted such fates as if they had no other say in the matter. But not him. Hank knew better. He had as much choice to reject such a future as he did to accept it. It was all a matter of choosing his path—the right path.

"But what is the right path?" he asked, as if expecting someone to answer.

Fixing his gaze east toward the closest mountain range, Hank marveled at the grooves and peaks. The snow was pretty much gone at this point. Here and there, Hank spotted a touch of white, but otherwise, a rich, dark green blended against the purple hue, suggesting a welcoming summer landscape. He found himself wondering what it might be like to ride up into those mountains and spend a week or two. The ride back from Virginia City had given him an experience unlike any he'd known. Even the times camping with his grandfather hadn't been as picturesque. Nor had they touched his soul the way that week with Gwen and Lacy had.

Hank shook his head and tried to force his mind on the task at hand. The first step was to find the stock certificates. The rules of the company demanded the physical stocks in hand in order to redeem them for cash. There was no hope of doing it any other way—the risk was too great that someone could show up at a later time with the stocks in hand and claim themselves to be the true owners. He needed those pieces of paper to give his mother the standard of living he'd promised her.

"But if I can't find them," he told himself, "I can provide for Mother. I could buy us a small place."

Even as he said it, however, Hank knew it was nonsense. His mother desired to live with her widowed sister. She wanted to travel and do all of the things that his stepfather had never had time or interest in doing.

Bozeman was a simple town, its main street varying in degrees of dust, mud, or muck. There were wide grooves in the now-dry roadway, as well as holes big enough to cripple a horse or break a wheel.

Hank picked his way carefully down the street, avoiding freighters, buggies, and pedestrians as he made his way to the bank. Just as Gwen had said, the place was closed up tight, but there was a sign that suggested where he might be able to speak with one of the owners. Hank secured the wagon, read the directions, then headed down the street. He had a feeling the trip would yield him nothing but additional questions, yet he had to try. He had to know the truth, even if the truth didn't resolve the problem.

Looking at the address and the name engraved on the door, Hank realized he'd come to the right place. The address was the law office of Mr. Kenneth Snyder. At least, that's what the gold-stenciled letters read.

Stepping inside the rather stuffy building, Hank pulled his hat from his head and looked to a clerk who sat buried behind stacks of thick, dusty books.

"May I help you?" the young man asked.

"I'd like to speak with Mr. Snyder."

The man looked at him oddly. "Do you have an appointment?"

Hank shook his head and steeled the younger man with a look that he knew to be quite intimidating. "No. I'm here, however, to discuss a matter that will not wait."

The clerk seemed to shrink behind the books. "I'll ask if he has time to see you. Wait here."

The man knocked lightly on the door to his right and quickly slipped inside. Hank waited for several minutes, feeling rather impatient at the amount of time it was taking. He found his mind returning to Gwen, against his wishes.

"Mr. Snyder will see you now," the man said, standing back from the open door.

Hank quickly entered the room. "Mr. Snyder, I'm Hank Bishop."

The older man looked up from his desk and leaned back in his chair. He threw Hank a smile. "What can I do for you, Mr. Bishop?"

"I've come here from Boston on family business."

"Seems a long way to travel. Where are you staying?"

"Actually, I'm at the Gallatin House. Are you familiar with it?"

The man smiled and nodded. "I should say. Most everyone is. Those girls have a reputation for some of the finest food in the valley, and you cannot match the comfort of their hot springs pool. So have a seat and tell me what this is all about."

Hank did as the man bid, giving a cursory glance to the office around him. Mahogany wood wainscoting lined the lower half of the wall, while the upper half had been painted a pale yellow. It was almost as if the designer, after seeing how dark the paneling had left the office, had decided to try to rectify the situation with a brighter top. The effect was not all that captivating.

There were two leather chairs positioned in front of a large mahogany desk. Both were a deep vermilion, which only served to make the walls and desk seem all the more reddish in tint. Hank lowered onto one of the leather chairs and found it surprisingly comfortable.

"So tell me about this family business."

"My brother came west some years ago. You may have known him. His name was Harvey Bishop. He married the elder Gallatin sister."

"Yes. I knew Harvey. Good man. I was sorry to hear of his passing." The white-haired man stroked a thick mustache and nodded as if remembering something important. "Mr. Gallatin thought highly of your brother. I was sad to hear of George Gallatin's passing, as well. A tragic accident."

"The Gallatin ladies tell me that their father borrowed money from your bank in order to expand his roadhouse. I wondered if my brother was involved in that venture."

"No," Snyder said, shaking his head. "George came to us in . . . hmmm . . . I believe it was two years now past to borrow the money. He already had the original property in place and had secured several contracts, so we felt it was a good risk. That note, however was sold to another bank when we closed our doors."

"What about my brother, Mr. Snyder? Did he have a deposit box or ask the bank to keep any stock certificates for him?"

"No. I would have known if he did." Snyder leaned forward. "Is that what this is about?"

Hank sighed and met the man's gaze. "Yes. My brother was in possession of some important family stocks when he came west. I'm now trying to locate the certificates. The Gallatins have been very helpful in assisting me. The elder Miss Gallatin had even suggested I come here to speak with you and see if Harvey had an account or some other arrangement for safeguarding the stocks."

"I'm afraid not. Harvey didn't have so much as a bank account here, as far as I can remember. George paid him, and he never seemed to have much need. I'm sorry I can't be of more use in the matter."

Hank felt the disappointment wash over him. "I'm sorry, too." He got to his feet. "If you happen to remember anything that would be useful, you can get word to me at Gallatin House."

Snyder got to his feet and extended his hand. "I'll keep that in mind, Mr. Bishop."

They shook as if making a deal, then Hank turned and walked out. He wasn't sure what to do at this point. Once outside, he looked up and down Main Street. There were a fair number of businesses lining either side. He thought of Gallatin House, out there in the middle of nowhere. Nick Lassiter spoke about the area expanding—about families coming to stay in the area to provide more services and needed commerce.

The Lassiter brothers' reputation was known from Bozeman to Butte, Gwen had once told Hank. There wasn't anything that Simon didn't seem to be capable of repairing, and Nick was talented in creating new devices for special circumstances. Folks were known to come to them from as far as eighty miles away, if the needs were important enough.

It seemed to Hank that a mercantile might do well in the area. With the Gallatin House serving the needs of the stage passengers and freighters, a mercantile might also benefit from such traffic. And the freighters were already making regular runs through the area, so getting supplies should prove fairly easy.

He considered the idea all the way to Sherman's Mercantile, where Gwen had directed him to pick up extra flour, sugar, coffee, and salt. There were also some smaller items needed, and she had written it all out for him in a very orderly list.

A bell rang overhead as Hank entered the sunlit store. There were rows of wooden shelves against two of the walls with a wide variety of items for sale. There were also counters with merchandise throughout the long, narrow room, offering everything from cookware to tools.

"Afternoon. Can I help you?"

Hank looked up to find a middle-aged man smiling in welcome. "Afternoon. I'm here on behalf of the Gallatin sisters, who own the stage stop. Miss Gallatin gave me this list of supplies." Hank handed over the list.

"I have everything they need," the man replied. He paused a moment and stuck out his hand. "I'm Brewster Sherman. This is my store."

"Hank Bishop."

"Bishop? Same as Harvey Bishop?"

Hank nodded. "He was my brother."

Brewster broke into a broad smile. "Well, I'll be. Your brother was a good friend. Played chess with me every Tuesday afternoon, if he could get away."

"Chess?" Hank had to chuckle. He'd tried for years to teach Harvey how to play chess, but his brother had never shown the slightest interest or aptitude.

"Your brother was the best for miles around. He beat out most everyone. Said his good friend taught him to play."

Hank felt a tug at his heart. "Aloysius?"

Brewster laughed and nodded. "Yessir. That Aloysius fellow sounded like quite the friend. Harvey spoke as if the man hung the moon and the stars. Never saw anybody who felt such allegiance to someone other than kin." Brewster looked at the list again. "I guess I'd better get this gathered up for you, or you won't make it back before dark."

"I do have a question," Hank said, remembering his thoughts about a store. "I've been considering staying around these parts—maybe open a store near the Gallatin House. Seems folks out that way could certainly benefit from having a regular supply of goods close at hand. After all, the freighters do pass right along that road. It would be easy enough to get whatever was needed."

"I've often thought of that myself," Sherman admitted. "It's a situation of having someone to run the store who actually wants to live out that far, however."

"I wouldn't mind living there," Hank admitted. "Perhaps we could consider a partnership. Maybe we could discuss it over lunch."

Brewster grinned. "I'd like that, Mr. Bishop. If you're anything like your brother, I know I'm going to like working with you." He started to leave once again, then turned. "How are you at playing chess?"

"I can hold my own," Hank said with a grin.

Nick and Simon sat at the Gallatin House table, finishing large pieces of buttermilk cake. There had been much conversation around the dinner table about Beth and the accident, as well as Hank Bishop.

"When has he decided to head back to Boston?" Nick questioned.

"There's no telling," Gwen replied. "He hasn't found what he's looking for, and until he does—or at least feels he's exhausted every possibility—he won't go. He planned to see the former bank owners while in Bozeman today. There's always a possibility that Harvey had an account I knew nothing about."

"I doubt that," Simon said, pushing back from the table. "Harvey would have told you about something that important."

Gwen frowned. "You mean like he told me about his family—his brother?"

Simon clearly felt awkward, and Gwen couldn't help but apologize. "I'm sorry. Sometimes it just overwhelms me. I'm sure Hank will leave before long."

"I wouldn't bet on it," Lacy said, getting to her feet. "I think Mr. Bishop has gone sweet on our Gwen."

"Truly?" Nick looked at Gwen and then back to Lacy. The grin on his face suggested Gwen was in for a great amount of teasing. "Did Harvey have any other brothers? Maybe you could just court them all."

"I'm not courting Hank," Gwen said rather defensively. "Now, if you two still want to say hello to Beth, I'll escort you upstairs."

She got up and headed toward the stairs. "Lacy, would you please clear the table?"

Without even looking behind her, Gwen knew the men were following her up the polished pine steps. Nick seemed particularly eager to see her sister. He'd talked about her nearly the entire time through dinner. With Hank still gone, Gwen had been glad for the chatter.

"Beth? Are you ready for visitors? Nick and Simon wanted to say hello," Gwen asked from her sister's bedroom door.

"Yes, please. I'm so bored here." They entered the room as she added, "I think I'd even be happy to talk with Rafe, himself."

Gwen laughed. "Surely not."

"We're a whole sight better company than Rafe," Nick declared. He crossed the room and drew a book out of his pocket. "I know you like to read, and I picked this up for you in Bozeman."

"That was very kind of you," Beth said, taking the book. "I'll treasure it."

"So how are you feeling?" Simon asked.

"Better. There is still a bit of pain, but it's far less. I see no reason to remain in bed for two weeks."

"I do," Gwen replied. "The doctor said to do it, and that's what you shall do."

"I'll get fat and lazy by then."

Nick laughed at this and gave her a wink. "You're not the type to ever be fat or lazy."

They chatted comfortably for a few minutes, and Lacy joined in, done with her chores. Simon then said something that drove the entire matter of curses back to Gwen's mind.

"You seem destined for a lot of accidents, Beth. I remember

last year when you fell in the river, and then a few months back, you slipped on the ice and went smack down on your—"

"Never mind the details," Beth cut in. "I'm just a bit clumsy."

"Well, this time it was definitely not Beth's fault," Gwen admitted. "Had I been watching where I was going, she wouldn't have gotten hurt. Sometimes I think both of my sisters would be better off moving away from me."

She saw the surprise on Beth's face, and the expression on Lacy's was much the same. Still, Gwen didn't back down. "I had mentioned my concerns to Patience, and she said if we sell the roadhouse, it might be possible for you to stay with her folks back East while you figured out what you wanted to do."

"What are you saying?" Lacy eyed Gwen. "Are you trying to get rid of us?"

"I'm just suggesting you both might be happier leaving Montana. You might even find eastern husbands," she said, smiling.

"What's wrong with Montana husbands?" Nick looked hurt.

"Well, I can answer that one," Lacy threw in. "They're like meringue pies without filling. They look good on the outside and may even seem sweet at first, but they have no substance to hold them together."

As if on cue, an angry voice bellowed from downstairs. "Lacene Gallatin, where are you? Lacy! You've got some explaining to do."

Lacy gazed toward the ceiling and let out an exasperated sigh. "As if I needed proof of my statement, it would appear the honorable Mr. Shepard is seeking my company."

"He sounds upset," Gwen said, following Lacy into the hall. "What have you done now?"

Lacy shrugged. "It seems my very existence is an irritation to Dave Shepard. I'm sure I needn't have done anything more than walk down the street."

Gwen nodded as her sister made her way downstairs, but something inside her told Gwen that Dave had more than a simple stroll against her sister. "I think I'd better see what this is about." She turned back to Beth's room.

"Nick and Simon, I must ask that you come with me. Apparently, Lacy is in some kind of trouble."

CHAPTER TWENTY-TWO

The trio made their way downstairs to find Lacy and Dave, nose to nose. Dave shook his finger at the young woman as he let her know exactly what the problem was.

"You're wearing my patience thin!"

"I have no idea what you're so fired up about, Dave Shepard, but if you don't lower your voice, I'll throw you out of here." Lacy put her hands on her hips and stood her ground.

Dave shook his finger at her as if reprimanding a wayward child. "You may think you've got the strength to take on the world, but I've got news for you."

"You've got nothing for me that I want to hear," Lacy said, surprising Gwen and the others by pushing Dave back a step. "Don't think you can come in here and bully me about."

"I have a complaint about you—a *formal* complaint."

"Oh, I do hope you have the proper clothes to wear for such an event," Lacy countered. "I've never seen you dressed in anything other than work clothes. Even for church."

"I didn't know you were keeping an account of my wardrobe, but right now that's neither here nor there," Dave replied, raising his voice. "You were in Rafe's Saloon."

Gwen gasped and stepped toward her sister. "Is that true?"

Lacy never even turned to face Gwen. "It's true, and no one's business but my own."

"It's my business." Dave folded his arms. "You know you aren't allowed in there. Rafe has a policy about not admitting women to the bar."

"I didn't go to the bar. I went to the tables around the bar."

"You know what I mean."

Lacy shook her head. "I doubt anyone really knows what you mean, Mr. Shepard."

"Then let me illuminate the matter for you."

"What's going on?" Hank asked as he strode through the front door. "I could hear you two yelling at each other from outside. I thought perhaps the place was under attack."

"Mr. Shepard is on the warpath," Lacy declared. "He really should check into joining up with one of the Indian nations."

"I'm gonna show you *warpath*," Dave said, moving toward her.

"Whoa. What is this all about?" Hank questioned again.

Gwen was thankful to see Hank. For reasons she would just as soon ignore, she was comforted by his appearance and moved toward him. "Lacy went to Rafe's the other day."

"The other night. The night when a bunch of the boys

from a neighboring ranch just happened to be there," Dave corrected.

"Hank already knew about it, and he didn't lose his mind over it like you are, Deputy Shepard!" Lacy kept her gaze fixed on Dave. "I wanted to see if any of them knew who might have killed our father. There's no crime in asking questions. Not that I'd expect any of you to understand that."

Gwen looked at Hank. "You knew about this?"

"I did. Lacy and I talked about it, and I had high hopes that she would give up her pursuits."

"You should have told me, Hank."

"No, he shouldn't have," Lacy protested. "I'm a grown woman, and I'll do as I please."

At this, Gwen stepped forward and took hold of her sister's arm. Lacy didn't want to turn but finally conceded. She met Gwen's gaze. "You have to stop this, Lacy. Pa is dead, and there is nothing we can do to bring him back."

"I know I can't bring him back, but we owe him justice," Lacy protested. "You seem quite content to forget it ever happened, but I can't. Pa was murdered, and no one wants to help me prove it."

"We *can't* prove his murder," Gwen told her sister. "There are just too many factors. Why not just let it go—and let Pa rest in peace?"

"Because he can't rest in peace so long as his killer is on the loose."

"What kind of theology is that?" Hank interjected. "Can God only give eternal rest to a man or woman whose death is completely understood?"

To everyone's surprise, Lacy's eyes filled with tears. "None of you understand. You never have. You're perfectly willing to take the easy way out and forget it ever happened. Well, I can't."

She turned toward Dave. "You go ahead and ignore the truth. Folks won't be safe in this area, but it won't be your problem." She turned back to her sister. "And you. Why don't you forget about sending Beth and me back East and go yourself? You don't care about us, and you certainly don't care about Pa. You only think about what's best for you."

With that, Lacy pushed past Dave and Hank and ran out of the house. Gwen felt as if a band were tightening around her chest and she couldn't contain the tears streaming down her face. How could Lacy believe she didn't care about anyone but herself?

"I think it would be best if Simon and I leave," Nick suggested. "We can unload the wagon for you, Hank. Night, Gwen. Thanks for supper."

"You're welcome," she whispered.

"Gwen, you know Lacy didn't mean it," Dave said, reaching out to touch her arm. "She's just speaking out of her fear. Fear that she'll never know the truth. Fear that once she does, it still won't give her the comfort she seeks."

"He's right," Hank said, stepping forward. "Lacy is desperate to ease the pain she feels, and hunting down your father's killer seems to be her only comfort. I apologize for not telling you, but I honestly didn't want to add to your worry. Lacy seems determined to pursue this until someone pays."

"I've done all that I could," Gwen said, sniffing. She wiped at the tears, but they only seemed more determined to fall. "I know I was a poor substitute for our mother, but . . ." She sobbed and buried her face in her hands. She had no idea Lacy hated her so.

"You've done a good job, Gwen. That's easy to see," Dave said softly. "I'll speak with my mother. Maybe she can talk some sense into Lacy. Maybe she can help her to understand your sacrifice."

"I don't care about that. I don't . . . care about what I've given up. I only . . . care that I . . . that I . . . not bring my sisters harm. I want . . . I want . . . them . . . safe."

"But you can't guarantee that," Hank said, coming alongside her.

"Lacy needs a firm hand," Dave said, meeting Gwen's teary gaze. "And frankly, I'm gonna give her one across her backside if she doesn't straighten up."

For some reason, this struck Gwen as funny. She smiled and her tears began to slow. "I'm sure you're just the man for the job," she murmured.

Hank laughed, and Dave shrugged. "We've all got our unpleasant duties," he told them.

This made Gwen laugh. She wiped at her eyes. "I'm sure my sister wouldn't take well to such an idea. Even Pa said it was best to leave well enough alone where Lacy was concerned."

"Your sister is half wildcat. She doesn't worry about protocol or her reputation. She just charges in without thinking, and one of these days she's gonna get hurt."

Gwen sobered. "I know. I'm not happy about her behavior, Dave. I just don't know what I can possibly do about it. She's a grown woman."

"And well I know it. So do those other rowdies who frequent Rafe's. Not to mention Rafe and Wyman. Your sister is going to get herself in a world of trouble if she doesn't stop this nonsense now."

"It's not really nonsense to want to see justice for our father," Gwen said defensively.

Hank interrupted. "I think it might be best if one of us had a talk with the cowboys who were at the bar the night Mr.

Gallatin was shot." He looked to Gwen. "Maybe it would settle Lacy down if she could see that we were actually making an effort to learn the truth."

"But I've been *trying* to learn the truth," Dave said, shaking his head. "They were drunk. There were at least eight men, all shooting off their guns. I've talked to the men, as well as to Rafe. No one even saw Mr. Gallatin in the midst of things until he was dead on the street. Some of them don't really even remember that. I just wish Lacy could understand that I've done my job. She's making it really hard for me, and now Rafe has filed a complaint with the sheriff and is demanding she be arrested if she tries to enter the saloon again."

Gwen heard the anguish in his voice. "I understand, Dave. Maybe getting herself arrested is what it will take. Maybe it will teach her a lesson. I just don't know."

"Well, I know good and well that if those men find Lacy alone, they'll teach her a lesson of their own."

Gwen shuddered. "I pray that doesn't happen."

Dave nodded. "I do, too." The clock on the mantel chimed the hour. "I need to get going."

"Tell your folks hello for me," Gwen said as she followed him to the door.

"I'll do just that."

She waited until he'd mounted his horse and headed down the road before closing the door. When she turned, she found Hank watching her. His gaze caused warmth to spread up her neck and cheeks.

"I'm sorry you had to be a part of that."

"You do realize that it may happen more and more, now that you're without a man to watch over you and your sisters."

Gwen met his eyes and lost herself in their blue depths for a moment. He seemed so concerned that it touched her. "I know this is a difficult territory, but we have people who care about us and watch over us. The Lassiters are good to check on us, and more people are coming to the area all the time."

"But more people may only mean more trouble. You spoke of sending your sisters back East, but what about considering the possibility of all of you moving?"

"I can't go. I'd never let Rafe have Gallatin House."

"What if someone else wanted to buy the place?"

Gwen shook her head. "I don't know of anyone, and I don't know that it would make a difference. I just don't know what I should do about anything. Even if we found a buyer, I wouldn't know where to go or how to get there. The girls and I have a good income with the stage stop, but I don't know that we could duplicate this success elsewhere."

"I could help you," Hank suggested. "I have friends who could offer their assistance, as well."

"Friends in Boston?" Gwen asked. It was unsettling to think about Hank leaving them soon.

"Yes, Boston is a large city and could offer a variety of opportunities."

"But a woman alone in the world will always find her opportunities limited. You know that well enough. You're here because of your mother's need."

"That's true, but my mother is without the ability or youth to make her way alone. You and your sisters are very talented. You're smart and young."

Gwen smiled. "You are kind to say so, but we both know the truth of it."

Hank raised a brow. "Which is?"

"Without husbands or male relatives, we will always be somewhat of a burden to society. The proper thing for a woman to do is to marry—whether love figures in or not." Gwen suddenly felt embarrassed by this declaration and moved toward the stairs. "If you'll excuse me, I should check on Beth."

Hank reached out and took hold of her arm. "What did you mean by that?"

Gwen tried to be nonchalant about her comment. "Only that women have very little say in what happens to them. No one really cares what we want. . . . or what we need."

"I care." Hank spoke soft and low, while his fingers gently stroked Gwen's forearm.

For a moment, Gwen lost herself in his gaze. She easily remembered the kiss they'd shared and wished against her will that he might kiss her again. She very nearly suggested such a thing when a bell rang out.

Gwen tried to pull her arm from Hank's grasp, but he wouldn't let her go. "That's Beth. I should see to her needs."

"But what about your needs, Gwen?"

She felt her heartbeat quicken. "I . . . uh . . . I don't know what you mean."

He pulled her into his arms and kissed her gently. Gwen was just losing herself in the moment when he pulled back. "Open your eyes."

She didn't want to. There was a part of her that hoped she was dreaming and could just go on doing so. Dreams weren't as dangerous as wakeful emotions.

"Gwen," he whispered. She could feel his breath upon her face. She trembled as his finger traced her cheek. "Look at me."

This time she opened her eyes. The intensity of his gaze caused her knees to go weak. Had he not been holding on to her, Gwen wasn't at all sure that she could have remained standing.

"Tell me what you need, Gwen. What would make you happy?"

The bell rang again, breaking the spell. Gwen straightened and drew a deep breath. "I have to go."

She hurried up the steps, afraid to delay or look back. Afraid, because if she saw the same desire in Hank's face that she felt in her heart, she might completely forget about Beth and tell him exactly what she needed.

Lacy sat on a rock by the river, not caring that the light was long gone or that a wild animal might appear to cause her harm. She felt overwhelmed by her feelings. She'd never meant to say such mean things to Gwen. She honestly didn't believe her sister was capable of being selfish, yet she'd accused her of just that.

Why did life have to be so complicated? Why did Dave have to be so mean? He only wanted to boss her around and make her miserable. He seemed to get some kind of strange pleasure in making her feel weak and stupid.

"I have a task to see through to completion," she said aloud. "I feel confident that I'm supposed to seek out Father's killer. But why must everyone stand against me? They treat me like a child. Like an addle-minded little girl."

Well, it had to stop. She gave serious thought to packing her things and leaving. She could live in Bozeman or even Butte. Both were big enough towns to have jobs available.

"But what would I do? I'm better at horses and hunting than I am at womanly chores. Who would hire me? Besides, I'd be too far away to really investigate Pa's death."

She felt such a severe sense of defeat that nothing offered

her any comfort. Well, there was the memory of Dave's kiss, but that certainly didn't qualify as a comforting thought. At least, she was determined that it wouldn't be such a thing. No matter how many times she found herself daydreaming about the way his lips had felt against hers, Lacy knew there was nothing but danger in such reflection.

"He's just trying to sidetrack me," she told herself. After thinking long and hard about why Dave had kissed her, Lacy was convinced that he had meant to distract her. Since Dave couldn't divert her attention from finding justice for her father in a threatening or nagging way, Lacy was convinced he meant to woo her into a state of cooperation.

"Well, he's wrong. He can kiss me all he wants. I won't change my mind."

At least, she didn't think she would.

She supposed another kiss might prove her theory one way or the other, but it was a terrible risk to consider such a thing. What if she was wrong? What if it *did* change her mind?

CHAPTER TWENTY-THREE

⁓

Hearing Major barking, Gwen looked out her bedroom window and was surprised to see Hank and Brewster Sherman on the property to the north of Gallatin House. Hank appeared to be walking as if measuring distance, while Mr. Sherman was writing something down. What in the world were they up to?

She watched for several minutes, seeing Hank extend his arms and point in first one direction, then another. Mr. Sherman stepped forward, nodding, and seemed to be making his own comments on the matter.

Hank wore the red shirt. He no longer seemed to mind the color, though he had come back from Bozeman with several new white shirts to add to his wardrobe. She couldn't help but wonder if he would take the dyed shirts back to Boston when he finally departed. Would he keep them as a remembrance of his time in Montana?

Gwen let the curtain fall back into place and finished making her bed. It was hard to imagine Hank leaving. And though it seemed almost ridiculous, she could no longer deny that she'd fallen in love with him. At first she'd thought it was some sort of infatuation—perhaps based on her loss of Harvey. But she knew better now. For all the good it did her.

Smoothing the pink-and-white flowered quilt over the sheets, Gwen knew she would be devastated when Hank returned to Boston. She reminded herself of the foolishness of caring about a man who would leave—who had never promised her anything.

He had said that he cared about her, but Gwen wasn't sure what that meant or to what depth she could rely on such a statement. Maybe Hank was simply concerned in the way a brother might be for his sister. But that kiss had been no brotherly bequest.

"I have to stop these thoughts," she chided.

Gwen finished with the bed and made her way downstairs. She had her chores to focus on. There was no sense in being silly or losing herself in daydreams that couldn't possibly come true.

She spied the stack of newspapers on the counter and remembered why there were there. They were intended for the outhouses. They weren't the most comfortable thing to use, but they served the purpose and were free. The stage drivers always brought the supply with them from whatever city they'd passed through on the way to Gallatin House.

Remembering the man who'd announced having torn paper from the wall of the men's outhouse, Gwen picked up a bottle of paste, also, and figured she might as well make repairs while she was at it. With Hank busy elsewhere and Rafe and his bunch still sleeping, the men's outhouse should be unoccupied.

A knock at the front door interrupted her plans, however. Gwen deposited her things once again on the counter and went to see who might be calling at this hour. Ellie stood on the other side, looking rather sheepish. She wore little more than a cotton skirt without benefit of petticoats and a camisole that did very little to hide her thin frame. At least she had a shawl with which to make the ensemble a bit more acceptable.

"I'm sorry to have bothered you, but I wondered how Miss Beth was doing. I heard she'd taken a fall."

Gwen noted the young woman's concerned expression before Ellie turned her gaze back to the floor. "Beth is much better. Why don't you come inside and see her?"

"Oh no," Ellie said, shaking her head. "Rafe wouldn't like that. He'll skin me as it is if he finds out I've been over here."

"But why? We're neighbors. He doesn't seem to restrict himself from coming over whenever he pleases."

Ellie's face flushed red. "He says you Gallatin girls are too high-and-mighty—too religious. He's afraid we might cause trouble for him if we talk to you too much."

Gwen laughed. "Rafe just feels guilty. He knows what he's doing is wrong."

"That's what Beth said. She mended some clothes for me while you were gone, and when she brought them back, she wouldn't take any pay. She said she couldn't take money that had been earned in such a manner. I felt awfully bad about it, but she said it wasn't anything personal."

"Of course not," Gwen replied. "We've often spoken about

how we might help you ladies…we just haven't found a simple solution."

"Oh, I know that well enough," Ellie admitted. She pulled her shawl close. "I tried to find a lot of other solutions before taking on this one. Believe me."

"I do." Gwen recognized the sadness in the girl's voice. She wished she could offer some kind of comfort, but what could she say that might take away the pain of her circumstance? "Are you sure you won't just slip upstairs and see Beth? You could do it quickly—even head back out on the side stairs. That way Rafe wouldn't see you leave the house."

Ellie seemed to consider this for a moment. "That might be all right. I mean, if he doesn't see me . . ."

"Ellie!" Rafe's gravelly voice boomed out as he approached the Gallatin House porch. "What are you doing over here? Haven't I told you not to be coming around here?" He walked right up and grabbed the girl by the arm.

"She's my neighbor, same as you," Gwen declared. "She has as much right to come calling as anyone else."

"I beg to differ with you. She's my property, and she has no rights. Not unless I've given them to her."

"I'm sorry, Rafe. I was just checking on Beth. She took a bad fall, and I wanted to see if she was recovering," Ellie offered.

"I don't much care what you wanted. Now get back to work. If you're up this early, you might as well make yourself useful. Help Cubby clean up the saloon."

Ellie nodded and Rafe released her. She hurried back outside, much to Gwen's disappointment. Rafe treated the women and his own son as if they were nothing more than slaves.

Rafe turned and offered Gwen a smile. "I actually came with a proposition for you."

"I told you that I'm not selling the place to you. I don't approve of liquor or prostitution." Gwen put her hands on her hips. "There is nothing about your attitude, demeanor, or vocation that I want any part of."

Rafe shook his head. "But winter is coming, Gwennie-girl. You and your sisters can't possibly hope to handle all of the needs of this stage stop. Why, the wood needed to heat the house alone will be difficult for you to collect and chop."

Seeing he had no idea of leaving, Gwen pushed past him and stepped out onto the porch. "I assure you, Mr. Reynolds, we Gallatins are cut from stout cloth. We will be quite capable of seeing to our needs."

"But along with the firewood, you'll need more water brought up. You'll need to make additional trips to town for supplies. Before winter hits, you'll have repairs to make and improvements to consider. I could help you with all of that. We could be partners."

"Partners? Have you heard nothing I've said?" Gwen picked up the broom and began to sweep. " 'What fellowship hath righteousness with unrighteousness?' "

"Oh, don't go getting all religious on me. I'm not such a bad sort. We could get married, if that made you feel better about things."

Gwen's jaw dropped. Had she really heard his nonchalant suggestion that they wed? He laughed and stepped toward her. Gwen backed up until she hit the wall of the house.

"I could show you a real good time, Miss Gwen. You wouldn't want for anything. We could run this place and my place together, but you could just stay here and run Gallatin House if you preferred."

Pushing at Rafe's chest, Gwen shook her head. "I would never marry you."

"What's going on here?" Hank asked.

Gwen looked up to see Hank and Mr. Sherman standing at the bottom of the steps. Relief washed over her and she hurried to step out of Rafe's reach.

"I was just reminding Miss Gwen that winter is coming, and she and her sisters will soon be hard-pressed to keep up with their work load. Their old man might not have been much of a businessman, but at least he was a man. They are three ladies on their own, and that doesn't bode well for them."

"And why would that be?" Hank questioned. "Given your gentlemanly nature, wouldn't you keep an eye out for their well-being?"

"That's what I was just suggesting. I proposed marriage, but Miss Gwen isn't of a mind to take my offer." Rafe pushed back his stringy hair and smiled. "Even though I could show her a real good time."

"I thought the point was to keep the ladies safe, not entertained." Hank stepped up on the porch and took a possessive stance beside Gwen.

"Like I said, those gals are gonna need help. Winter is sure to be fierce, and they'll need more wood and water, not to mention supplies."

"And marriage to you would somehow change that?" Hank asked rather sarcastically.

Rafe squared his shoulders. "I made her a good offer. Any single woman should be honored to have a man ask for her hand. It weren't like I was expectin' her to live in sin."

"Of course not," Hank said, turning to Gwen. "So he proposed a legitimate offer of marriage, but you denied him?"

Gwen nodded, and Hank looked back to Rafe. "You have the lady's answer, Mr. Reynolds."

"Come winter, she'll be sorry. Especially when she or her sisters have to drive out for supplies."

"Well, that's the beauty of it," Hank said with a smile. "She won't have to. You see, Mr. Sherman and I have just struck a deal to open a new store here to the north of Gallatin House."

Gwen's stomach tightened. What was he saying? Was he planning to live here, or would he simply be a long-distance partner living in Boston while owning a piece of Montana?

"You got the VanHoutens to agree to sell you a parcel of land? I've been after them for months, and they wouldn't even entertain the idea."

"Perhaps they didn't like your plans for the property," Hank replied. "They seemed quite enthusiastic upon hearing plans for a general mercantile."

Rafe bit at his lower lip for a moment, then stomped down the porch steps. "It really don't change a thing. The Gallatins will still find themselves in need of help, and they won't get it from me." He paused and turned to look Gwen in the eyes. "You mark my words, you won't last the winter."

"Is that a threat?" Gwen asked.

Rafe laughed and continued on his way. "It's just the facts of life in Montana. You've spent winters here before."

"Such a pleasant fellow," Mr. Sherman said once Rafe had returned to his saloon.

Gwen shook her head. "He'll no doubt go back there and take his anger at me out on everyone else. Ellie came over to check on Beth's condition, and he found her here. He was none too happy. I wish I could do something to make her life better."

"You can't save the world, Gwen," Hank countered. "It's much too big a place."

"I don't want to save the world," she replied. "Just maybe make my corner of it a little better."

⁂

Rafe stormed through the saloon and into his office. He'd had more than he cared to of those self-righteous Gallatins. Now they had a new friend in Hank Bishop, and the man was planning to stick around.

He barely saw Wyman following behind him before slamming the door shut. "What do you want?" he called out.

Wyman pushed open the door hesitantly and peered inside. "Problems?"

"You could say that," Rafe said, turning back to his desk. He took up a nearly empty bottle of whiskey and drank down the contents before slamming it back on the desktop. "I've had it with interference to my plans."

Wyman shook his head. "Who's interferin'?"

"The Gallatins and their uppity city-friend Bishop. Do you know that he plans to open a mercantile on the other side of the stage stop?" Rafe looked at Wyman and could see from the man's expression that he hadn't heard the news. "That's right. He plans to put in a store. Next thing you know, this whole area will be teeming with law and order."

"I hadn't heard about the store, but I did know there were several new homesteaders in the area. He probably heard about that, too. Seem to be new folks in the area every summer."

"I don't so much mind the homesteaders," Rafe admitted. He leaned back against his desk. "They usually bring me business and yet aren't so close as to be a nuisance. But a store and other businesses will put demands on us—probably drive us out altogether and make this a temperance town."

"Ain't too many of those in Montana," Wyman said with a laugh. "Sure, there's always a few, but folks around here like their whiskey too much."

"They like it enough to just head over to Bozeman or elsewhere."

Rafe dropped down on the chair and shook his head. There had to be a way to slow down progress. He'd done his best to discourage the railroad fellows when they'd come through to survey. He and Wyman had both regaled them with stories of flooding and other problems, mostly fabricated. Unlike most folks who saw the railroad as a boon to business, Rafe had other plans. He knew that with all the area ranches, he could expand his business. He could have gaming and even bring in entertainment from the bigger cities. He saw Rafe's Saloon as an oasis in the middle of an isolated land. And if he could just get rid of the Gallatin girls, he'd have a first-rate place to set up a large brothel—maybe the largest in the territory.

"There has to be a way to convince those girls to go."

"Maybe if the dangers seem to increase in the area, they'll leave," Wyman suggested. "If that youngest one noses in over here again, something unpleasant could happen to persuade them."

Rafe nodded. "I had considered that. The only trouble there is, the law would be sure to get involved. They don't take well to women suffering such fates in these parts. Someone'd be strung up for sure."

Wyman folded his arms and nodded. "Well, there's bound to be a solution. We just ain't thought of it yet."

"Yeah, well, now we have to deal with Bishop, as well," Rafe said in disgust. "If it ain't pious, saintly women, it's dandies. They're ruining this country."

"A store would be a great addition," Patience Shepard said. "We have enough new families in the area, and more are sure to follow, what with the railroad planning to come through here."

"Have they decided the route?" Gwen asked. She had taken time out of her busy schedule to ride over to the Shepards' on the pretense of needing cream and butter. What she really hoped to address was the issue of Lacy.

"No, but Jerry thinks they will come through this way. After all, it's well traveled, and there's plenty of water for the train engines." Patience smiled and offered Gwen more tea. "Of course, the best news of all has been the circuit rider. I can hardly believe we'll get to have regular services. Well, at least every third Sunday. The rest of the time Jerry has gotten several of the men to agree to lead us. It will almost be like having a real church."

"I know. Beth and Lacy will be surprised when I tell them. Maybe even more so after I explain that I've volunteered Gallatin House for the meetings," Gwen said, taking a sip from her cup.

"It's a very generous offer and more centrally located than our ranch. I think we'll see an even bigger turnout that way. Jerry said if you have the space for the piano, he'll have it brought over as soon as possible. With the girls gone, no one plays it anyway."

"He can bring it over anytime. We'll put it in the front room, but we'll need to find someone who can play it. None of us ever learned how."

"I think Mrs. VanHouten plays. Perhaps she'd be willing. If not, I'm sure someone will come along in time."

"I can hardly wait to get to know everyone," Gwen said. "I remember when we lived elsewhere, Sunday was such a wonderful day of worship and visiting. I'd like to see us all share meals and just enjoy the day."

"I'd like that, too," Patience admitted. She put her cup aside and smoothed down her skirt. "But why don't you tell me why you really came here today? I can see that something is troubling you."

Gwen nodded. "It's Lacy. She's continuing to put herself in danger because of Father's death."

"I know. Dave had a talk with me." She gave Gwen a sympathetic smile. "Your sister knows no fear. That's a dangerous state to be in."

"I know enough fear for the both of us, to be honest. I'm worried that something really bad will happen to her." Gwen put her cup and saucer aside and leaned toward Patience. "With a rifle at her side, Lacy thinks she can take on any man. But I fear they may harm her virtue."

"It's true. There are a great many rowdies and ne'er-do-wells. I'd hate it to become so bad that a woman couldn't ride around on her own without fearing danger."

Gwen swallowed hard. The idea of Lacy being hurt was almost more than she could bear. "I have suggested what we talked about—you and me."

"About sending your sisters to my folks?"

"Yes. Perhaps I broached the subject poorly, for neither one wanted to hear anything about it. But I can't help but wonder if it wouldn't be best. It might lessen their problems."

"What about you?"

Gwen shook her head. "Sometimes I think I'm their biggest problem of all."

"You can't possibly be serious. You've mothered them and nursed them when they were sick, been a help and a companion. You are far too important to them, Gwen." Patience frowned. "This isn't still about your thoughts on being cursed, is it?"

"I try not to believe myself to be cursed, but then something like Beth's accident happens and I'm full of doubts." Gwen knew Patience wouldn't approve of her confession, but it felt good just to admit to her struggle. "If I hadn't been racing up the stairs without paying attention, Beth would never have fallen."

"You aren't cursed, Gwen. You have to accept that truth, or you very well may bring worse trouble upon yourself."

Gwen stiffened and eyed Patience intently. "Why? What do you mean?"

"Only that sometimes we bring these things upon ourselves by willing them to be. If you decide that you're cursed and continue to act as though you are, you very well may find enough problems in life to convince yourself that you're right. Then you'll miss out on the liberty and victory you could have had—the joy and happiness. There is something to be said about thinking on the positive side of life. Remember, the Bible also tells us to think on pure and lovely things."

Gwen nodded, knowing Patience was right. "I'm trying. I suppose I get anxious about working out all the details. I know being anxious is wrong, but I love my sisters and hate to think they might somehow suffer because of me."

"Darling girl, everyone suffers from time to time. Continue to trust that God will see you through this, and pray for His guidance."

Gwen drew a deep breath and sighed. Why did someone always have to remind Gwen of such a simple thing as trusting God and praying? *How weary the Lord must grow of me and my lack of faith.*

CHAPTER TWENTY-FOUR

"Just hold on. I promise I won't drop you," Hank told Beth as he carried her downstairs.

"I'm going to close my eyes," she said, pressing her face against his shoulder. "This just doesn't seem at all safe. You should have waited for help."

Hank laughed. "I assure you, I can manage. You hardly weigh anything at all."

He met Gwen's amused gaze as he came to the bottom of the stairs. "I believe your sister doubted my abilities to assist in her delivery to the breakfast table."

Just then, Nick and Simon bounded into the foyer. Nick looked at Hank and frowned. Well, perhaps it was more of a scowl, Hank decided.

"What's going on?" Simon asked.

Beth looked up and smiled. "Gwen said I could come downstairs today. But while I've finally had enough days in bed to merit the opportunity to sit up for breakfast, I apparently am not released to climb up or down the stairs. I keep telling her I feel fine, but she won't listen."

"You need to follow the doctor's orders," Gwen interjected. "He's due to come back and visit you in a couple of days. We'll see what he says then."

Beth rolled her eyes, and Hank laughed. Gwen meanwhile motioned them all to the dining room. "Breakfast is getting cold."

Nick and Simon stepped back to allow Hank to pass by with Beth. Hank couldn't help but feel that they were watching his every move. It was clear that the Lassiter boys felt possessive of the Gallatin sisters, but perhaps even more so of Beth. They waited until Hank deposited her on a well-padded chair before taking up residence on the seats on either side.

Lacy poured coffee for the men but said very little. Hank could see she was still nursing hurt feelings; she'd hardly said two words all morning.

Gwen offered grace, then passed a plate of scones to Hank. He smiled, remembering his English cook in Boston. Scones were one of his specialties, but Hank had a feeling these would taste every bit as good.

"Are you truly feeling better, Beth?" Nick asked. He took a huge slice of fried ham but kept his gaze on the woman at his side.

"Oh goodness, yes. My back hardly bothers me at all. I feel like a pampered princess as I lie about all day, doing nothing but reading." She looked at Gwen. "Perhaps you and Lacy should take your turns after I'm up and about. Of course, I would recommend leaving off with the fall down the stairs."

The men chuckled at this, but neither Lacy nor Gwen so much as smiled. Hank knew Gwen was quite touchy on the subject of her sister's fall. He also knew he had played a role in it. Had he not upset her, Gwen would never have gone running without giving thought to others in her path.

"Have you thought to soak your back in the hot springs?" Nick asked. "I'd be happy to carry you down there, if you thought it might help."

Beth's cheeks turned slightly red, but it was Gwen who answered. "We've brought hot water to the house and helped her soak here in our tub. No doubt it has aided in her recovery." She picked up a bowl of berries. "Would you care for some?" She held the mixture out to Nick. "Lacy picked them just yesterday, and they're quite delicious mixed into your oatmeal."

Hank eyed his bowl of oatmeal with some amusement. He looked up to catch Beth watching him. She grinned, and he couldn't help but chuckle. "I think berries sound delicious."

Nick helped himself to the berries, then offered them to Hank. "So we hear tell that you're planning to build a mercantile, Hank."

"That's right. Brewster Sherman and I discussed the potential for a store here on the stage route and decided it would do well." He spooned the berry concoction onto his cereal and passed the bowl back to Nick.

"Bruce ought to know." Nick turned to Beth and handed her the berry bowl.

"He does know a great deal about the valley," Hank said, stirring cream into his oatmeal. "There are already several new families in the immediate area, and after further investigation, we've learned that many others have applied for homesteads."

"Maybe it won't be all that long before we can have a regular town," Simon said. "I, for one, would like to see us grow."

"I'm sure Rafe would be less than enthusiastic," Lacy said, joining the conversation for the first time. "He would hate to see real law and order come to this place."

"I imagine that's true," Hank said, meeting her gaze. "Still, I think we'll have more folks in the area wanting it than not."

"Well, I hope you'll carry smithing supplies," Simon threw out.

"That's a good idea," Hank agreed. "I hadn't fully considered what all to carry. Bruce and I discussed it and knew there would be a great need for everyday things like lantern oil, matches, candles, food items, canning equipment, and so forth. We also figured to have gardening and ranching supplies."

Nick waved his fork as if to emphasize his words. "You'd do well to lay in feed and seed."

"Sounds like quite a large store," Gwen remarked.

Hank buttered a scone and smiled. "It seemed a sound investment, what with the traffic this area sees." He bit into the scone and marveled at the taste of cinnamon and cloves. "Mmmm, this is delicious."

"Gwen has always been the best baker in our family," Beth said with a giggle. "The first time I tried to make scones, I nearly set the house on fire, remember?"

"Remember?" Lacy questioned. "I can still smell burnt cinnamon in my sleep."

Gwen smiled. "You were only twelve, Beth. You shouldn't be so hard on yourself. You can make an excellent scone these days."

"I have a cook who came to me from Manchester, and he can certainly make nothing better than this. Of course, I won't mention that to him. It's likely to send him packing. He's a very sensitive sort," Hank told them.

"A fellow who does the cooking, you say?" Simon looked at his brother. "See? I told you there was nothing wrong with a man taking responsibility for the kitchen."

Hank laughed. "Some of the best chefs in the world are men."

"I'd rather work with horses," Nick said, shaking his head. "And eat here at Gallatin House. I figure, why bother to cook when the girls are just across the way?" He grinned at Beth and added, "They're a whole sight prettier, too."

"Than what?" Lacy asked. "The horses?"

Everyone laughed at this while Nick's face turned beet red. Simon seemed to take pity on his brother and questioned Gwen. "How's your garden working out this year?"

"Better, but only marginally. We've had a good show with some of the greens and the beans. Hank suggested maybe I could get some better soil from one of the local ranches or farms to mix in with our ground and see even better results next year."

"Sounds worth a try," Simon said, nodding. "Maybe even move it closer to the river. Your property runs all the way back."

"That's true, but it puts me quite a ways from the house." Gwen turned to Lacy. "Would you mind getting the coffee?"

Lacy got up and did as she was asked. Hank wondered if the sisters had worked out their differences yet. He knew Lacy's harsh words had deeply wounded Gwen, but she wasn't one to hold a grudge—not that Hank could see.

"So I'm sure you've heard by now that we'll have Sunday services here a week from Sunday," Gwen announced.

"I would imagine you ladies have missed having a church to regularly attend."

Gwen looked at Hank and nodded. "There are a variety of churches we could travel to attend, but often the distance makes it unrealistic. It will be so nice to just have services here."

Hank began to envision the future for this community. More people would mean the need for schools and doctors. And if the railroad came through the town, it would definitely bring more business and settlers.

"I heard there were also plans for a sawmill," Simon said. He downed the last of his coffee and waited patiently for Lacy to make the rounds and fill his cup. "I know Jerry Shepard said there was some thought to have it to the south of here, but I told him to encourage it coming closer. We could definitely benefit from a sawmill."

Hank nodded. "I believe the man in question has been approached and is considering the changes. Not only that but one of the new couples in the area have experience in running a flour mill. Given the wheat that is grown in the area, I believe this would serve us well."

"Just think, Gwen—we could build on to Gallatin House and make it even bigger," Beth said excitedly. "Maybe we could even employ Ellie and the others and get them away from Rafe."

Gwen seemed to consider that thought for a moment. "That would definitely have been in keeping with Pa's desire to expand."

"Well, first things first," Simon said. He pushed back his plate. "Tell us what you and Sherman have figured out for the store."

The conversation once again focused on Hank's plans, and

for several minutes the conversation dealt with thoughts on location and positioning of the actual building.

"Will we see the store in place before winter?" Simon asked.

"It's my desire to see a small structure up before the end of summer," Hank replied. "Bruce believes he can get the manpower to start cutting and stripping logs. We'll start small and keep building so we can make it a profitable business right away."

"And you plan to remain here and run it?" Simon asked.

Hank nodded. "Of course."

"I thought you came here on another task," Beth said softly. "You were searching for your mother's certificates, as I recall. What about that?"

"And what about Boston?" Gwen asked.

Nick eyed him intently. "Yeah, why would you move here?"

Hank laughed. "Because I've fallen in love."

Everyone looked at Gwen, who looked at Hank as if he'd lost his mind. He laughed. "It's true I came here with a different purpose, but Montana has wooed me and won my heart," he said, grinning. "That, along with other things, seems to make moving here not only reasonable but necessary. I still haven't found the certificates, but I can sell my Boston businesses and help my mother. In fact, I've already wired to start the process of finding a buyer."

Beth looked at him as if trying to size up the truth in his words. "You'll find life here to be very different from Boston. There are many more dangers and problems to be had."

Hank couldn't be sure, but he thought there was an edge of warning to her tone. "The city has its dangers, too," he admitted.

"But I find when you care deeply about something, you need to risk it all—take a chance to be a part of what you love."

Simon pushed back from the table and turned to Beth. "Looks like you've finished. How about I carry you back upstairs?"

"Oh no, you don't," Nick argued. "I'll carry her."

"I'll flip you for it," Simon said, pulling a coin from his vest pocket. "Heads or tails."

"Heads." Nick watched intently as the coin slipped end over end. When it finally landed, it was heads. He grinned at his brother and then turned his attention on Beth. "Looks like I win."

"I don't know that you'll feel quite the same after you lift me," Beth declared. "I've just eaten enough for three men."

Gwen was already gathering the dishes. She looked uncomfortable, and Hank hoped they might be afforded a few minutes alone when she instructed Lacy to go along with Nick to turn down Beth's bed.

Simon got to his feet as Nick gathered Beth in his arms. "I'll come, too. That way I can keep an eye on Nick."

Hank laughed, but his thought was on how to explain his heart to Gwen. When he looked up to comment, however, Gwen was gone.

The only thing Gwen wanted was to escape the table and all those curious stares. She hadn't expected Hank to declare his love for anything, but when he'd made his comment, she found herself both terrified and hopeful that she might be the recipient of his affections.

"You seem upset."

Gwen turned, her arms still full of dishes, and saw Hank

watching her. "Upset? Why would I be upset? I'm just busy. I have a lot on my mind."

He walked toward her with determined steps. Gwen felt her knees weaken as Hank reached out and took the dishes from her. "Like what?"

"What do you mean?" she asked.

He smiled, and Gwen felt her breath quicken. "Like, what's on your mind? What has you so preoccupied?" He put the dishes in the sink and turned back to take hold of her hands.

Gwen stared at him in dumbfounded silence. What could she say? She really couldn't explain to him that her emotions were so jumbled, she couldn't even hope to sort them out.

"Well?" he asked.

"I . . . uh . . ." She licked her bottom lip. "I . . . have the dishes."

"And they require washing but are hardly worthy of your thoughts." He stepped closer, all the while stroking his fingers across the back of her hand. "Gwen, you have to know that I've fallen in love with more than just Montana."

"Ah . . . I . . ." She looked at her hands and found it mesmerizing to watch the pattern Hank traced upon her skin. She might have continued to watch this indefinitely, but Hank stopped and lifted her chin.

He bent forward ever so slightly and pulled her face toward him. Their lips touched for just a moment before Nick and Simon called out from the front of the house.

"Thanks for breakfast, Gwen. We'll see you later."

Gwen startled and pushed away from Hank. She hurried into the front room just as the door closed behind the two men. Turning abruptly, she found that Hank had also followed her. He pulled her into his arms.

"I've fallen in love with you, Gwen, and I think you've

fallen in love with me, as well." He looked at her with such passion—such desire—that Gwen couldn't even form words, much less thoughts.

"You don't have to say anything. Just promise me that you'll think about it."

Gwen shook her head. "Think about what?"

He let her go and stepped back with a grin. "About loving me."

CHAPTER TWENTY-FIVE

Lacy saw the trio of cowboys on the road below well before they spotted her. She was on higher ground and able to watch them for some distance before sending her mare down the path to ambush them.

Pulling up short of the lead man's gelding, Lacy faced them with a sense of false bravado. "I want to talk to you," she announced.

The men eyed her, more out of curiosity than concern. The one whose horse now stood nose to nose with hers pushed back his hat a bit and smiled. "You're that nosy little Gallatin gal who's been asking all the questions about her dead pa, aren't you?"

"I'm Lacy Gallatin, and yes, I'm asking questions about the night my father was murdered."

"Hey, now," one of the other men declared. "I heard that was just an accident. Some of the boys were whooping it up, and it just got out of hand." He nudged his gray closer to Lacy's mare.

She didn't like the feeling of being boxed in as the final man made his way forward and came up on her left. His flaxen chestnut seemed none too happy about the arrangement, either, and tried to dance a step to the side.

Trying hard to appear unaffected by the men's actions, Lacy leaned back in her saddle. "There are those folks who say it was an accident," Lacy admitted, "but even accidents of such a careless nature should merit some kind of punishment."

"I was there that night," the man on her left said. "Nobody knows whose bullet hit your pa. We were careless, sure enough, but no one would have wanted to see it cause the death of anyone. Fact is, I've made a pact with myself to leave the guns at home when I go drinking from now on."

Lacy shook her head. "It's too little, too late."

The man cocked a brow. "Would you have us all hanged instead?"

"You need to leave off with this, Miss Gallatin," the first man said. "No one is going to admit to killing your father, even if there was a way to know whose gun did the deed. We're powerful sorry that such a thing had to happen, but nothing can be done about it now."

"Even the sheriff said it was a closed case," the man on her right added.

Lacy fumed. "Oh, he did, did he? That doesn't surprise me. However, it's not a closed case to me. The sheriff and his dim-witted deputies can rot, for all I care. I intend to find the man responsible and see him pay."

The man on her left shook his head. He had a kind expression, and Lacy could see that he was neither angry nor amused.

"Miss Gallatin, again, what is it that would suffice as pay? Do you honestly want to see another man die because he made a mistake?"

Lacy was taken aback for a moment. She didn't know what to say. She didn't advocate an eye for an eye—not really.

"I suppose it would help me a great deal if the man would just admit to what he's done," she finally said. "I don't want any more killing, to be sure, but my sisters and I are alone now. The least he could do would be to accept some sort of responsibility for what happened and try to make it up to us—to help us."

The man nodded. "I suppose that would be only fair. My name is Ben. Ben Mills. Why don't we just say that my bullet was the one that struck your pa?"

"Did it?"

"I don't think so, but let's just say it did."

Lacy shook her head. "Why? Why should I say that if it's not true?"

"Because I'm trying to take your point on the matter. I'll come and help you and your sisters when I can get away from the ranch. Right now we're rounding up strays, but I should have some time tomorrow."

"I don't want your help," Lacy said, looking at him oddly. His dark eyes seemed to penetrate her façade of calm. "I want justice."

"You want something that can't be had," Ben replied softly.

"Ben, you don't want to be committing yourself to help those women," the lead man declared. "You'll never hear the end of it. They'll have you doing their fetching and odd jobs for the rest of your life."

"Slim's right," the other man threw in. "There's no sense in paying the price for something you didn't do."

Ben's gaze never left Lacy. "But isn't this more about the need of the Gallatin women? They've been left without a man to do the hard work around the place."

"No!" Lacy declared. "I mean, yes, we're without a man, but no, it isn't about our need. It's about justice for my father."

"Justice?" Ben asked.

Lacy nodded. "It's about the right person paying for what they did."

"But I'm willing to stand in his place."

The concept only served to confuse Lacy all the more. She didn't want to admit that, seen in this light, her quest seemed almost silly. What did she really want from all of this?

"It's unacceptable to have an innocent man take the blame for someone else's evil," Lacy said, squaring her shoulders.

Ben smiled. "Good thing Jesus didn't feel the same way as you."

"Jesus? That's entirely different."

"Not if we're supposed to live like Him," Ben countered.

Now Lacy was really disturbed. His words made too much sense, and they caused her to rethink everything she'd been so sure of since losing her father. "It's not the same," she muttered and pulled on the reins gently. The mare backed up several paces, and Lacy turned her to exit the enclosure the men had created. "If you'll excuse me, I'm going to be late."

She kicked the mare into a hard gallop and raced down the road, not even looking back to see what the men were doing. Her mind whirled with a hundred thoughts, and none of them made any sense. She felt as though Ben Mills had stolen her purpose.

Heading toward the Shepard ranch, Lacy tried to think

through the situation, but there was no comfort in any conclusion she made. If Ben was right, then she needed to put aside her hunt and accept that he was willing to help her family.

"Like we really need help," she muttered and slowed the mare.

The girls had been doing most of the work around Gallatin House. Their father was useful in his own way, but he never seemed quite organized enough to see anything through to completion. He might start chopping wood, but as soon as he saw Simon or Nick, he was off to talk and discuss any news they might have about the area. Lacy was usually the one who would pick up where her father left off. Her sisters had teased that she was the son her father had always wanted, but Lacy knew the truth of it.

The only son in the Gallatin family had died trying to be born, and it was Lacy's fault that he hadn't made it. If she could have found their father in time, he would have been able to come and help their mother with the delivery.

Lacy hated trying to remember the past. So much had gone wrong after the death of her mother. Their lives had been forever changed with her passing, and the good times were few and far between. The pain and sadness that followed had been so great that Lacy had worked with all of her might to forget it all. The only trouble was, Lacy found forgetting the bad also required forgetting a great deal of the good. Her mother was one of those good things. Lacy couldn't remember her face or her voice. They didn't even have a picture of her, but their father had often said that Lacy resembled her greatly. It was funny how Lacy could stare in the mirror for hours and never see it.

That was maybe the worst of it. Letting go of the sorrow had also robbed Lacy of the joy and tenderness she'd known.

She had asked Gwen over and over to tell her stories about their mother, but it never really helped her to remember.

Thinking of Gwen, Lacy felt a terrible weight of guilt. She had been cruel to Gwen, and even now, two weeks later, she had done nothing to make things right between them. It wore at Lacy like a rock in her boot.

The Shepard ranch house came into view, and Lacy urged her mare to pick up the pace once again. Patience Shepard was the one woman Lacy thought might very well help her to understand what needed to be done to make things right—especially with Gwen.

Gwen had never been so glad to see a stage leave as she was that morning. With Beth back on her feet but still taking it easy, and Lacy mysteriously gone for the day, Gwen had found herself overwhelmed with the work required. Even though it was nearly noon, she felt she'd hardly made a dent in the list of things to do.

Of course, she might have been more efficient at her tasks had her mind not been wrapped up in thoughts of Hank and his declaration of love. He had left her alone—in fact, he had very nearly avoided her, choosing instead to spend far more time away from Gallatin House than in it.

At first Gwen had been relieved, but as the days stretched into weeks, she found herself watching for him—waiting for him to reappear. She kept meals warming on the stove for him and continued to clean his room, even when he was gone for several days. So it only seemed reasonable that she be startled half speechless when he surprised her by walking into the kitchen as if he owned the place.

"Afternoon," he said casually. He smiled and made his way to the stove. "Mind if I have a cup of coffee?"

"No," she managed. She stood frozen to the spot, not even attempting to help him.

Hank pulled a cup from where they hung and poured himself some coffee. "I suppose you're wondering what I've been up to these last few days."

Gwen started to deny this but finally nodded. She leaned back against the sink and tried not to remember how his lips felt when he kissed her.

"I've been making arrangements. Bruce has managed to get the details settled on the construction of the building, but there have been many other things to see to."

"You seem . . . well . . . to have it under control," Gwen managed to say.

"I do. I feel confident of the way things are coming together." He drank the coffee down in one long gulp, then smiled. "You're beautiful, you know."

She turned to pick up a wet platter and dish towel. "When will you go back to see your mother? You'll have to tell her about Harvey."

"I know. I figure I'll need to head out in a few days."

"How will you tell her?" Gwen asked softly. "How will you explain not finding the certificates?"

He said nothing, and this caused her to turn. Hank seemed to be considering the matter. "I suppose I'll tell her that Harvey either lost them or hid them away. Then I'll tell her about you."

"Me? Why me?"

He grinned. "She ought to know about you—don't you think?"

Gwen shrugged. "I suppose. I am, after all, the hussy who married your brother."

Hank laughed, then sobered almost as quickly. "You are the beautiful woman who won my brother's heart. Just as you've won mine. I have a feeling you'll be an important part of my family for a very long time. Therefore, my mother needs to know all about you."

Gwen felt her face grow hot. She gave a nervous laugh and tried to make light of his statement. "Is that a proposal?"

Hank put the cup aside and crossed his arms. "That depends."

"On what?"

"Would you like it to be?"

For a moment, Gwen wasn't at all sure she could draw a breath. She had thought of this moment for a long time. In her daydreams, she had imagined telling Hank that she loved him and wanted to be his wife. She had thought of what her sisters might say—what their friends might say.

"Well?" Hank asked, tilting his head slightly to one side.

The cat made an appearance at that moment and looked up at Gwen as if also awaiting her answer. He gave a single *meow*, then looked at Hank.

"I believe Cal would also like to know what your reply might be."

Gwen smiled in spite of herself. "Calvin already knows my answer. I've spent enough nights discussing the matter with him."

"And just what did he have to say about it?"

Gwen met Hank's eyes and felt the wall around her heart crumble into dust. "He said I'd be a fool not to return your love."

"I don't want it returned. I want it shared," Hank said softly. "For the rest of our lives."

Gwen nodded. "I'd like that, too."

∞

Lacy sat at the Shepards' kitchen table and tried to explain her dilemma. "I don't know what to do. I don't know why I can't think clearly."

"You've suffered a great loss. It only stands to reason that you would struggle to come to terms with it all."

"But everyone else seems to be adjusting just fine. Why should I be the only one who continues to be haunted by Pa's death? I keep having nightmares. I see him dead on the street—I hear him plead with me to find his killer."

"And what good would it do to find him?"

Lacy looked at Patience and shrugged. "I don't know. I used to think it would ease my hurt, but now I'm not so sure."

"And why is that?"

"Well, like everyone keeps saying, it won't bring him back. I guess it's just that if I don't find the man responsible, I will have failed my father again."

"Again?"

Lacy nodded. "Like when my mother died."

Patience came to sit beside Lacy. She reached out and took hold of the younger girl's hand. "You didn't fail him then. There was nothing you could have done, even if you'd found him before she passed on. You have to accept that and let the past go."

"I can't. I just know that if I could have found Pa, he would have known what to do. I don't care that the doctor said otherwise. I just know things would have been better. He never said

305

so, but I know he blamed me for failing him. I could see it in his eyes."

"If he blamed you, Lacy, then he was wrong. You weren't responsible for your mother's death or for his absence at her side. You were a little girl—five years old. You did what you could."

"But it wasn't enough. It's never enough—just like now." She put her hands to her head. "I've said awful things to Gwen, and I just know she'll never forgive me."

"It hardly seems reasonable to judge without at least first attempting to receive forgiveness."

Lacy looked up with tears blurring her vision. "I said that she cared only about herself. Nothing could be further from the truth."

"So tell her that." Patience put her arms around Lacy and hugged her close. "Be reconciled with your sister, Lacy. She loves you, and she grieves for you. And, I know without a doubt that she will also forgive you."

∞

Lacy waited until everyone was in bed that night before lightly tapping on Gwen's bedroom door. She hadn't bothered to put on a robe or slippers, and the chill of the floor was making her uncomfortable. Maybe she should just go back and wait until morning. She had just turned to go when the light from Gwen's room spilled into the hall.

Gwen seemed surprised to see Lacy there, but she opened the door wide to usher her inside. "I thought you'd gone to sleep."

"No," Lacy admitted. "I was waiting until you came upstairs so I could talk to you."

Gwen sat down on the edge of the bed and patted a spot beside her on the mattress. Lacy shook her head. "No, I'll just stand here. I came to apologize. I know I said some mean things, Gwen. Things that weren't true. I spoke out of anger and pain."

"I know that, Lacy."

"But I hurt you, and I'm sorry. I never wanted . . . never meant . . ." Lacy's voice cracked. "Please forgive me."

"I already have," Gwen replied, holding out her arms.

Lacy leaned in to her sister and allowed herself to be enfolded in a tight embrace. She sobbed against Gwen's shoulder for what seemed a very long, comforting time.

"I love you, Gwen. I want to do what's right, but it always seems like I do what's wrong."

"We all have that problem from time to time. Even Paul spoke of it in the Bible."

Lacy straightened. "But I feel like I'll never overcome it. I just don't think I'm strong enough to do it on my own."

Gwen smiled and gently wiped Lacy's face. "Who ever said you'd have to do it on your own?"

"But I feel alone. I feel like I'm the only one who cares about Pa's death. I feel like the law has given up and so have you and Beth."

"Lacy, I don't see things the same way you do. Pa is dead, and I feel terrible that he's gone. I miss him so much sometimes. He was a great comfort to me after Harvey died, and now he lies in a grave right next to him. It's hard to see that grave and know that he's gone."

"It just seems to me that if we could find the man responsible, then . . ."

"Then what, Lacy?" Gwen looked at her with such

compassion that Lacy felt surely this must be the kind of tenderness their mother would have had for them.

"I don't know," she finally whispered. "I just keep thinking it would help me."

"But how?"

Lacy pulled away and got to her feet. "I really can't say. I can't explain it, but it just seems to drive me."

"It terrifies me, Lacy." Gone was Gwen's tender expression. In its place she wore a look of panic. "I think about what might happen to you, and it kills me inside. Men can be so cruel. I fear that you'll get yourself in a situation where you won't have help—where someone will hurt you."

For the first time, Lacy felt grieved over her actions and attitudes regarding their father's killer. "I'm sorry. I've been very selfish in all of this."

"I'd just like for you to leave off with this search. At least for now. We need time to heal from our hurt—not cause more of it."

Lacy felt a band tighten around her chest. She didn't want to promise anything but knew that she'd come here in hopes of making amends with Gwen. The only thing she truly had to offer was her willingness to stop investigating their father's death.

"I'll try, Gwen. I don't want to say that I won't mess up, but I'll try to let it go. I don't want to cause you further worry."

Gwen got to her feet and went to her sister. Pulling Lacy into her arms, she hugged her tight. "Thank you. Thank you so much. I know what a sacrifice this is to you."

Lacy forced a smile as they separated. "I guess I'd better get back to bed. Morning will come soon enough."

"I'm sure we'll both sleep a whole lot easier with this behind us," Gwen said as Lacy opened the door.

Outside in the hall, Lacy pulled Gwen's door shut and hurried back to her own room. She closed the door and slid the latch into place to keep out the world and all its woes.

"If only I could lock away my thoughts as easily," she muttered, knowing that while Gwen's mind had been eased, hers was far from settled.

...

CHAPTER TWENTY-SIX

Gwen had already determined to say nothing to Beth or Lacy about Hank and his proposal of marriage. She thought of her decision as she worked around the kitchen. There was always the possibility that once Hank went east, he would remember his life there and want to recapture it. She could hardly expect to hold him to his proposal if he found that life in Boston was what he really longed for.

I could be nothing more than a diversion, she thought.

And if she was only that, Gwen had no desire to work her sisters into a frenzy planning a wedding that might never take place. She also didn't want to worry about their future. After all, she and Hank had scarcely discussed what that future would hold. If he did return and desired to continue with his plans for the store, then perhaps things could go along as they always had. Maybe there wouldn't need to be any big changes to their lives.

She opened the oven door and took out a tray of plump cinnamon rolls. The aroma nearly enticed Gwen to sneak a bite or two. She remembered that when Lacy was little, she would often walk right in and grab up freshly baked cookies and gobble them down. Gwen told her that stealing was not acceptable, but Lacy merely countered with her childish reasoning that if she was doing the deed right in front of Gwen, it wasn't stealing at all.

We always have our ways of reasoning out our wrongdoings, Gwen mused. She put another pan of rolls into the oven, then checked the fire and added a few more pieces of wood. She had just finished when Beth appeared.

"Smells mighty good. Can I help you frost those?"

Gwen nodded. "They're all yours."

"Did you see that Hank and Brewster Sherman are working to mark out where the store will be?" Beth asked as she tied on an apron.

"No, I hadn't noticed. I'm surprised Mr. Sherman is here so early. That's quite a ride from Bozeman."

Beth shrugged and took up the bowl of frosting Gwen had already prepared. "Maybe he stayed at one of the ranches. He drove his wagon, so he might have brought out supplies for someone."

"I suppose that makes sense."

Just then Lacy came running in through the back door. She was breathless and her hair flew wildly around her face. "We have . . . there are . . ." She bent over to draw her breath.

"What is it?" Gwen asked, hurrying to close the back door behind her sister in case she'd been running from a bear.

"The survey team is back," Lacy managed to gasp out. "They're coming for breakfast."

"Oh goodness," Gwen said, looking around the kitchen rather fretfully. She'd made no plans for a large breakfast. On days when it was just the three or them, or four including Hank, she had a rather slow-paced meal of oatmeal or flapjacks. Today she had actually decided to get up early and make the cinnamon rolls, but they had been planned for tomorrow morning when she knew she'd have at least three of her regular freight drivers coming through.

Beth put down the bowl of frosting. "I'll get the eggs and bacon." She headed for the cellar door and called over her shoulder, "Or would you rather I bring up the last of the ham?"

"The bacon is fine." Gwen motioned Lacy to the rolls. "They're still warm, but go ahead and frost them. Then set the table. How soon will they be here?"

"They were seeing to their horses and gear over at the Lassiters' place. From what I heard, they plan to head out again after they eat."

Gwen took up the coffeepot. It was still pretty full, so she relaxed a bit. "I guess we'll start them on the rolls, and by then we should have some eggs and bacon ready."

The hubbub that followed was something akin to a circus gone amok. The men were more than grateful to be taken in and cared for, but they were smelly and dirty from their weeks on the trail. Adrian Murphy suggested they all wash up prior to descending on the girls' breakfast table. This suited Gwen just fine, as it gave them extra time to prepare the food, but it also added the problem of seeing everyone had supplies for bathing.

"Why don't you have them go wash up in the stream where the hot springs overflow pours out of our pool?" Beth suggested.

"I'll get them several bars of soap, and there are fresh towels ready and waiting on the back porch."

"That sounds like the perfect idea, Miss Beth," Adrian said, giving her a smile. "I should have known a beautiful young woman such as yourself would also be smart."

And so the chaos continued. The men lined up and headed out to the hot springs, with Adrian bringing soap and towels for everyone. Meanwhile, Gwen and her sisters went back to work preparing breakfast. By the time the men shuffled back into the house, they were fairly clean and half starved.

Adrian Murphy seemed as enthralled with Beth as he had been during their last trip. He was ever so concerned to hear about her fall but glad that her subsequent recovery had been a quick one.

"We had to send one of the men home," he told them, "after he took a fall into a ravine east of Bozeman. He was busted up pretty bad."

Gwen shuddered at the thought that such a fate could have been Beth's, as well. "We are grateful to God that Beth was spared any breaks."

"But you can be sure I'll hold on to the rail when descending the stairs from now on," Beth added.

The men ate their fill amid discussions about the Northern Pacific Railroad. Gwen found it all rather fascinating to hear how routes were chosen based on the availability of water, the quality of the ground, and the ease of the passage.

"Folks often think we plot out the line based on the available towns along the way, but that's not necessarily so. Most towns do have a good water source, which is absolutely necessary to the railroad, but if the location is too isolated or difficult to reach, we have to look at a better route. If we have to do a great deal to prepare the land in order to lay tracks," Adrian told them, "it will send the railroad over budget and cause another stall."

"And I suppose until the railroad is actually running trains, they can't make any money," Gwen commented.

Adrian smiled and picked up a piece of crisp bacon. "They do make some money in bond sales and investments, but once the line is actually moving freight and passengers, then you will have regular revenues. One of the smartest things the railroad has done is extend the line from Tacoma to the coal fields in Wilkeson, Washington. They found four good-sized veins in the foothills of the Cascades, and now that coal is being sent south to the Central Pacific in California and earning the Northern Pacific some much-needed revenue."

"Has the route been decided through our area?" Lacy asked.

"No, but we're coming closer to finalizing ideas for some of the trickier passages. You have to remember, there are a lot of mountains to deal with in this area. Building into Bozeman or Butte is going to test the patience of even the most saintly man."

"That's for sure," one of the other men agreed. "When you have to add in blasting through rock and diggin' out tunnels, it starts adding up real fast."

Gwen nodded. "I can well imagine."

"Would you happen to have rooms available for us?" Adrian asked. "We'll be scouting the area for the next couple of days and figured this would be a nice place to call home. We'll be gone through the day and not back until evening, so we would need you to pack a lunch of sorts for us."

Considering the six men at her table, Gwen calculated the work involved and nodded. "I believe we could handle it, Mr. Murphy, although the packed lunches would be simple fare.

At this time of year, with the heat and all, we don't keep a lot of fresh meat."

"That's quite all right. We can hunt whatever else we need—even bring you some of the kill, as well. It would just be nice not to have to live off canned beans and jerked meat."

"We can give you a little better fare than that," Gwen said with a smile. The extra money would definitely help them to lay up supplies for winter. Maybe she could even pay Cubby to come cut wood for them.

"Well, if you'll show us where to stow our extra gear, we'll be on our way." Adrian got up from the table, and his men did likewise. He smiled at Beth. "We'll take care of ourselves for lunch today, so there's no need to concern yourselves."

"I'll show them to the big room upstairs," Beth declared.

Gwen nodded. "That would be good. There should be enough space for everyone there."

The man who had approached Gwen on their previous trip about tearing newsprint from the outhouse wall came to her again. "I see, ma'am, that the damage I caused in the outhouse has not yet been repaired. If you would give me some glue and paper, I'd be happy to rectify that before we head out."

He seemed so concerned and sincere, that Gwen couldn't help but smile. "That's quite all right. I've meant to get to it all along but figured with the weather good, it wasn't much of an issue. Please don't concern yourself about it. I already have plans to see to it."

"If you're sure."

"Come on, Barnaby," Adrian called from the doorway, "let's get a move on."

With Lacy and Beth hard at work and the men on their way to other projects, Gwen thought it the perfect time to see to the outhouse papering.

316

"I'm going out back to see to the men's outhouse," she told her sisters. Gwen took the glue bottle down from the cupboard and headed out the back door. She picked up a stack of newspapers on the way and glanced to the north to see that Hank and Mr. Sherman were still hard at work staking out the dimensions of the store. Major followed Hank from one end of the property to the other. He certainly had taken to Hank.

"Well, it's only fitting, since I have, too," Gwen said with a laugh.

It would definitely be nice to have a mercantile next door. How handy to be able to just go a few feet, instead of having to drive all the way into Bozeman. She supposed that once she and Hank married, they would continue to live at Gallatin House, but she couldn't be sure. After all, they hadn't ever discussed their living arrangements.

Gwen propped the outhouse door open with a rock to allow fresh air and sunshine into the stall. She quickly noted the large spot where the paper had been ripped away. She put the stack of newspapers down and opened the bottle of glue. It would be a quick and simple job, and then she could put that poor Mr. Barnaby's mind at ease.

Lifting the brush to apply the glue, Gwen stopped short. Beneath the torn edges of the newsprint was something white. Although dusty and not clearly visible, it looked to be paper of some sort. She put the brush back into the bottle and reached up to pull back more of the newsprint.

"What in the world is this?"

Part of the newspaper peeled away, while other parts stuck to the paper where it had been glued. Gwen carefully pulled at the edges of the white paper and found that only the corners had been glued to the wall of the outhouse. Her heartbeat quickened as she eased the paper loose and turned it over.

It was a stock certificate bearing the name of Martin Bishop.

She reached up and pulled away more of the newspaper and could clearly see that there were a number of the white pages beneath.

"Oh, Harvey," she whispered.

It was clear to see that Harvey had hidden the certificates away from her, but for the life of her, Gwen couldn't figure out why. Why all the deception? Why had he not felt he could trust her?

Tears trickled down her face. It had all been a lie. The life he'd said he'd lived—the childhood dreams and friends—the parents he'd lost.

"And probably our love," Gwen said, shaking her head. "All lies."

She turned from the wall, stock certificate in hand. There was no sense in trying to repair the mess. No sense in trying to repair anything. She choked back a sob and raised her apron to her face. She couldn't let anyone else see her crying. They wouldn't understand. Her sisters would tell her to rejoice—the lost was found. Hank would be beside himself with joy, because now his mother would have the future she so desired.

But seeing the stocks so carefully hidden away on the out-house wall destroyed a part of Gwen's heart. She couldn't pretend that the stocks had merely been mislaid and forgotten. Harvey had intentionally kept them from her. He'd gone out of his way to lie to her.

"And why should Hank be any different?" she muttered and sniffed back tears.

Bitterness edged her emotions. All men were liars. Pa had lied about what a great future they were going to have. Harvey had lied. Hank was probably lying, as well. She couldn't trust anyone.

"I'm cursed, and this just proves it. Well, so be it," she said angrily.

Her anger stifled her tears and gave her a false sense of strength to face Hank. At least a false sense was better than nothing. She marched across the yard to the north, tightly gripping the stock with one hand and wiping away the last evidence of tears with the other.

Hank was standing there talking to Mr. Sherman when she approached. He had rid himself of his coat, vest, and tie and had even rolled up his sleeves.

"Come to inspect our work?"

"Not exactly." She held out the paper. "You need to see this. I think you'll find it's what you've been looking for."

Hank took the piece and inspected it. His eyes widened, and he looked up at her with such an expression of joy that Gwen nearly burst into tears anew.

"Where did you find this?" He grabbed her and whirled her in a circle. "This is so wonderful. Truly answered prayer!" He put her down. "Show me where you found it."

"Apparently Harvey hid them in the outhouse."

Mr. Sherman looked at her oddly, as did Hank. Hank glanced at the stock once more, then shook his head. "I don't understand."

"Come with me, and I'll show you."

She led the way, not even waiting for Hank to acknowledge her. *I have to stay strong,* she told herself over and over. *I have to be brave.* Opening the door to the outhouse, Gwen pointed and looked back at Hank and Mr. Sherman.

"He papered the walls with them and then covered them

over with newsprint." She gritted her teeth. *It shouldn't matter that this is one more thing he omitted to tell me about.*

Hank entered the outhouse and studied the situation. He pulled at the strips of newspaper to reveal even more of the stocks than Gwen had exposed.

"Well, I'll be." He turned to Gwen. "This is amazing. It's the last place any of us would have thought to look."

It's also the last straw. The last hope I had—that maybe, just maybe, Harvey had somehow forgotten who he was and who his family was.

"I guess I have my work cut out for me. Leave it to Harvey to do something like this."

Yes, leave it to Harvey to betray us all.

Hank pulled another certificate from the wall and marveled at the thing as if it were a treasure map. "This is so wonderful. Everything will be better now."

Everything but my life.

Gwen's anger continued to mount. She held her tongue and stared on with clenched fists as Hank worked loose one certificate after another. If she remained here much longer, she would surely explode.

"I'm leaving now." She turned to go, but Hank reached out to stop her.

"Wait, is it just in here or does the ladies' outhouse have the same thing?"

Gwen shrugged. "I have no idea. I didn't get any further than this. I came to repair the paper and saw that there was another layer of something underneath. I knew we hadn't planned it that way, but Harvey was the one who built and papered the outhouses." She looked past him as her eyes began to fill with tears. "It would seem his ability for hiding the truth knew no end."

She pushed back Mr. Sherman and stomped off toward the house. The last thing she wanted to do was get into a discussion about Harvey and his deception. Gwen stumbled up the back porch steps and made her way blindly into the kitchen.

"Watch out!" Lacy said as Gwen flew through the back door. "I nearly got this bacon grease all over you."

"Sorry," Gwen muttered, but she didn't stop.

"What's wrong?" Beth asked. She stepped in front of Gwen to block her passage. "Something's happened."

Gwen looked up at her sister. "Yes. I found the certificates."

"You did? But that's wonderful." Beth looked at Gwen for a moment as Lacy came up to join them. "It is wonderful, isn't it?"

Gwen began to cry in earnest. She had honestly thought she was all cried out years ago, but now the flow didn't seem to want to stop. "I'm glad . . . we found them," she said. "For Hank's sake, and his mother's."

"Then why are you crying?" Lacy asked. She seemed completely shocked to see Gwen fall apart, but Gwen couldn't do anything about it. *Let them be shocked,* she thought. *Let them see that I'm only human.*

"Because it only serves to prove Harvey's deception. He intentionally kept their existence from me. All the time he was making up stories about his life—all the things he said to me—it was a wall between us. I loved him so much, but everything he told me was a lie. It's all been nothing more than lies."

She pushed past Beth and raced through the dining room and up the stairs.

Beth thought to go after her sister, but when she looked up and saw Hank standing in the back doorway, she decided against it. She wasn't sure how much he'd overheard, but apparently he'd been there for at least the last of it.

"I should go talk to her," he said, coming forward.

Lacy and Beth turned to face him. Beth put out her hand. "No. Let her have some time alone. She's really hurt over this."

"But she knew the past wasn't what Harvey had told her," Hank said, shaking his head. "I was proof of that."

"Maybe so, but the certificates left no doubt. Gwen could have pretended that Harvey spent the certificates before we met him or lost them on his journeys, but the fact that he purposefully hid the certificates . . . well, that pretty much says it was all intentional."

"It's hard for her to face that someone she loved could lie to her so completely," Lacy added.

Hank drew a deep breath and nodded slowly. "I suppose I can understand that."

"Which brings us around to you," Beth said, crossing her arms against her chest. "Exactly what are your intentions, now that you've found the stocks?"

He looked at her oddly for a moment. "The same as they've always been. I'll recover the stocks and take them back to my mother. I had planned to go at the end of the week, due to helping Bruce set the design of the store, but now I think I must go as soon as possible."

"And what of our sister?" Lacy questioned. "What are your intentions where she's concerned?"

Hank raised a brow and smiled. "They're the same as they've been now for some time."

"Which are what?" Beth asked.

He chuckled. "Well, to marry her. I've talked it over with

Major Worthington and Calvin J. Whiskers, and I've even asked your sister for her hand."

Lacy looked very doubtful. "And she said yes?"

Hank looked from Lacy to Beth and nodded. "She did."

Beth narrowed her eyes and squared her shoulders. She hoped she might look intimidating but doubted her ability to do so. "And does finding the stocks change things?"

"Of course not," Hank replied. "It makes things much better for me, in many ways. I can leave my mother to her adventures with a clear conscience and the knowledge that she has more than enough money to care for her needs. It also frees me, once I deliver the stocks to her, to return sooner. I was going to have to stick around Boston and see to the sale of my various businesses, but now that won't be necessary. I can have my accountant handle it all for me."

Beth considered his comment for a moment, then asked, "Does Gwen know this?"

"I didn't tell her that in so many words," Hank said. "I didn't get much of a chance to say anything. She commented about Harvey being good at hiding the truth, then stormed off. I followed after her and heard what she said to you and Lacy. That's why I want to talk to her."

Beth could see the sincerity in his eyes and hear the concern in his voice. She'd always found Hank Bishop a bit of a mystery, but one thing she could clearly recognize and understand was that this man loved her sister.

CHAPTER TWENTY-SEVEN

"Gwen, we need to talk." Hank stood facing the closed door and continued to call out. "Open the door, please."

"Go away, Hank. I've nothing to say."

"Well, I do. Now open the door."

"Just go."

"If you don't open the door and let me in, I'll kick it down," Hank warned. He waited a moment, then heard her footsteps on the floor.

Gwen opened the door only enough to reveal her tear-streaked face. "You can't be here, it isn't appropriate."

Hank pushed back the door as gently as he could without allowing her to oppose him. "There are a lot of inappropriate things in the world, but this isn't one of them. I know you're hurt by what Harvey did, but keeping me away isn't going to help the matter at all."

Gwen shook her head and moved across the room to her rocking chair. She took a seat and pulled her shawl close. "I don't want to hear any more lies."

Hank stood watching her for a moment. She looked as if she were trying to protect herself from the world—from whatever blow that might come. She looked helpless and terrified, and he hated that he had any part in the matter.

"I've never lied to you, Gwen. That was Harvey."

"You're brothers."

"Yes, and two entirely different men. How do you get off thinking it's fair to blame me for the actions of someone else?"

She barely raised her face. "I don't want to talk about it. Say what you feel you must and then go."

Hank shook his head. How could he get through to her? What should he say to make her understand? "Look, I can't say that I fully understand what you're going through, because I don't. The truth of the matter is, Harvey lied to me, too. He also betrayed me and our family by denying our existence. It hurts—no doubt about it. Still, I thought you'd accepted that Harvey lied and that, for whatever his reason, he thought it was the best thing to do. Maybe he thought he was protecting you."

"Ha! He was protecting himself, most likely. He didn't care about me, or he never would have lied in the first place."

"I agree that he shouldn't have lied, but I can't imagine that he didn't really care about you. He'd been through a lot and probably wasn't thinking clearly." Hank gritted his teeth. Making excuses for Harvey wasn't the reason he'd come here.

"No matter what he thought or felt, that's no reason for you to go on so."

He bit his tongue on that one. He hadn't meant to make it seem like it was her fault. Hank paced for a moment. "That didn't come out right. I just meant to say that Harvey's lies had nothing to do with you—with us."

"They have everything to do with us. You wouldn't even be here if not for Harvey and his lies. You came here to find the hussy who'd married and killed your brother. Well, here I am. You came here to find the stock certificates that my esteemed husband stole. You've found them. Your mission is complete, so now you can go back to Boston and the life you knew there. Just don't lie to me and tell me Harvey's lies had nothing to do with you or us."

Her voice was raw with emotion, and Hank knew that while his first thought was to counter with denial, Gwen would never receive it. He stopped and stared at her until Gwen lifted her gaze once again.

"All right. I won't tell you that Harvey's lies had nothing to do with us. Harvey obviously put them between you and him, and you're putting them between you and me."

"That's not true. I'm not responsible for what happened. I knew nothing about his past. I'm just as surprised as you to find my outhouse papered in hundreds of dollars of stock certificates."

"But don't you see?" he said, coming closer. "We have both been duped by Harvey. We've both been hurt by the decisions and choices he made. Let us use it to unite our cause rather than destroy us."

"There is no us," she countered. "Everything has been built on falsehoods. I can't trust that this is the end of it just because the stocks were found. For all I know, Harvey may have married someone else and have a family elsewhere. He might have been running from them, as well."

"But that has nothing to do with you and me. I love you, Gwen."

She raised her head fully. "Don't. I want to set you free from our engagement." She sighed, and it was as if some of the life left her with that single breath. "I can't explain why this hurts me so much. I know it seems silly to you, but I can't help it. I have to sort through all of this and figure out what I need to do next. All I know for certain is that you shouldn't feel obligated to me."

"I don't feel obligated. I love you. I don't want to be released from our engagement."

"But you need to go to Boston. Once you're there, you will probably find that your old lifestyle is more appealing than the idea of living in Montana."

"If you really think that of me, then you don't know me at all." He was getting frustrated. How dare she suggest he could so easily cast aside their love for the comfort of the familiar?

"That's my point. I don't really know you. You don't know me. If you did, you would know that I only cause pain and suffering to those I love. You would know that I'm destined to be alone."

"This is about that curse again, isn't it?" He looked at her, and though she didn't answer, he could see the affirmation in her eyes.

"The real curse is that you're blind to the truth," he said, heading for the door. He knew if he didn't leave he would say something in anger that he might regret. "You'd do well to read that Bible of yours—if you want to know what the answer is."

Gwen heard the survey team return for the evening and realized she'd wasted the entire day in her room. Beth had tried to talk to her about eating lunch, but Gwen had begged her to just go away for a few hours. She knew she'd hurt Beth's feelings, but she couldn't even begin to talk to her or anyone else.

Now, given the shadows in her room, Gwen knew that it must be quite late. The summer sun in Montana was up sometimes until nine-thirty or ten. Seeing the fading light made her realize she'd lost all track of time, doing nothing but rocking and contemplating her life.

Why did it have to be like this? Why was she so naïve about people and the things they said and promised?

I am a poor judge of people, she told herself. *I believe most anything, only to be disappointed when reality hits.*

Still, the things Hank had said made sense, she reasoned. But so had the things Harvey told her.

She knew she had lost the ability to trust. There was no way she would set herself up for that kind of hurt again. Trusting in men had proven her downfall. Didn't it make sense to protect herself from the possibility of it happening again?

Her thinking might be unfair to Hank, but Gwen sincerely felt he'd be better off without her. At least now, before the store actually began to be built, Hank could cancel his plans and return to Boston, unfettered by ties, either emotional or financial.

It really will be better this way.

A knock at her door caused Gwen to stiffen. Had Hank come back to try again? "Who is it?"

"It's Patience Shepard. May I come in?"

Gwen realized she'd not bothered to lock the door again after Hank left. "Go ahead," she called and straightened in the chair.

Patience smiled sympathetically. "Your sisters told me you weren't feeling quite yourself."

"That's putting it mildly, I suppose."

Taking a seat on the bed, Patience reached out to take hold of Gwen's hand. "Why don't you tell me about it."

With defeat settling over her like a wet blanket, Gwen didn't know where to begin. "I can't believe Harvey lied to me all those years. I can't believe he continued to lie to me right up until his death. I feel like my entire life has been based on lies, and the worst of it is, I lied right along with everyone else."

"How did you lie?" Patience asked.

"I lied to my mother when I promised not to go to the fortune-teller," Gwen said, staring at her lap. "I lied about what I had done at the fair when she asked me after we'd returned home. I've lied to my sisters when I told them everything would be all right—that Pa's only problem was the fact that Mama had died and he was sad and lonely."

"But he *was* sad and lonely. There's no doubting that. You couldn't possibly lose a mate and not be."

"I know, but Pa was always chasing one dream or another. He dragged us around when Mama was alive, and he kept dragging us around after she died. He was restless and could never find anything that satisfied him. If he'd lived, we would have found ourselves selling out to Rafe and moving within a matter of a year or two."

"Why do you say that?"

Gwen looked at her friend. "Because he talked about it. I never told anyone else, and you mustn't say anything to the girls."

"But why?" Patience squeezed Gwen's hand. "Why would he have ever wanted to sell to Rafe? This stage stop has been a tremendous success."

"But Pa was never satisfied with anything for long. Besides that, he told me that we girls would soon be married and gone, and he couldn't run the place by himself. I assured him that I wouldn't go and that, together, we two could keep Gallatin House going, but he said it would never be fair to me."

"He probably felt he'd forced it upon you."

"That's what I tried to convince myself of, but I know it was a lie. Just one among many." Gwen pulled her hand away from Patience and got to her feet. "Like I said, my life has a foundation of lies, and while I understand that Pa couldn't help his wanderlust, it doesn't make it any easier to deal with."

"But why should it matter now that he's dead?"

Gwen looked at her in disbelief. "Just because they're dead doesn't mean their lies don't live on. Harvey told me he loved me. He told me how important my love was to him, because he'd never had anyone's love. That was a lie. His brother and mother loved him, even if his stepfather didn't—and who's to say that he didn't? And if he could lie about his family like that, why wouldn't he also lie about his feelings for me? I feel like such a fool."

"And that's what really bothers you about all of this, isn't it?"

Gwen shook her head and began to pace. "I don't know. I don't know what bothers me most about this."

"How does Hank figure in?"

"He asked me to marry him," Gwen admitted. Patience smiled, but Gwen held up her hand. "Before you comment on that, you should know I just broke the engagement. I can't marry him if I can't fully trust him."

"But why?" The older woman was clearly puzzled by this declaration. "Hank has done nothing wrong."

Gwen went to the window and stared out at the darkness. "We found the stock certificates that Hank had come looking for. I found them in the outhouse. Apparently Harvey had taken them and hid them there, under the newsprint." She turned back and leaned against the sill. "That's when all of this really sank in. Harvey had those certificates, and he knew he had to keep them from me. Otherwise, I'd know that everything else was a lie.

"Hank came here for the sole purpose of recovering those certificates and the jewelry Harvey had taken. Hank lost sight of it by allowing his emotions to get in the way by feeling sorry for me, and for a time, I think the stocks no longer mattered."

"You think Hank fell in love with you because he felt sorry for you?"

"Well, maybe not completely, but now that he has his stocks back, he needs to deliver them to his mother. He also has to tell her of Harvey's death. That won't be easy for a mother to hear."

"No, I don't suppose so," Patience admitted.

"Especially if he tells her about all the lies." Gwen buried her face in her hands for a moment. After several moments she looked up. Tears blurred her vision. "I love Hank, but I loved Harvey, too. I guess I just wasn't a good judge of character or of love. What I thought I had wasn't real."

"Gwen, I believe Harvey really did love you."

"If he loved me, then why couldn't he just trust me?"

"Why can't you trust Hank, if you really love him?"

Gwen wiped at her eyes with the edge of her apron. "Because I don't want to get hurt again. I can't bear the thought of being such a big fool. What will everyone think of me when the truth is told?"

Patience got to her feet and came to Gwen. She put her hands on Gwen's shoulders and took on a stern expression. "Your heart is bitter because you feel that you look foolish. You feel vulnerable and silly for having learned that your fairy tales were not true. Harvey was human—fallible and capable of making the wrong decisions. But, Gwen, so are you. So am I. That's the fallen way of man. You must decide for yourself— but in my eyes, you will only be foolish if you allow pride to make your choices for you."

She abruptly turned away, leaving Gwen to stand there, rather stunned by the declaration. Patience exited the room without another word, and Gwen found her own voice would not come. The lump in her throat made speaking impossible. Was this really all about her pride? Was she about to lose her chance at happiness and love because she was too afraid to look silly?

CHAPTER TWENTY-EIGHT

Lacy saw Hank working with his black gelding and knew that he was packing to leave. Knowing that Hank had proposed marriage to her sister, Lacy wondered now if he'd called it all off on account of the stocks and Gwen's strange mood. Would he head back to Boston and stay there?

"I see you've decided to leave us," Lacy said, leaning back against the fence rail.

Hank looked up and nodded. "I need to return my mother's property to her and let her know about Harvey."

"And will you come back, or have you given up on that idea?"

He looked hard at Lacy for a moment, then turned his attention back to his saddlebags. "I plan to come back."

"I see."

He chuckled. "Don't sound so disappointed."

"I'm not," Lacy countered, pushing off the fence to come closer. "I might not have liked you much in the beginning, but I've come to respect you. And you love my sister and plan to marry her."

"I did plan to marry her."

"You've changed your mind?" Lacy rubbed the black's face and waited for an answer.

"I didn't, but she did." Hank finished with the bag and turned back to face Lacy. "She told me she doesn't want to marry me—that I'd be better off without her."

"And would you?"

Hank's expression softened. "No. I can't even imagine life without her."

"Then don't give up on her that easily."

"I hadn't planned to give up on her at all, Lacy. I'm just sort of nursing my wounds and trying to rethink my plans. Maybe going away will give her time to regret what she's done and change her mind. Then again, maybe it won't."

Lacy could see he was troubled by the very thought of leaving. "Gwen's had a hard life. She's the oldest and always felt responsible for Beth and me. She even stopped going to school in order to take care of us. She loved school, and I knew it was a real sad thing for her, but I was so young, I couldn't do anything about it." Hank seemed puzzled, so Lacy waited for him to pose the question on his mind.

"Why did your father allow her to quit school? Surely he knew how hard it would be on her. Didn't he care?"

Lacy shrugged and moved away from the horse. Hank followed her and they walked for a ways down the road. She wondered how she could possibly explain her father to Hank.

"Our pa was what our grandparents called a restless spirit.

My grandmother once told me that from the time he was born, Pa was a wanderer. She lost him on so many occasions that it became the running joke in town. People were always looking for him.

"Grandmother said that was just the way it was with some folks. She never figured he'd marry and settle down, so when he did, they thought maybe God had answered their prayers and taken away Pa's desire to always be moving from place to place."

"But He hadn't?"

"No. They moved all the time before I was born and even after I joined the family. I was three when they settled in Texas for a time. Pa tried his hand at several jobs, and around the time I was nearly five he landed a job at a ranch, wrangling horses. That's how I learned to ride so well. Sometimes he'd take me with him when he was breaking a new horse. The rancher took a liking to me and taught me to ride while Pa worked."

"Then your mother died. I suppose it was too hard to remain there after that happened."

"Yes, I suppose," Lacy replied. "But if my memories of that time—what few there are—serve me well, I believe we were already making plans to move. I only remember bits and pieces. Arguments I overheard. Gwen would be able to tell you for certain. Anyway, after Mama died, we went from place to place, leaving dead relatives in our wake." She laughed at Hank's surprised expression. "Don't worry—they died of illness or natural causes. We didn't kill anyone."

He laughed and paused to take in the glorious view of the mountains to the east. "I didn't figure you had. It was just a funny way of putting things."

"I'm that way. I always manage to shock folks. Truth is, I think I could be a lot like Pa. I didn't mind moving around.

Beth hated it. She used to cry and cry. All she ever wanted was for us to stay put."

"What about Gwen?"

"I can't really say. Being the oldest, I think Gwen felt she had to grow up and distance herself from Beth and me. Don't get me wrong—we're all very close. Gwen wanted to fill the void left by our mother, but she couldn't. I remember telling her I just wanted her to be my sister, not my mother."

"But she didn't understand?" Hank turned from the mountains and looked at Lacy.

"I don't think she did. I felt bad and stopped saying anything about it, because I thought she figured I was saying that nothing she did was good enough. It was never that. I always knew the sacrifice Gwen made. Like I said, our pa was never good at much of anything. From the time we were young, we girls knew we had to pull our weight and earn what we could to make things run smoothly. Gwen was always sewing for someone or doing their laundry. She wasn't educated, but she was industrious."

Hank pulled out his pocket watch. "I should be going. I have directions and instructions from Nick and Simon, and if I want to get to my first stop, I will need to get on the road."

Lacy nodded. "I'll miss having you around, Hank. I hope you'll be back."

"You can count on it. I'm not finished with your sister, and you can tell her I said so." He grinned, and Lacy couldn't help but laugh.

"I have a feeling you've both met your match. This should be one interesting marriage."

Gwen was hard at work cleaning the house with Beth when Lacy returned. Gwen asked them to sit a moment so she could apologize.

"I need to tell you that I'm sorry. The way I acted was completely uncalled for. I've been foolish and prideful, and I never should have taken it out on you two."

"We're just sorry . . . that . . . well . . . things were so hard on you," Beth replied, a slight hesitation in her voice. "I know you're upset about so many things, but I also don't know what I can do to help."

"You can't do anything. Patience was good to show me last night that I was being a spoiled child in many ways and simply prideful in others. I wanted to hide away from the world so I wouldn't have to deal with anything, but that was completely unfair to you two."

"It's not like we aren't grown women who can handle things for ourselves. You've put yourself in the role of being our caretaker for too long, and I think it should stop," Lacy declared.

"I do, too," Beth agreed. "You need to have time for yourself. In fact, Lacy and I have decided to take on more responsibility around here so you can have some time to enjoy yourself."

Gwen was touched at their concern for her. "I don't know what I'd do without either one of you. I hope when I apologize to Hank, it goes even half this well."

"If you're going to apologize to Hank," Lacy said in an urgent tone, "you'd best get over to the stables right away. He's leaving."

"What?" Gwen looked at her sister and then rushed to the window. "He's leaving now?"

"Yes. He and I were just talking, and he said he needed to

leave right away in order to keep to some schedule Nick and Simon suggested."

Gwen rushed for the door. "He can't leave without me telling him I'm sorry. I've been so foolish, and now I may have lost the man I truly care about."

She hurried down the porch steps and hiked her skirts. She ran as fast as she could to reach the Lassiters' place. A prayer was on her lips that Hank might still be there—that he might forgive her and listen to what she had to say.

"Where's Hank?" she asked Nick.

"He's gone, Gwen. He rode out just a few minutes ago."

"Saddle my horse, please, Nick. I have to catch up with him. Which way did he go?"

Nick let her know Hank's planned route before hurrying to do her bidding. As he brought her saddled mount, he shook his head. "How are you going to ride? You aren't wearing a split skirt."

"There's no time to change," Gwen told him. "I'll just have to be a bit inappropriate." She pulled her skirt over her knee in order to fit her foot in the stirrup. It was probably the most unladylike pose she'd ever struck, but she couldn't stop now to worry about it. Goodness, but she was glad she'd chosen to wear a short corset today.

Nick looked politely to one side as Gwen revealed the laced edges of her bloomers and petticoat. She hoisted herself quickly into the saddle, then hurried to arrange her skirts.

"I'm decent now," she said. Nick looked up to reveal his reddened face. He held the leather reins up to her and quickly looked away to avoid eye contact.

Gwen took the reins from him and kicked the horse into action. Poor Nick had probably been completely scandalized by her lack of decency in mounting, but she knew she could always apologize later. Right now the only thing that mattered was finding Hank and letting him know she still cared—that she'd been wrong.

The horse easily handled the dry road at a full gallop. Gwen began to worry when she didn't immediately spot Hank on one of the first straightaways. Perhaps he'd pushed his horse to make up for lost time. Maybe she'd end up riding all the way to Ennis before she'd find him. Her mind whirled with thoughts.

I have to let him know how stupid I've been. I have to tell him that I don't want him to release me from our engagement.

She rounded a bend in the road and saw dust whip up ahead on the trail. Not far beyond this she could see a black horse and his rider. They were moving fast. Urging her gelding to pick up speed, Gwen bent low against the horse's neck and gave no thought to the way the wind whipped at her gown.

Apparently, the sound of her horse approaching at such a high rate of speed caused Hank to stop and turn as if to make way for more urgent traffic. Gwen pulled up just short of sending her horse into the side of the black. During the ride, the wind had wreaked havoc with her hair, and the pins had pulled out. When she straightened in the saddle, waves of golden curls fell over her shoulders and down her back.

Hank shook his head and grinned. "And I used to think you were the more demure of the Gallatin sisters. Clearly, I was misled."

Gwen smiled and relaxed her grip on the reins. "I came to apologize."

"Funny way of doing it."

She could hear the amusement in his voice and knew he'd already forgiven her. It made the situation a little easier. "I'm sorry, Hank. I've been a fool. I was so worried about looking silly and being thought naïve that I took it out on you."

He sobered. "I hated having you push me out of your life like that."

"I know. I was wrong. I'm so afraid, and it got the best of me."

His eyes narrowed. "Afraid? What are you afraid of?"

Drawing a deep breath, Gwen found the strength to be completely honest. "I'm afraid of caring too much about you, only to find that you don't care about me. I'm afraid that I'm so vulnerable and dim-witted that I can't possibly know when people are being honest with me or playing me for a fool. I don't like feeling like that, Hank. I don't like knowing that the man I thought loved me—who married me and shared the stories of his life with me—had been lying all those years. Do you know how that feels?"

"I think I do. Even though he never told me the same lies, in a way I was just as much a victim of his stories as you were. But, Gwen, I don't think Harvey lied about loving you."

"Why? Why would he have stopped there?" She shifted in the saddle, and the horse nickered softly.

"Because if he felt even a fraction of what I feel for you, then he couldn't have lied about that. Gwen, I've waited all of my life to find a woman like you. My mother despaired of me ever marrying, but the women I knew were simply not suited to me. Now I know why. I belong here—I belong with you. I can't lose that. Not after a lifetime of trying to find it."

Gwen nodded. "I feel the same way. I can't lose you."

Hank stepped down from the horse and came around to hold Gwen's mount as she slid down. He embraced her and held her as if he would never let her go. The strength of his arms around her left Gwen no doubt that this was where she belonged. She buried her face against his neck and sighed. For several minutes they simply stood there holding each other.

Finally Hank loosened his grip, and Gwen looked up to find her face only inches from his.

"I love you, and I will come back to you."

She nodded. "I know you will. Take the time you need. Your mother will need you to strengthen her once she learns about Harvey."

"I've a feeling my mother already suspects the worst, but you are kind to care about her needs. If she can't bear to be without me, I'll simply bring her along."

"Gallatin House will always have a place for her," Gwen replied.

"I hope there will be a place for me, as well," he said softly.

Gwen took hold of his face and touched her lips to his. It was the first time she'd initiated a kiss, but it felt right. "There will always be a place for you," she whispered against his mouth.

⟨∞⟩

That night as Gwen sat alone in her room, she warmed at the thought of Hank's parting kiss. She touched her lips and smiled. A lifetime in the arms of such a man would never be boring or without its pleasures.

She climbed into bed and pulled the lamp closer on the nightstand. Taking up her Bible, she turned to a passage Patience had once shared with her from Romans eight.

" 'There is therefore now no condemnation to them which are in Christ Jesus, who walk not after the flesh, but after the Spirit,' " she read aloud.

Patience had told her that curses and condemnation ended when Gwen gave her heart to Christ. *"God has set you on a new path,"* she had told Gwen the morning after the fire. *"If you choose to go back to the old path, how is that His doing? Instead of blaming God for somehow letting you down or allowing you to be cursed, why not just get back on the right path?"*

She was right, and Gwen could finally see it for herself. There was truth in the Word of God. Truth that would never let her down and never leave her to wonder if she was being deceived.

Rafe stepped out the back door of his saloon and stared at the darkened structure of the Gallatin House. It was nearly two in the morning, and he knew the Gallatins were safely tucked in their beds. He knew, too, that Hank Bishop had gone. Cubby had told him that much. Apparently, Bishop had found some valuable papers his brother had brought to Montana and was now heading back East.

Cubby didn't know if Bishop planned to return but said that Nick and Simon felt sure he would. They offered two strong reasons to suspect this. One was the store Bishop was building. The second was Gwen Gallatin.

Rowdy laughter came from behind him as someone bellowed out that Lady Luck was his tonight. This was quickly followed by several lewd comments and more laughter. Rafe narrowed his eyes and continued to stare at the Gallatin property. He'd never wanted anything so much in his life as he did that operation. He already had additional girls heading to Montana from a cathouse in Seattle. There was great potential for what he could do, if only he had that house and land.

"Something wrong, boss?" Wyman called from behind.

Rafe turned and nodded. "I don't own the Gallatin House yet—that's what's wrong."

Wyman laughed. "It's just a matter of time, and you will. Those ladies aren't going to want to stay around once they see how difficult life can be without a man. We'll have them so defeated and worn down, they'll be asking you for a job."

Rafe chuckled. "Now, that would be something—the Gallatin girls working for me. I can't say I'd mind that one little bit."

"Didn't think you would," Wyman replied.

"Still, we need a plan."

"I've been thinking on that, boss. I'm thinkin' that with those extra girls you have coming, and the fact that we have additional ranches setting up in the surrounding area, things could get mighty destructive around here. Who's to say what might happen?"

"I don't much care what happens to those girls, but I want that house in one piece. There's no sense in going to all the trouble to get the place if there isn't a place to be had."

Wyman nodded. "Oh, there will be a place, all right. Maybe two places, if that store goes up right away. Mark my word, we'll make life so miserable around here that those ladies will pack their bags and head out on one of the stages they've catered to."

Rafe yawned and pushed past Wyman to head back into the saloon. "You'd better be right. We can't afford to let this place grow any more respectable."

CHAPTER TWENTY-NINE

Gwen looked out the front door of Gallatin House and sighed. Major Worthington gave her a forlorn look, then followed her gaze down the road. They were both wondering when Hank would return.

"He's been gone two months," she told the dog. "I thought he'd be back by now."

The harvest was rapidly coming together in the valley. Lacy's twentieth birthday had come and gone earlier in the month, and Calvin had become father to a litter of Lassiter kittens. So much had already taken place without having Hank near to share it.

Of course, he had sent a letter to let her know he'd made it back to Boston and would soon head to Rhode Island to see his mother. The letter, which came exactly one month to the day

347

of Hank's departure, had been brief. He wrote of how much he missed and loved her, then offered reassurances that he'd return to Montana as soon as his business was concluded. But since then, there'd been nothing more. Gwen knew the mail ran slow and knew, too, that Hank might have been too busy to write. Still, she couldn't help but worry.

She stepped outside, and Major got to his feet. He followed her from the porch to the north side of the house. There, Gwen gazed upon the simple log structure that was to be Hank's mercantile. It had been finished and waiting for him for over two weeks. Brewster Sherman had come several times with wagons full of merchandise. He, too, was anxious for Hank's return so the store could become operational.

He wasn't the only one. Most of the community was enthralled with the idea of a store opening. It seemed someone stopped in at Gallatin House almost every day to ask when the mercantile would be open for business.

"I wish I knew," Gwen murmured.

She looked down at Major and smiled. "Come on, boy. Wishing won't make him get here any sooner." They made their way back to the house, where Major resumed his vigilant position on the porch, while Gwen made her way inside.

"Did you know we've managed to save nearly twenty dollars?" Beth asked as Gwen joined her sisters in the kitchen. She placed a handful of coins in a metal box. "Those surveyors really added to our business."

"If we keep going at this rate," Lacy said, "we'll have the loan on Gallatin House paid."

Gwen nodded and went to the cupboard to take down a bowl. "It would be nice to have all that debt gone."

Beth closed the lid of the small strongbox. "The survey team said they'd be back before winter set in, so that might see us profiting another few dollars, depending on how long they stay with us."

"Could be," Gwen agreed. She went to a stack of potatoes she'd brought up earlier from the cellar. "Of course, there are a few things we need before winter sets in. We should pay someone to cut a supply of wood. And it might not hurt to have some new blankets. The old ones are getting pretty threadbare."

"Hank can cut wood for us when he gets back," Lacy said.

"He'll be busy running the store," Beth countered.

Gwen smiled. "You are both so sweet to have such faith that he'll return. I know you're doing that to encourage me."

Beth put the strongbox in the cupboard and turned. "I only say it because I believe it. If I didn't, I wouldn't lie to you. This family has endured enough of that."

Gwen nodded. "I agree, but I'm thankful, nevertheless. You are the best sisters a girl could have." She picked up a paring knife and began to peel the potatoes. "Lacy, will you be able to ride over to—"

"I'm sorry to just walk in," a weak voice called.

Gwen looked up and found Ellie standing in the doorway. She held a blood-soaked cloth to her throat. "What happened? Beth, get her a chair. Lacy, get me some hot water and towels." Gwen hurried to the woman's side. "Why are you bleeding?"

Ellie turned her pale face upward and grimaced with pain. "I got cut. That's really all I dare say. Rafe won't send for the doctor. He said it would take too long and cost too much. He suggested I come here and see if you couldn't patch me up."

"Here, sit," Beth said as she positioned a wooden chair behind Ellie.

Unladylike words regarding Rafe were on the tip of her tongue, but Gwen held them back. She took hold of the cloth, and Ellie's hand fell away as if she were too weak to continue holding it in place. She sank onto the chair, and Beth steadied her shoulders when Ellie started to lean to one side.

Pulling the cloth back gently, Gwen could see that the cut on her neck, while not all that long, was deep. "It will have to be stitched." She met Beth's worried expression. "Get the laudanum."

"Oh no," Ellie said. "Rafe would never allow for me to be drugged. I'd be no use to him."

"I can't sew you up without giving you something for the pain," Gwen countered.

Ellie bit her lower lip, then drew a ragged breath. "I can bear it. Just do it quickly."

Gwen thought the woman looked so defeated—so haggard. Her blond hair was stringy and dirty and her face, pale from the trauma, was gaunt. A rage built inside Gwen that threatened to spill over at any moment. She forced it down and prayed for peace and calm in order to handle the task at hand.

Lacy returned with a stack of towels and a bucket of hot spring water. "I brought this, too," she said after setting the other items down. She pulled a small bottle of whiskey from her apron pocket. It was the alcohol they kept for medicinal purposes.

"Good thinking," Gwen said. She took the bottle and motioned to one of the dining room tables. "Beth, get a cloth to cover the table. We'll let Ellie lie down while we work on her wound. Lacy, run get my sewing basket."

The girls quickly accomplished their tasks while Gwen began to clean the cut. "Who did this?"

Ellie closed her eyes. "It doesn't matter."

"It does to me. I intend to see the man punished."

"The table's ready," Beth called.

"Come help me with Ellie." Gwen put a makeshift bandage over the wound. "Can you hold it just for a few seconds, Ellie?"

"I think so."

"Once we get you to the table, you can rest." Gwen helped Ellie place her hand in the right position before getting the girl to her feet. She quickly realized that Ellie was so light, she hardly needed Beth's help—the girl had wasted away to nothing in the last few months. It pained her to see how poorly Rafe cared for them.

Ellie closed her eyes the second they helped her to lie down. It was clear she had fainted, and Gwen thought it a gift from God.

"Let's work fast; maybe she won't regain consciousness before we finish." Gwen opened the bottle of whiskey. "Lacy, after I pour some of this on the wound, you thread a needle with the stout quilting thread, then soak all of it in some of this whiskey."

Her younger sister nodded. Gwen cleaned the wound and was grateful to see that the bleeding was slowing considerably. Beth held Ellie's head in place, just in case she woke up during the stitching, while Lacy took the whiskey and poured some over the needle and thread.

As soon as she was satisfied that she'd done all she could to cleanse the cut, Gwen went to work stitching. Ellie didn't so much as move, which almost caused Gwen more alarm than satisfaction. She feared the poor girl had probably gone into shock, yet there was little Gwen could do to help her.

Lacy stood ready with the scissors, clipping the thread after Gwen tied off each stitch. As Gwen finished with the seventh and final stitch, she looked to Beth. "Tear two strips of cloth.

We'll make a bandage with one and secure it by wrapping the other piece around her neck."

Ellie rallied just as they finished. She looked up, rather confused, then recognition flooded her face. "Are you done?"

"Yes," Gwen said, smiling. "Are you sure you won't have some laudanum? I could talk to Rafe and tell him that it was necessary—that it was my doing."

Struggling to sit up, Ellie shook her head. For a moment, it seemed she might faint again, but she fought against it. "I have to get back to work." She put her hand to her head. "I'm a bit dizzy."

"Lacy, get her a glass of buttermilk. That should give her strength."

Ellie smiled ever so slightly. "My mama used to give me buttermilk. I haven't had it in ever so long."

Gwen pushed back Ellie's hair and smiled. "You are welcome to come have a glass with us anytime you like. In fact, I'm really worried about you. You've lost a lot of weight, and you don't look well. I think I speak for my sisters when I say we'd like you to come stay with us. At least until you're well again."

"I can't," Ellie said, resignation in her voice. "Rafe owns my contract. He says I've cost him way too much money to let me go."

"No one owns anyone," Beth declared. "The War Between the States settled that. Slavery is against the law."

Bringing the glass, Lacy steadied it while Ellie downed the contents. "I feel better," she assured Gwen. She got to her feet and swayed a bit. "Really, I'm all right."

"Ellie! Where are you?" Rafe bellowed from the front room. He blasted out a string of obscenities, then looked around the corner into the dining room. "I told you to get fixed up, not move in."

"She's sick, Rafe. Can't you see how thin she is?" Gwen stepped toward the saloon owner. "Not only that, but she's in shock from the loss of blood. How in the world can you treat these women so poorly?"

"It ain't your business."

"I'm making it my business," Gwen said, moving so close she was nearly nose to nose with the man. "I hope you at least had the decency to take care of the lowlife scum who cut her."

Rafe threw back his head and laughed. Gwen stepped away a pace in surprise. "I'm the lowlife scum," he announced. "She got lippy with me, and I showed her the price for bein' mouthy."

"You? You cut her?" Gwen asked in disbelief. "You're an animal, Rafe Reynolds. I knew you could be mean, but I had no idea you were this cruel."

"Lady, you have no idea what I'm capable of."

By now, Ellie had come to stand beside Gwen. "They patched me up, Rafe. I'm all done now."

"She's weak and in pain," Gwen said between gritted teeth.

"I don't care." Rafe shrugged. "She brought it on herself."

"I'm going to speak to the sheriff about this," Lacy declared.

Rafe laughed. "You do that. You'll have about as much success with this as you had in findin' your pappy's killer." He reached out and grabbed Ellie. "Get back to the saloon."

She went quickly and without a word, which caused Rafe to smile. "Now, that's the kind of obedience that keeps a woman from getting cut."

"You are . . . you're a . . ." Gwen doubled her fists. "Oh, I can't think of anything bad enough to call you."

"It wouldn't matter," Rafe said, laughing. "I've been called far worse than anything your sweet little Christian mouth could come up with." He turned to follow Ellie out but stopped when Gwen made her next announcement.

"We want to buy Ellie's contract."

He turned and looked at the trio. Gwen could feel the full weight of his glare upon her as he fixed his gaze on her.

"She's worth too much money to me."

"How much?" Gwen asked.

"Two hundred dollars."

Beth and Lacy exchanged a look with Gwen. Her heart sank. They could never raise that amount of money. "That's outrageous. You could buy a house for that."

Rafe laughed. "Yeah, if I wanted one. Oh, come to think of it, I do want one. I want Gallatin House. How about we make a trade?" He eyed her quite seriously. "You give me this place, and I'll give you Ellie."

"You know I can't do that."

He shrugged again. "Your loss. Either way, this place is going to be mine soon enough. You girls will never last the winter without a man, and it doesn't look like that Mr. Bishop is coming back anytime soon."

"Oh, I wouldn't be so sure of that."

Gwen looked up to see Hank standing in the doorway. "Hank!" He looked tired but otherwise so very handsome and happy. She ran to his arms and held him tight.

"Hello, beautiful," he whispered against her ear.

"I stand corrected," Rafe said. His sarcasm was clear. "The prodigal son has returned."

Gwen pulled back but remained at Hank's side. "You need to go, Rafe."

"I suppose I've worn out my welcome." Rafe moved toward

the couple. "Probably wouldn't be a good time to ask if you had any extra pies for sale."

"From now on, you aren't welcome here, Rafe. If your girls are hungry and want to eat, they are welcome to do so," Gwen said, narrowing her eyes. "The same goes for Cubby, but you and Wyman are not welcome."

Rafe put his hand to his chest as if struck. "Now, that hardly seems Christian." He laughed and gave a mocking bow. "Wyman and I have bets on you, Mr. Bishop. We're betting you won't make it to Christmas."

Hank shook his head. "At this rate, if I were a betting man, I'd have to say that you're the only one who may be gone by Christmas. I just guided two new families here who want to set up business in this area. Funny thing, though: none of them are very fond of saloons. First comment they made when they arrived was how they'd love to see you run out of business."

"That'll never happen," Rafe growled. He shoved past Hank and left the same way he'd come, muttering obscenities and stomping.

Gwen looked up at Hank and sighed. "I can't believe you're finally here. I was so worried."

He kissed her lightly on the forehead. "I figured you might be. I tried to hurry." He smiled. "Believe me—no one wanted me back here more than I did."

"How's your mother?"

Hank sobered. "She's fine. She's deeply saddened over the news about Harvey, but as I had suspected, she already believed this would be the outcome. She was happy to have the stocks returned and made me promise I would bring you to see her someday."

"She . . . approved . . . of me?" Gwen asked hesitantly.

"Of course she did. Not only that, but I told her how much

you had loved Harvey and how you were there for him right up until the end. That comforted her to know he died being loved and cared for."

"I'm glad. It means a great deal to me to know she doesn't oppose our marriage."

Gwen noticed that Beth and Lacy stood silently at the other end of the room. She nodded toward her sisters. "Now you'll just have to work on getting their approval."

Hank laughed. "I brought them both presents from Boston. I'm hoping it might persuade them."

"Presents?" Beth said, looking at Lacy. "You think you can buy us off?"

"Not exactly." Hank grinned. "I just figured my sisters-in-law would like something new to wear. Something befitting a wedding. Then I thought they might enjoy some new reading materials."

"Books?" Beth gasped. "You brought books?"

Lacy rolled her eyes. "Clothes and books. That will hardly win me over, Mr. Bishop."

"I didn't suppose it would," he admitted. "That's why I brought a new bay mare with me. She's young and spirited and kind of reminded me of you, except she's expecting a foal in the spring."

Lacy looked at Beth and then to Hank. "A horse? A spirited horse?"

"I thought you might want to start your own horse-breeding venture. The stock at the Lassiters could use some new blood."

"Now you'll have them both eating out of your hand," Gwen said with mock exasperation.

"Wait," Beth interjected. "I want to know what you brought Gwen."

"Me too," Lacy admitted. "Horses are great, but my sister's happiness is more important."

"I don't need anything else," Gwen declared. "I have Hank, and he's all I want."

"Well, I did bring you something else," Hank admitted. "In fact, I have several presents for you. But this one is very special."

He pulled a small box from his coat pocket and opened it. Inside, Gwen saw a beautiful gold ring with a diamond and several red stones. "This belonged to my grandmother," he told her. "My mother suggested it might make a good wedding ring."

Her sisters rushed forward to see for themselves. They made several comments, but Gwen couldn't register any of them. Her heart felt as if it might burst from the wonder of the moment.

Gwen fought back tears as she lifted her face to Hank's. "It's beautiful. I have never thought of owning anything half so lovely."

"It's not nearly as beautiful as you. I've done nothing but think of you since the day I rode out. You've been in my thoughts, my prayers, my every waking and sleeping moment." He bent down on one knee and took hold of her hand. "Gwen Gallatin, will you marry me?"

She looked at Beth and Lacy, who to her surprise were both crying. Beth was nodding her approval, while Lacy was more vocal. "Well, tell him yes!"

Gwen laughed and looked down at Hank. "I thought I already had."

"Well, tell him again," Lacy prompted.

"Yes," Beth insisted. "Tell him."

Hank smiled, and Gwen thought she would never, ever

grow tired of those beautiful blue eyes staring deep into her soul. "Yes, Hank. I will marry you."

He laughed and got to his feet. "It's a good thing. Otherwise, I don't know what I would have done with my mother's wedding dress."

CHAPTER THIRTY

The morning of October fourth dawned bright and clear. The air was chilled with the taste of snow that Gwen associated with the new dusting upon the mountaintops. It was a perfect day. A beautiful, perfect day.

It was her wedding day.

The circuit rider had come in last night and planned to ride out shortly after the wedding that, by Gwen's calculations, would take place in a little less than four minutes.

Beth came hurrying through the door, as if to confirm what Gwen already knew. "Everyone is here. They're all in place. It's time." She was followed in by Lacy, who seemed rather pleased with her new gown and ran to the mirror to take one last look.

"I never thought I'd like dressing up, but I have to say this gown makes me feel quite special."

"And it's not even your wedding day, Lacy," Beth declared, joining her sister at the mirror. "But I agree. I love this gown." She twirled and watched the pale pink silk ripple. "Isn't it amazing the way the material almost seems to be moving like a waterfall?"

Lacy touched the bodice of her lavender gown. "I've never owned anything so lovely. I hope Dave eats his hat when he sees me in this."

"What?" Gwen asked, moving to the mirror to check her hair. "Why would you care what Dave thinks?"

"Because he's always telling me I need to dress more lady-like. With the cut of this bodice and all this lace," she said, turning to cast a teasing grin, "he'll know very well that I'm a lady."

Gwen laughed. "I suppose now would be the perfect time to let you both in on a little secret."

"Only if it's quick. We need to get downstairs," Beth declared.

"Had you wondered at all about the color of your gowns?"

Beth looked at Lacy and then to Gwen. "No."

"Not really," Lacy admitted.

"Hank told me he chose the colors because they reminded him of the shades of shirts you two graced him with when he first came here."

Beth flushed. "I had no idea. Oh dear. That must mean he still holds it against me."

"I only hid the blue dye," Lacy protested. "The lack of proper amounts might have turned the pink shirts purple, but that was hardly my doing."

Gwen laughed. "He's not mad at either of you, and neither does he hold it against you. Rather, it endears you to him. He remembers how defensive you were about me—how you both worked to protect me from him."

She touched a hand to her upswept hair. Ringlets of spun gold curled down around her face. Beth had secured a few dried flowers at the top of Gwen's head and piled curls of hair around them. The effect was of a flowery tiara.

Stepping back, she smiled. "I'm ready."

Her wide, belled gown of white satin was antiquated in its fashion but precious to her because it had once belonged to Hank's mother, Matilda. The lace sleeves flared out to fall just below her elbows, and the bodice, though revealing of her neck and shoulders, was modestly cut and trimmed in lace.

"You're beautiful," Beth said, coming to hug her sister. "I'm so happy for you. It's just like a fairy tale. The beautiful princess and her handsome prince."

Gwen laughed. "I don't know about that, but I am happy, and Hank is a prince among men."

"And he's not half bad at picking out horses."

"What?" Gwen and Beth both said in surprise.

Lacy's eyes widened. "I didn't mean that you're a horse, Gwen." She giggled and hurried forward to embrace her older sister. "I think Dave is right about one thing. I'd do well to think about my words before letting them fly out of my mouth."

The main room of Gallatin House was filled with visitors for the wedding of Aloysius Bishop and his bride, Gwendolyn Gallatin. Hank paced nervously beside the fireplace. He'd chosen Jerry Shepard to stand up with him. Jerry had been faithful to help Hank with questions he had about the Bible, not to mention offering advice on dealing with the local folks and becoming a Montanan. He stood at Hank's left and offered him a reassuring smile. Major Worthington sat at Hank's heel and seemed to grant his approval, as well.

When Lacy first appeared on the stairs, Hank quickly pulled back to stand beside the circuit rider. He heard Dave Shepard draw in a sharp breath and smiled. Lacy certainly had cleaned up well. Her cinnamon hair was worn long in waves of curls and fashionably pinned to drape on either side of her head. She looked quite elegant, and Hank pitied Dave Shepard for not taking a little more care in his costume.

Beth walked down the stairs behind Lacy. She looked radiant and happy, yet Hank couldn't help but notice that she cautiously held the banister while descending. She glanced behind her, then cast Hank a smile as if to assure him the best was yet to come.

The white satin material of his mother's wedding gown draped first one step and then another, until Gwen was finally in view. It was Hank's turn to suck in his breath rather abruptly. He thought his heart might stop, it was pounding so laboriously. Gwen smiled at him, fixing her gaze on his face and never turning away.

He couldn't help but smile. *She's mine. She's mine forever.*

The girls stood on either side of their sister, and when the preacher asked who was giving the bride, they announced that they both were. Then they surprised Hank by kissing him on the cheek before giving him first Gwen's right hand and then her left.

"Guard her well," Lacy whispered.

"Love her always," Beth followed.

They paused and in unison added, "Or you'll answer to us."

Those close enough to hear chuckled. As they moved away to take their places, Beth met Hank's eyes and grinned.

"Nice white shirt, Hank."

He barely contained his laughter. "Lovely pink gown; purple's nice, too."

Beth giggled and slipped in beside Lacy.

The rest of the service was somewhat of a blur to Hank. He knew there were people—friends and neighbors who watched as he spoke a jumble of vows he would never be able to repeat verbatim but would always hold fast in his heart. He was also well aware of the beautiful woman at his side. When the preacher finally announced Hank should kiss his bride, the fog lifted and his new life seemed to dawn before him.

Gwen lifted her face to him and smiled. "Congratulations, Mr. Bishop."

"And to you, Mrs. Bishop."

Gwen watched as her dear friends cast smiles her way, then turned toward the bounty of food to be shared during the reception. She couldn't help but wish that her father were here to join in this blessed day. She smiled. He would have been in his element, telling stories and sharing in the revelry. Gwen couldn't help but believe he'd be pleased with Hank as his son-in-law. She stepped forward to follow the guests, but Hank tugged on her hand and brought her focus back to him. He took hold of her face in his hands. "I love you so very much, my dear Gwen."

Gwen smiled, and joy radiated from her eyes. "I love you too, Hank. I never thought I would love again. The wounds of losing Harvey ran so deep . . . but with you and God, I found healing."

"Amoris vulnus idem sanat, qui facit," he whispered against her lips. "Love's wounds are cured by love itself." He kissed her long and tenderly.

Gwen sighed against him and felt all of her fears drift away. Hank had given her a promise to believe in. Love had not only healed her wounds; love had given her the strength to let go of the past and look forward to the days to come.